"You are as in
protected w

"But there I am not tied to a man!" She yanked the rope for emphasis, but the movement did not budge him.

"Become accustomed to it, Melissande," he counseled. "You will be tied to a man once you wed Roarke, or any other man who kills for a living." Crossing her arms, she stared at him in rebellion.

Lucian's gaze fell to her crossed limbs.

No, she realized, to her chest.

Her defiant action succeeded only in squeezing her breasts together and thrusting them upward in vulgar display.

His gaze did not budge from her body for a long moment.

When he did look up, his gray eyes glittered with an unfamiliar light.

"Nevertheless, Angel, you certainly were not meant for the convent…!"

* * *

The Wedding Knight
Harlequin Historical #694—February 2004

Praise for new Harlequin Historical author
Joanne Rock

"Joanne Rock's talent for writing passionate scenes
and vivid characters really sizzles in this story.
Even the hot secondary romance has chemistry!"
—*Romantic Times* on *Wild and Wicked*

"A fresh voice in fiction with warmth and wit,
Joanne Rock's page-turner
sparkles with electric sizzle."
—*Romantic Times* on *Wild and Willing*

The Wedding Knight

Joanne Rock

HARLEQUIN®

TORONTO • NEW YORK • LONDON
AMSTERDAM • PARIS • SYDNEY • HAMBURG
STOCKHOLM • ATHENS • TOKYO • MILAN • MADRID
PRAGUE • WARSAW • BUDAPEST • AUCKLAND

ISBN 0-373-29294-5

THE WEDDING KNIGHT

Visit us at www.eHarlequin.com

Printed in U.S.A.

Available from Harlequin Historicals and
JOANNE ROCK

The Wedding Knight #694

Other works include:

Harlequin Blaze

Silk, Lace & Videotape #26
In Hot Pursuit #48
Wild and Willing #54

Harlequin Temptation

Learning Curves #863
Tall, Dark and Daring #897
Revealed #919

Please address questions and book requests to:
Harlequin Reader Service
U.S.: 3010 Walden Ave., P.O. Box 1325, Buffalo, NY 14269
Canadian: P.O. Box 609, Fort Erie, Ont. L2A 5X3

In joyous celebration of the historical romance writers who have preceded me, this book is dedicated to one writer heroine in particular. For fabulous Teresa Medeiros, whose medieval stories transported me hundreds of years in a matter of minutes. Many thanks for the wonderful tales and personal inspiration!

And for Kentucky Romance Writers, an endlessly talented and supportive group. Thank you, ladies, for sharing your wisdom on everything from plot development to Derby Day recipes. I am eternally grateful.

Chapter One

Spring 1250

If Lucian Barret had been a righteous, God-fearing man, he might have trembled at the thought of kidnapping a nun.

Fortunately his faith in God had died two years ago, along with his foster father in a stale sickroom. Stealing Melissande Deverell posed no moral dilemma for him now.

Lucian dragged in a breath of thin mountain air and pulled a length of white muslin from his saddlebag to wrap around his face. Although he would reveal himself to his captive eventually, he didn't want her to recognize him too soon and inadvertently betray his identity.

The good sisters of St. Ursula's would not appreciate his plans for Melissande.

He peered through the generous chink in the loose rock enclosure to spy on the young nun. After spending days observing the rituals of the convent's inhabitants, Lucian had narrowed his focus to this particular female.

Studying her profile as she read from her book, he searched for affirmation that she was the object of his quest.

The graceful woman in the severely cut habit bore no similarity to the hellion he recalled from childhood.

Her demeanor radiated contentment and fulfillment, as if divinely called to life behind silent walls.

The Melissande Deverell of ten years ago had screamed herself hoarse the day her parents announced she would enter a convent. She'd been rumored to have sobbed halfway to France once she departed England.

Confirmation of her identity came when playtime began.

Lucian watched his quarry frolic with three children in the sun-filled gardens. The scene reminded him of his childhood with his brother Roarke and their neighbor, Melissande—two boys and one mischievous girl to lead them on a merry chase. After reading to the little sprites for most of the afternoon, Melissande now allowed them to run and romp. Flashes of his old devil-may-care friend became apparent as the young woman tumbled laughing to the ground under the gleeful attack of her small charges.

A glimpse of vivid red hair peeped from beneath the black wimple when she sprawled on the new spring grass. The grin playing about her lips spoke of vibrant life trapped within her Spartan cloak.

Melissande.

There could be no mistaking the woman Roarke had demanded he retrieve from her convent hideaway in the secluded French Alps. The same woman whose deliverance would fulfill Lucian's long debt to his brother.

Roarke would not be disappointed.

As beautiful a maiden as he had ever seen, Melissande had blossomed into a prize who merited stealing. If Lucian were worthy to carry on the Barret family line, he would leap at the chance to possess such a wife to bear heirs.

But that job he left for Roarke. Lucian would continue to pay his penance for the life he had taken with his sword.

In spite of those who had labeled the deed an accident, he blamed himself.

Remembering the need for swiftness in his plan, Lucian jerked the fluttering white muslin about his head to secure it.

A sudden stillness permeated the convent garden.

He wrenched his gaze back to the happy group sprawled on the ground and discovered Melissande had gone stiff and wary while the little ones continued their play. She peered with intent eyes toward the crevice in the wall, as if she saw beyond the fractured rock to the danger lurking there for her.

I am saving her, Lucian told himself, needing that peace of mind to counteract the contented picture she presented as a nun.

Obviously startled by whatever movement she might have detected, Melissande spoke in a hushed voice to the children, hurrying them indoors.

The time had come to act.

Melissande Deverell had known many lonesome moments in her convent exile, but until now she had never known fear.

Heart racing as she struggled with her skirts and willed her children safely inside the sturdy walls of the schoolroom, her hands foolishly gripped the leather binding of the book she'd been reading to them.

Suddenly another set of hands gripped *her.* Impossibly big, strong hands.

No.

She tried to scream, but one of the massive paws smothered her mouth while the other reached around her belly to slam her backward into a rock wall.

"I will not hurt you." The rock wall spoke.

She kicked and jerked at her captor, wondering how a human body could be made of such hard substance. Even as she feared for herself, she winged a prayer of thanksgiving heavenward that at least Andre, Emilia and Rafael had made it safely inside.

Oblivious to her struggles, the man who restrained her scooped Melissande up as if she were no more than a feisty kitten. Still flailing any portion of her body that would move, she watched in growing panic as her tormentor kicked open the convent gate and left the towering protection of St. Ursula's in their wake.

My babes! Melissande's heart wrenched at the thought of those three dear faces waiting for her in the schoolroom. She fought even harder, screaming behind the hand smothering her mouth and nose.

Her shouts reverberating in her brain, Melissande didn't hear her abductor's commands whispered into her ear. All she could think of was the pain and disillusionment her absence would cost the three little orphans who were finally learning to love and trust again.

The madman who held her released her mouth, apparently needing a free finger to aid in the whistled call that now pierced the air.

"Please!" Her sudden cry rang out with startling conviction in the quiet Alpine forest.

Hesitating only a moment, Melissande launched into a torrent of urgent pleas to the man she still couldn't see. "I am the guardian of three young children. I must not leave them. I am their only stability, their—"

A horse galloped out of the woods, a fleet-footed gray beast with a dappled body and black mane. "They will be taken care of," a deep masculine voice growled in her ear, the rumble of which Melissande could feel against her back. He spoke slightly accented French, as though a foreigner to the land.

She screamed. A blood-chilling, forest-shaking screech that scared birds from their perches and caused the gray horse to rear in displeasure.

If the nuns were alerted to Melissande's absence soon enough, the abbess could possibly track her down before any harm came to her. Abbess Helen commanded a modest army, after all.

And if shrieking helped Melissande escape her captor, then by Ursula's sainted slipper, she would raise a holy terror.

"Quiet!" the voice behind her ordered, though the man could not cover her mouth while his one hand was sorely taxed to hold on to the nervous horse. Yet before she could shriek again, Melissande was hefted high onto the frightened animal's back, her forgotten burden ripped from her arms.

"My book!" It occurred to her she might have fought him off with more success if she'd dropped the manuscript.

"You cannot hold it while you ride," the man returned, shoving the heavy volume into a saddlebag.

"I do not know how to ride," she protested, though her hands instinctively sank into the thick mane when the animal reared again.

"The hell you don't," growled the voice.

Shocked, both at the curse and at the man's risky assumption that she would be able to keep her seat on a temperamental horse, Melissande braved a glance backward to look at him.

The flash of white, she realized, taking in the intricate wrapping of the man's exotic head covering. She had spied the material through the crevice in the convent wall.

Steely gray eyes stared back at her. A long, textured scar

from his temple to ear gave him a sinister visage. Dark skin around his eyes and his uncovered hands conjured an image of a desert sheikh.

Was she being abducted by an infidel warrior?

Terror clenched cold fingers around her stomach and squeezed. She knew the bloodthirsty ways of men who chose to kill for a living.

Perhaps her captor read her renewed commitment to escape in her eyes, for he suddenly materialized at her back, mounting the horse quicker than a blink. Shouting to the animal, the warrior kicked the gray mare's sides, launching them headlong into the forest.

"No!" Wiggling in her seat, Melissande cried out, thinking it would be better to fall from the mare than to submit to the heathen.

Yet as she slipped in the saddle, one strong arm caught and lifted her, yanking her down onto her captor's lap with amazing speed.

"Be still," he rasped. "You'll hurt yourself."

His muscular arm anchored her against the broad expanse of his chain-mailed chest. The tiny links of the metal tunic pulled at her woolen habit while his hand clamped the narrow space between her ribs and hip.

She had scarcely been touched in her ten years at the convent. To be held thus now seemed cruel fulfillment of her secret wish for human contact.

True to his warrior nature, the beast used his strength with reckless abandon. Melissande could not move if she tried.

"You're hurting me," she gasped, her words breathless with the effort.

To her surprise, his grip softened at once, though the heathen still made certain she could not fall—or jump—from the galloping mare.

Perhaps he was capable of listening to reason. If he would relax his hold at her behest, mayhap she could still convince him to release her altogether.

"You're making a grave mistake, sir. I belong to a holy order of women who—"

"I know who you are."

The husky whisper sent tremors down her spine.

"Then you know I must go back to the cloister where I belong." She breathed deeply, steadying herself against the nervousness his presence wrought. Melissande had not so much as spoken to any man save a priest these last years. And never had she touched a priest's body in such a manner.

"You will not be going back." His words fanned over her ear, his cool assurance at odds with the warmth of his breath.

Never see her home again? Anger surged through her, keen-edged and volatile as the fear she'd felt earlier.

Before she could frame a suitable response—a scathing tirade to put the heathen in his place—the stranger spoke again.

"But you will thank me one day." Scarcely slowing the horse as the forest grew more dense, he rode the rough terrain with reckless speed.

"Thank you? I would be hard-pressed to ever forgive you!" Outrage filled her. "You've stolen a novitiate right out of her convent!"

"You are not an avowed nun then?"

The hopeful note in his voice made Melissande regret she had not yet taken her final vows. "I will be *very* soon."

"No, lady. You will not."

He held her more tightly than strictly necessary as the landscape passed in a blur. Perhaps he'd given some credence to her claim that she could not ride after all. She'd never been so firmly anchored to another person, as if they'd been hewn of the same stone in a living statue atop the huge horse.

They were pressed so close she didn't need to turn around for him to hear her words.

"Yes, sir, I will. My abbess is one of the few to command her own army. She will hunt you down and demand my release." Or so Melissande hoped.

"My research found the good abbess heads a minimal force of men to protect her convent, but perhaps you know something I don't." The crinkles in the corners of his eyes deepened as if he smiled.

He knew the abbey's resources? He'd obviously exercised more forethought to capture her than she'd first realized.

Indignation brought a hot flush to her cheeks.

"Hellfire awaits you, sir. I hope you know that. This act denies your access to the Kingdom of Heaven for all eternity."

The man's gaze shifted to hers above the clean linen hiding his face.

"Then I shall add this to my long list of sins, Angel."

Chapter Two

Silence reigned in the aftermath of Lucian's declaration. Perhaps Melissande was finally so shocked she couldn't speak.

Good.

The last thing he needed was someone asking the whys and wherefores of his past. Better that Melissande be intimidated enough to leave him alone until they reached the time for him to unveil himself. Then there would be no hurry.

Although she sat still and outwardly tranquil, Lucian felt the tension reverberate through her slender form. Her stiff posture reminded him of the fear she surely struggled to hide.

She's frightened.

A moment's regret whispered through his consciousness, stirring a bit of emotional empathy he'd thought long dead. It seemed rather cruel to allow Melissande to suffer under the delusion he was a faceless stranger with harmful intent. He should reveal himself so her mind might be eased. Once she knew who held her, and for what purpose, she would willingly submit herself to his protection. Indeed, she would no doubt be grateful to him for rescuing her from a life of isolation.

Yet, Lucian waited.

Putting distance between her and St. Ursula's was critical to his success. The powerful abbess did indeed possess a small army for her personal use and would no doubt dispatch men to find Melissande.

If Lucian wanted to keep his prize, he needed to move quickly. That meant Melissande would have to remain ignorant of his identity awhile longer.

A contrary part of his brain reminded him that once she knew who he was, he would have no cause to ever hold her this way again. The knowledge should not have bothered him half so much as it did. Melissande was to be his brother's wife, not his.

Yet he would have to be a dead man not to notice the sweet curves his hands cupped beneath her coarse habit.

He was a damned man for so many reasons. Lusting over a convent-bred bride meant for another man would be a small transgression compared to his other sins.

How would she react when he revealed himself? Would the darkness of his soul be all too apparent to one as pure and unspoiled as her?

He could not pretend to be the Lucian Barret she had known. When confronted with the truth of his identity, she might be disillusioned at the stark changes. She might question what had turned the quiet boy into a cold, hard man. Worst of all, she might pity him.

And that, he could not bear.

Her youth and innocence brought to mind the life he might have had if his sword had not found its way into his foster father, Osbern Fitzhugh. Perhaps Lucian would now be securing a bride such as Melissande for himself instead of his brother.

Cursing foolish thoughts, Lucian dismissed all notion of marriage and Melissande from his mind. He could not alter the fact that in the heat of anger, he'd raised arms against a man who'd loved him like a son. Nothing would erase Lucian's sins—or erase the debt he owed his younger brother for safeguarding his most grave secret.

For now, he longed to shorten the distance between his captive and England as much as possible. The quicker he delivered Melissande to the man who awaited her, the sooner he could return to his penance and the savagery of war.

'Twas what suited him best.

The sun sank early in the mountainous forest region, leaving in its wake a brisk evening and a journey fast growing hazardous in the approaching dusk. A vast outcropping of rock closed in on them to one side, while a cliff dropped off to nothingness on the other.

Melissande's sore body and chilled skin cried out for rest, yet she feared sliding off the horse and having to face her captor once again.

Her back ached as if it would break under the strain of keeping her body away from the beast who held her. Though she could do nothing about the heavy arm wrapped around her waist, she found she could avoid more intimate contact with the silver-eyed man if she remained ramrod-straight in front of him.

In spite of her best efforts to evade his touch, however, she could not escape the brush of his strong thighs bracketing hers as they rode. The smooth leather of his braies slid against the coarse wool of her gown in a most unnerving manner.

He reined in their horse abruptly, slamming her backward against him.

In a heartbeat, he righted her in the saddle, forcing the space between them again as if he desired it as much as she did. But he showed no inclination to dismount. Instead he lifted his head into the wind, like an animal scenting danger long before its arrival. A predatory stillness came over him.

"We are not alone, lady." Though whispered through the layer wrapped around his face, his words were distinct in her ear.

The road they now traversed accommodated little more than horseback travelers or perhaps a rugged cart. Melissande had given up hope they would meet any passersby on the route, but in the distance she heard the drum of quick hooves.

Someone to save me. She opened her mouth to scream, but her captor's muffling hand stifled the sound.

"You do not want to do that, Melissande. Trust me."

After a long moment, the sound of her name penetrated her brain. *He knows me.*

Cautiously she turned and raised her eyes to his, her lips still covered by a huge, warm palm. Drawing still closer, the echoing hooves beat an urgent rhythm to her fears. She watched, fascinated, as her captor reached to unwind the concealing layers from his face.

"I am your friend." His features revealed, he looked more European, less foreign somehow. His hair grew as dark as any infidel's, yet its shorter length was the same as that favored by many Englishmen. The sound of horses beating the hard ground closed in on them. "Your former neighbor."

Yanking the rest of the cloth from his head, he stared back at her with intent gray eyes. The hard planes of his face, the quiet intelligence of his gaze, loomed above her with haunting familiarity.

Lucian Barret.

Recognition hit her a scant second before the other riders came into view around a mountainous pass. Though she did not see the newcomers, her peripheral senses alerted her to their presence as she gazed dumbfounded into the eyes of a childhood friend.

A boy she'd once fancied her hero.

Her relief lasted only an instant before fury took its place. How dare he steal her away?

The horses halted on the dirt path in front of them. Lucian's hand slid from her mouth before he turned to the riders. The touch struck her as more intimate now that she knew her captor's identity. Her lips burned with the touch.

She fumed silently though her curiosity compelled her to greet their visitors. "Good evening to you, gentle knights."

They wore the sign of the cross, Melissande noted, yet they had that haggard look of long travel about them. Their beards were dirty and unkempt, their shields dulled with lack of recent care.

Crusaders.

"Good eve to you, sir." The first knight directed his words to Lucian, then turned to Melissande. Noting her habit, he bowed his head more deeply. "And you, Sister."

Now was her chance. All she had to do was to say something. Anything. Decry her abductor, proclaim her captured status.

Yet despite their pretense of respect, the men looked at her with disturbing boldness. Some demon lurked in their brazen stares, as if they would gobble her up at the first opportunity.

Never, in all her years at St. Ursula's, had she met a warrior knight whom she admired. The battle hungry sought shelter on their way to war. The battle weary sought food on their way home from war. If they did not bring obvious bloodlust to the convent table, they brought vain-glorious tales of their prowess on the field. All of them brought boorish manners and lice.

She'd been aware of their bawdy ways, but none had dared lust after a nun. Warrior knights were apparently more bold outside the convent walls.

Melissande nodded in acknowledgment of their greeting, holding her tongue until she determined the best course of action.

"You go to Acre?" Lucian asked the question naturally enough, but Melissande could feel the edge of tension in his body where it surrounded hers. The thighs embracing hers no longer seemed like cold stone. The knowledge that this hard masculine form belonged to Lucian Barret infused the limbs with warmth.

Or was it her limbs that grew so heated and…aware?

"Outremer." The first man answered in French, though the second knight never took his attention from Melissande.

She shook off her odd response to Lucian to take note of her situation. The Crusader's silent appraisal deflated all hope that she could ask the newcomers for help. The devil she knew, at this point, seemed safer than the two she didn't know.

Even if the known devil seemed to be causing a quiet inferno within her already. She edged forward slightly, needing the extra space between her and Lucian.

"Your king has great need of you," Lucian told them, tightening his grip on Melissande's waist before she could go far. "His wars do not go well."

As twilight fell, the men spoke of faraway battles and the French king's recent captivity at the hands of the infidel. The exotic place names and foreign events held little meaning for Melissande, though she had read many Eastern texts in her work as a copyist at the abbey.

One thing became quite clear from the exchange, however. Lucian himself had been a Crusader.

It didn't recommend him, in Melissande's eyes. In fact, it made her all the more wary. But he was still Lucian Barret, for St. Ursula's sake.

He must have some compelling reason for taking her. News of her family, perhaps. Maybe one of her sisters needed her. Once she explained to him how much she belonged at the convent, he would return her. He had always been an honorable person, even as a young man.

With a respectful nod, the first knight spurred his horse forward to ride past them to the south into the dark swell of forest. "God speed you, sir."

"God speed," Lucian returned, his gaze falling to Melissande now that the threat of danger had diminished.

Distant gray eyes seemed to forbid her unspoken questions, inspiring Melissande to shiver with their blatant lack of human warmth.

"Lu-Lucian?" Her voice caught in her throat. It seemed silly to fear an old friend—an honorable one at that—yet anger for what he had done still boiled in her blood.

"We need to ride a bit farther, Melissande." The terseness in his tone cut off any hope of further interaction. "We'll talk then."

Ordinarily, Melissande would not have submitted to a high-handed directive, especially from a man who'd kidnapped her and purposely kept his identity a secret knowing it would have lessened her fear to know it.

But by now she was so cold and uncomfortable she had little thought for anything other than a warm fire and a seat anywhere but perched atop the mare.

Inky darkness surrounded them by the time they reached a vacant cottage in the middle of nowhere. Ice already forming in her veins, Melissande knew she would not sleep a wink in such drafty quarters with naught but thin wooden walls between her and the frigid night air. As Lucian helped her from the horse, Melissande slumped with weak relief into his arms.

"You are unwell?" Lucian asked, carrying her into the cottage.

"Only tired, I think." There was no need to mention her susceptibility to lung fever. The years of hard Alpine winters had given her more cases than she cared to count.

He looked skeptical as he settled her on a low bench before a dank fire pit in the one-room shelter.

"And sore. I have not ridden a horse in many years." Her legs ached with the truth of the statement.

"You will be warm in no time," he promised, though she hardly heard him through the veil of fatigue that quickly overcame her.

She didn't realize she'd slept until she awoke a short time later.

True to his word, Lucian had supplied a brightly burning fire for Melissande while she'd slumbered. One heavy woolen blanket covered her. Another was propped beneath her head with a thin sheet of white muslin thoughtfully tucked between her cheek and the scratchy wool.

Running idle fingers over the muslin, Melissande recognized Lucian's head covering from earlier in the day.

The tender care evident in her warm cocoon eased Melissande's spirit. Lucian Barret did not seek to harm her, even if he was a warrior.

Lifting her gaze to his seat a few hand spans away, Melissande watched him unwrap a linen sack and pull out a loaf of bread and some cheese. A large wineskin followed.

"Has my family asked you to seek me out?" Her voice sounded throaty and thick with sleep.

Lucian stared at her for a long moment, keen gray eyes

roving along every detail of her missing wimple and bed-rumpled hair.

A curious prick of heightened awareness darted through her, faintly akin to embarrassment, but not quite.

This was only Lucian, after all.

She had never been shy with the boy who had taught her how to fish and never pulled her braids. Although he was much bigger and infinitely more intimidating than the skinny boy she'd known ten years ago.

"Drink this." He thrust the wineskin in her direction.

Melissande shook her head, determined to learn the truth behind his scheme to abduct her. There must be some vital reason he had frightened her half out of her wits. "Is it one of my sisters? Are they—"

All the other Deverell daughters had been married off long since. Only the youngest had been destined for the convent. What if one of them had taken ill or had trouble birthing or...

"I do not know the status of your family since your parents died. I didn't come on behalf of your kin." He cut the cheese into smaller portions as if it were the most important task before him, as if he didn't have a woman hanging on his every word, waiting to know her fate at his hands.

Melissande struggled for a measure of calm, recalling Abbess Helen's favorite admonishment from the Book of Proverbs. *The fool blurts out every angry feeling, but the wise subdues and restrains them.* "Then why?"

Handing her a portion of cheese and bread, Lucian regarded her with stern eyes. "Eat well, Melissande, and I will explain as much as I can."

She tore off a small piece of bread and ate, too tired to be contrary.

Lucian took a deep breath, then raised the wineskin in

casual tribute. "I have saved you from a life behind the cloister walls so you might marry the man you love."

Saved me? Melissande tried not to panic as she pulled her blankets more closely about her shoulders, watching Lucian drink deeply from the skin. The muscles of his neck contracted in intriguing rhythm with his swallow. Melissande found herself fascinated to watch him.

A man.

"And who might that be?"

Lucian raised a dark brow at her ignorance. The thin, pale scar near his eye caught her attention in the flickering firelight. A jagged line that marred his temple from brow to ear, the mark was one of the reasons she had not recognized him earlier.

"You've forgotten the man you claimed you'd love until your last dying breath?"

Heat flooded her cheeks as Melissande recalled the horrible scene she had caused the day she'd left for the convent. She had screamed like a harridan, ranting and raving that she did not want to be a nun, that she would find a way back home…and that she would love Roarke Barret until her dying day.

"Roarke?"

Lucian almost smiled. Amusement definitely quivered around the corners of his lips before his face fell into more serious lines once again. "Aye, lady. Roarke."

"You traveled all through Europe and braved the Alps to retrieve me…" The thought staggered her, knowing how difficult the roads were. "For Roarke Barret?"

"I hope you are well pleased," he managed to say between bites of his apple.

Her curiosity quenched, Melissande's good sense returned. She snatched the fruit from his hand. "Nay, I am not pleased, sir. I demand you return me to my abbey at daybreak.''

Only the crackling of the fire broke the stiff silence of the room.

"You do not wish to wed Roarke?" His voice told her he was genuinely surprised.

"Of course not.''

At his look of utter confusion, Melissande sighed.

"How many things did you yearn for at eight years old that you no longer want or need as a man full-grown?''

"None.'' He grabbed his apple back and devoured half of it in one crunching bite.

Recalling the serious sort of boy Lucian had been, Melissande realized he probably spoke the truth. "Well, you are unusual. Most people have unobtainable dreams during childhood.''

He furrowed his brow before he schooled his features into the mask of patience a teacher might use with a difficult child. "Your dreams are not unobtainable.''

"But they are no longer my dreams!'' Melissande heard her voice reverberate through the cottage with satisfying volume. When was the last time she had raised her voice? "Don't you see? I am happy at the convent, Lucian. I care for the abbey's orphans. I read books few people in the western world will ever lay eyes on. It is a blissful life!''

"Blissful?'' He took back the wineskin from where it lay forgotten in her hand and sipped its contents thoughtfully.

The warm brush of his hand unnerved her.

"Yes, blissful.'' In the most secret regions of her heart, she knew that might be stretching the truth, but she loved St. Ursula's. She certainly would not chain herself to a knight who would be off fighting ten months of the year, and then train her sons for the same dangerous profession.

"Fickle woman."

"Pardon?" Melissande could not have heard him properly.

He pinned her with a cold steel gaze. "You are most fickle, lady, to claim you love Roarke and to pledge yourself to him in tortured screams as you left England, then decide you do not love him and want to live in a convent."

"I was eight years old!"

"Old enough."

Could he be serious? "I can assure you it is not uncommon behavior for a child's passions to alter as he or she grows."

"And I can assure you with equal authority that some people possess the same passion their whole lives."

She flushed, although she wasn't sure why. His words confused her, taunted her in ways she couldn't understand.

"I am sorry you have changed your mind, Melissande. The fact is, I am bringing you back to England to marry Roarke."

"I will not go to England and I will not wed anyone." Melissande might just as well shout into the Alpine wind for all that he seemed to be listening.

"Ah, today you do not wish to wed, but who is to say what you will feel tomorrow?" He brushed a weary hand through his hair. "I am hoping your fickle nature will turn to my advantage by the time we get home."

Dear God, he was serious. A small twinge of panic shot through her. "Lucian, I cannot go with you. I won't."

"You can and you will. I have promised Roarke you will arrive in England by midsummer."

"But—"

"And I always keep my vows." Hints of pride and warning mingled in his voice, his cool gaze level with hers.

Melissande stared back at him, feeling no glimmer of

friendship or empathy with the man across the fire from her. Similar to his childhood self only in his quiet seriousness and obvious intelligence, Lucian Barret had changed drastically in the past ten years.

The raven's-wing hair he used to keep so closely shorn now touched his collar. The sharp planes of his face seemed even more dramatic now that his visage had lost all traces of youthfulness. Of course his huge warrior frame bore little resemblance to the lanky youth she remembered.

Darkness pervaded him, where once Melissande could tease a grin from her somber friend. He kept her at arm's length now, as if being too friendly might shake his resolve to accomplish his own goals.

His utter commitment to those goals, even if it involved kidnapping a woman devoted to God and ignoring her pleas for return, unnerved her. Ruthlessness lurked behind his words. And no wonder—he was a warrior. He would do whatever necessary to drag her back to England.

Yet Melissande could not allow him to proceed with his scheme to "save her."

She gauged her opponent, wondering how best to attack as he stored the leftovers of their dinner. Firelight danced over his intimidating form, making him appear even larger and more forbidding in the tiny cottage.

With little hope the ploy would work, she tried one last time to appeal to the heart he seemed to be lacking.

"Three children depend on me to care for them—"

"There is an abbey full of kindly nuns to watch over them." He did not even bother to glance in her direction as he settled a few feet from her. His protective armor hit the dirt floor with a dull clink where he laid upon it.

The man slept in chain mail?

The impropriety of their closeness struck her, but her

main concern remained with the children, not Lucian's unorthodox proximity.

"I must go back in the morning," Melissande informed him, hoping with all her heart he would agree but knowing he would not.

With him or without him, she would return.

"Go to sleep, Mel." He yawned.

Though he used the nickname from old habit, it brought to mind the loving way her little charges called her Mel. Or Angel Mel. Or Rafael's ridiculous combination of AngMel.

Her heart lurched with a sudden, empty pang. Her arms ached for her children. Could any mother love them more, these babes of her heart?

"Don't you want a blanket?" she asked, realizing he meant to sleep on the hard floor with no covering to warm him. As soon as she asked, she felt embarrassed by her solicitous concern.

"Nay."

Her maternal nature forced her to pull off one of her numerous woolens and toss it over him anyway.

He flung it back with angry impatience. "I said nay, lady." Then, as if realizing his appalling manners, he managed a stiff, "No thank you."

Odd.

Melissande watched him close his eyes, one hand propped under his head for a pillow. He had to be excruciatingly uncomfortable, but she would certainly make no move to offer him any reprieve. She left the blanket he tossed aside between them, however, just in case he changed his mind.

As she watched and waited for his breath to even into the smooth pattern of sleep, she wondered what had happened to Lucian to turn him into the cold, hard man before her.

She prayed she could be stealthy in her escape, because she had no doubt his wrath would be formidable when he discovered her missing the next morning.

Chapter Three

Perhaps he had been too hard on her, Lucian thought, listening to Melissande fidget in the pallet he'd made for her. She'd been raised to become a nun, after all. A sheltered, delicate creature, she would be unacquainted with the harsh side of life. She did not deserve his continual reminders that she could not return to her convent. Since leaving England, he had lost all notion of how to deal with a woman.

Maybe not quite all, he amended, recalling the faceless females who had slaked his most basic need for feminine flesh over the past two years. But he no longer possessed the finesse necessary to deal with a sensitive noblewoman, let alone a cloistered would-be nun.

Regret stole through him when he thought of his crass refusal of the blanket she'd tossed him. Of course she wouldn't understand his deep-seated need to suffer, to sleep on the hard floor, to allow the cold to permeate his skin in the early morning hours.

Her action had been thoughtful and he'd rewarded the effort with boorish behavior. She was a sweet soul, incapable of understanding the darkness driving him to his acts of penance, acts of guilt.

Even now another kind of guilt flooded him for the inappropriate thoughts he'd experienced in regard to his brother's future wife. The coarse woolen habit she wore didn't begin to hide the pleasing form of the woman Melissande had grown into. She looked like a walking sacrilege with those voluptuous curves straining her habit in all the right places.

But in spite of Lucian's poorly placed fantasies, Melissande Deverell would wed his brother by the moon's next cycle, and she deserved Lucian's polite respect. He wouldn't be caught leering at her like the lecherous Crusaders they'd met on the forest road.

As his future sister-in-law, Melissande deserved a bit more freedom under his protection. He didn't need to watch her as if she were his prey.

She wasn't a prisoner, but a bride.

Breathing deeply, Lucian promised himself he would relax his watch just a little. Heaven knew his tired body cried out for a good night's rest. He had not slept in two days, and fitfully on the road before that. She did not need him breathing down her neck, and Lucian could use some sleep.

Melissande shivered in the warm nest of woolens Lucian had given her. Now she shuddered not from the cold but from her fear and unease at the thought of escaping him.

Certainly he meant her no harm, in spite of the fright he'd given her when he'd stolen her from St. Ursula's. He would be furious to discover her defection, but there could be no help for it. Lucian would just have to tell Roarke she didn't want any part of marriage.

Slipping silently from her blankets, she waited for any change in his breathing.

Nothing.

Steady, even sighs greeted her ears.

The intimacy of the sound wound around her, drawing

her back to where Lucian lay with hypnotic pull. Long accustomed to nights spent in a hard bed with naught but her own thoughts and a warming brick to keep her company, Melissande found the experience of lying in the warm cocoon between a fire and Lucian oddly comforting.

For years Melissande could not sleep at the convent. After sharing a room with two older sisters at her home, she had found it impossible to slumber alone in the darkened cell at St. Ursula's when she'd first arrived. How peculiar that she would rest easily in the company of a warrior knight.

She would leave in a moment, she told herself. Now, gazing on the dark mass of chain mail and muscle lying in a perfectly straight line on the cottage floor, curiosity consumed her.

Would Lucian look as cold and forbidding in sleep as he did awake?

Driven by the innate inquisitiveness ten years of convent education still hadn't overcome, she knelt beside the knight who had stolen her. Fading firelight played over his features, casting half his face in shadow. The scar glared; the one patch of white in an otherwise deeply bronzed complexion attesting to long battles fought under a scorching desert sun. Brow furrowed even in sleep, he still bore an aspect of cold harshness.

Instinctively, Melissande reached to touch the vaguely wrinkled place across his forehead. He radiated warmth despite the chill of the room. Amazingly, the skin beneath her fingers smoothed as she touched it. Lucian's whole countenance slowly relaxed into a less fearsome visage.

She drew her hand back, surprised at the change in him, but even more astonished at her brazenness.

Immediately the furrow returned to his face. His breathing hitched.

Oh, no.

She counted each measured inhalation to assure herself he would not awaken. Finally she tiptoed away, tying her loose habit more snugly about her.

The sooner she left behind the strange pull of Lucian Barret, the better.

With slow caution, she lifted the heavy blanket over the shelter's one window and hopped across the sill. Replacing the rock that secured the covering over the opening, Melissande prayed she would not regret her action.

Many hours later, as first light hovered, Melissande murmured proverbs to herself as her tired body longed to collapse in a heap on the frosty ground.

The way of the lazy is a thorny hedge, the path of the honest a broad highway. She hoped her determination to do the right thing would render her path more highway-like and less thorny.

A village had to be around the next rise, although she had told herself the same thing for the last fifteen hills she'd climbed.

A stranger to such grueling exercise in the thin mountain air, Melissande knew her lungs would burst from her efforts. The thought of returning home to Emilia, Andre and little Rafael kept her feet moving in spite of the burning in her chest.

"You need help, Sister?" a small French voice called out in the hazy light of predawn.

Dragging her eyes up from the ground, Melissande caught sight of a young girl, no more than eight or nine, with a large bucket in her arms.

Blinking in surprise, Melissande wondered if she hallucinated.

"Yes!" She thought she'd weep with relief.

After helping the girl procure a bucketful of water from a nearby stream, Melissande accompanied young Linette to her family home, which really was just over the next rise. A simple wooden structure, the house was a neat square with two plain windows flanking the doorway like eyes in a face. The stubs of empty rose vines poked through the snow at intervals across the front of the dwelling, and Melissande could envision the cottage as it must be in the summer, covered with roses and sweetly fragrant.

"My papa is away until next week, but you may speak with my mama." A dark-haired imp full of energy despite the early hour, Linette spoke musical French that warmed Melissande's heart.

Melissande helped the girl open the door to the sparsely furnished home. A single chair graced the one room dwelling, a prized possession for the family, no doubt. Several other wooden objects filled the small cottage—a set of spoons hung on the kitchen wall, a polished box near the fireplace that probably contained a store of salt and a carved cross above the table.

"My papa is a carpenter," Linette told her proudly. "Would you like to sit in our chair?"

Linette's mother hurried over from her sewing beside the window, the worried lines in her face telling Melissande she looked a sorry sight. The woman—a sturdy blonde whose Nordic features seemed at home in the wintry landscape—appeared scarcely older than Melissande herself.

"I apologize, ma'am," Melissande began, gratefully accepting the arm the taller woman held out to her.

"Just rest, Sister," the lady of the house admonished as she guided Melissande to the chair before the fire. "I am Mistress Jean, but we may speak later."

Heaven. The chair, the warmth, the generosity of Linette and her mother…Melissande could think no further. She closed her eyes, overcome with fatigue and gratitude now that she sat still for a moment.

She needed to relay her story to these strangers, but grogginess overwhelmed her after the unaccustomed exertions of her snowy trek. The cold weather had never agreed with her...

Melissande didn't realize she'd drifted off to sleep until a small gasp awakened her with a start.

"A knight approaches, Mama!" Linette's childish tone grew shrill in her excitement, prompting Melissande to lift an eyelid.

"And he rides the most beautiful speckled horse!"

Melissande's eyes flew open, her fingers clutching the smooth wooden arms of Mistress Jean's lone chair. Cold dread sank down her spine.

Lucian.

How could he have found her so quickly? All hint of exhaustion evaporated. She jumped to join the girl in the doorway.

Sure as she breathed, there he was—a walking weapon of war come to impose his will upon her. Why did he insist she marry Roarke? For that matter, what did Roarke care about a woman he hadn't seen since childhood?

"You know this man," Mistress Jean observed, her assessing blue gaze flicking over Melissande.

"He stole me from St. Ursula's convent yesterday, but I escaped him." Melissande dug into the small sack tied around her girdle and removed a tiny cheesecloth parcel.

If there had been a man in the home to help her, she might have called upon him to protect her. But she could not put Linette and her mother at risk. They had been so kind.

"We could hide you," Mistress Jean suggested, her eyes

already flitting about the inside of the cottage for a suitable place.

"He will know. My footprints must be obvious for him to have found me already." She pressed the small bundle containing a short missive and a signet ring into the woman's hand as they watched Lucian vault from the gray mare's back. "But if you know a way to get this to Abbess Helen at St. Ursula's, I will be forever in your debt."

They locked gazes over Linette's head. Melissande could see the woman's hesitation. Yet at the last moment, just before Lucian reached the doorstep, Mistress Jean withdrew the bundle from Melissande's hand and shoved it into a pouch among the folds of her gown.

Her words were a tense whisper beneath the heavy fall of Lucian's boots on the cobblestone walkway. "I will try, Sister."

Melissande breathed a sigh of relief. Even if Lucian dragged her away with him again, she could at least count her mission somewhat of a success. If the abbess received the note and signet ring, she would launch a search party. Failing that, the abbess could always proceed straight to Barret Keep in England. Melissande had revealed her captor's final destination.

"Good morning, mistress," Lucian called from the doorframe, his uncommon height filling the entry. "Good morning, Melissande."

Although he kept his tone utterly neutral, there could be no mistaking the anger seething just below the surface.

"I have come to escort you home." His gaze froze her in place. "I trust you do not want to cause a frightening scene in front of the little one."

Linette looked back and forth between them with wide, scared eyes. Mistress Jean skittered closer to her daughter and looped protective arms about the girl's shoulders.

Lucian certainly knew how to wield a weapon effectively, Melissande thought. Just like a man who killed for a living.

The beast.

He couldn't have put her in motion any faster than by threatening that sweet girl with a scare.

Melissande made a move to stand beside him, but he halted her with one raised palm.

"First, I'd like to see you dressed in more appropriate travel clothes." Glaring at her habit with disdain, he pulled a sack from the belt at his waist. "Perhaps you have something, madame?" He jingled the coin-filled sack as he turned inquiring eyes toward Mistress Jean. "I am willing to pay handsomely for warm garments to replace the habit."

The woman glanced nervously between Lucian and Melissande. "I could spare her a few things if she really wants them—"

"She does." He gave Melissande a prodding shove. "We need to hurry, Melissande, to recover the time you've cost us." Turning his back, he waited just beyond the cottage door.

Gratefully, she accepted the comforting squeeze Jean gave her as she steered Melissande toward the wardrobe. Blinking back her frustration, Melissande concentrated on the small wooden chest and not her disappointment.

The thought of removing her habit after all these years both troubled and tempted her. It symbolized everything she held dear, and she valued its practical warmth. Yet, as Linette and her mother dug through the clothes, Melissande could not help a rush of pleasure to see colored garments in less coarse material than her woolen habit.

She crossed herself and prayed for forgiveness for her worldly wants.

Soon, Melissande stood outfitted in the modest but pretty garments of a merchant's wife. Although not richly decorated, her new surcoat boasted a finely woven wool in a dull shade of forest-green.

The white undertunic brushed her skin in a silken caress, its soft muslin fabric the most decadent material to touch her skin in ten years.

She noticed Lucian with his back still turned and hesitated. A flush stole through her as she realized she had never faced a man without the barrier of her habit in place, at least not since she had become a grown woman.

Melissande cleared her throat to gain his attention. "I'm ready."

"Very well then, we—" He stared at her. His gray eyes widened as he took in every detail of her new garb.

Self-conscious under his scrutiny, Melissande hurried to drape a shawl about her shoulders.

With a soft clink of silver, Lucian laid a bag of coins in the woman's hand and turned to leave. "Come, Melissande."

"I apologize for the intrusion," Melissande murmured to her hostess, following Lucian out the door into the cool morning air. "And thank you."

"God go with you, Sister," the woman returned, her blue eyes sympathetic.

Lucian tugged Melissande's arm, obviously impatient to go. She longed to fling herself around Mistress Jean's neck and to plead for shelter from her fate, but she did not.

With the submissive grace pounded into her at every opportunity at St. Ursula's, Melissande allowed Lucian to pluck her from the ground and seat her before him on the horse.

Again.

"Goodbye, Sister Melissande," Linette called from the doorway of the cottage.

Melissande waved and made a vain effort to smile even though her thoughts strayed to her children at the abbey who never got to say goodbye to her.

Now she sat trapped between Lucian's thighs; the leather of his braics against her new, soft garments did nothing to ease her jumpy nerves.

"Children seem fond of you, lady," Lucian remarked as he spurred the horse to a run.

"They are trusting souls."

"I, however, am not." Gray eyes flickering with an anger he didn't bother to hide, Lucian looked down at her.

"I am sorry I could not go with you willingly." As soon as the words were out, Melissande regretted having said them. Why should she be sorry? "But you must understand my refusal to wed."

"I do not understand it at all," he remarked as he reached behind him to pull a length of rope from a satchel "But I do know I cannot allow you to roam the forest unprotected."

Words clipped, movements tense, Lucian radiated impatience. Tying the horse's reins around the pommel, he allowed the mare to choose their path while he adjusted the rope, tying and retying it. What in St. Ursula's name could he be trying to accomplish?

"Can I help?" she offered, growing nervous when the horse raced beneath a particularly low branch.

"Give me your hand."

With one wary eye still cast toward the mountainous trail, Melissande reached to assist him.

No sooner had she extended her palm than the heavy rope looped around her wrist.

"What?" She jerked back instantly, but she was too late.

The bond held her fast. Its other end, she now realized, had been secured to Lucian's waist. "Just what do you think you are doing?" Outrage simmered in her veins.

"Protecting you." With methodical movements, he untied the bridle and regained control of the mare.

Man and horse alike seemed to relax, their tension dissipating now that Lucian held the reins.

Melissande, however, had never felt further from calm.

"Your idea of protection is imprisonment?" Her well-modulated convent voice evaporated. She shouted like a termagant.

"I gather yours is, too, lady, if you are so fond of your home at St. Ursula's." Ruthless control back in place, Lucian glared at her. "You are as imprisoned as you are protected within the cloister."

"But there, I am not tied to a man!" She yanked the rope for emphasis, but the movement did not budge him.

"Become accustomed to it, Melissande," he counseled. "You will be tied to a man once you wed Roarke, though mayhap not with such a tangible bond."

Over my dead body.

"I will never marry Roarke, or any other man who kills for a living." Crossing her arms, she stared up at him in rebellion.

Lucian's gaze fell to her crossed limbs.

No, she realized, to her chest.

Unaccustomed to her new garments, Melissande had not taken into account the more snug fit and low cut of secular clothing. Her defiant action succeeded only in squeezing her breasts together and thrusting them upward in vulgar display.

Embarrassed to her toes, Melissande let her arms fall to her sides, though his gaze did not budge from her body for a long moment.

When he did look up, his gray eyes glittered with an unfamiliar light.

"Nevertheless, Angel, you certainly were not meant for the convent."

Chapter Four

This was all Roarke's fault.

If Roarke hadn't been so hell-bent on having Melissande Deverell for a wife, Lucian could have crossed Europe at his ease. He fumed as he picked their way toward the Alpine lowlands, trying to ignore the sweet scent of Melissande's hair beneath his nose.

If not for Roarke, Lucian wouldn't even be returning to England. Why should he? He'd given up his claim to the Barret lands long ago. There was naught for him there anymore.

Melissande shifted sleepily in his arms, her feminine curves brushing against him with startling clarity now that she wore regular clothing instead of the flour sack she called a habit.

His request that she trade in her convent attire ranked as his most stupid move of the day. He had a difficult enough time keeping his eyes off her when she remained dressed as a nun.

But now…

Lucian gritted his teeth as his sleeping passenger finally settled her head on his chest, burrowing as close to him as humanly possible upon horseback.

Damn.

Lucian had known, even as a boy, that Melissande would transform into a raving beauty one day. Her unruly red braids and freckles hadn't fooled him. Her ready smile and warm brown eyes had won his heart the first time she'd clamored to go fishing with him.

Roarke had been the dolt who'd never noticed her. No matter what tricks little Mel tried, Roarke had ignored the youngest Deverell daughter, oblivious to her tender feelings for him.

Until now.

Roarke had written to him during the wars and asked Lucian to retrieve Melissande on his way home from the fighting. He had not planned to go home at the time, but couldn't refuse his brother's request.

And the more he thought about it, the more he realized Roarke must have finally come to his senses. Melissande was a noble lady and a strong woman. She would make any husband proud. Although the idea of her as Lady Barret inspired a small twinge of jealousy, Lucian enjoyed the notion she would help rule their family lands.

Reaching a small clearing in the trees, Lucian reined in his mount. He still needed to hunt for their dinner and to build a shelter of some sort. Alpine nights were none too forgiving to unprepared travelers.

As they stopped, Melissande lifted her head from his chest. The late-afternoon air felt more chilly without the warmth of her body against his, his arms strangely empty without her in them.

"Where are we?" The throaty rasp of her voice reminded him of a lover's morning greeting.

"We're camping here tonight." Shoving aside the inappropriate thoughts, Lucian slid from underneath her and jumped off the horse.

Melissande looked bereft atop the animal. "Here?" she squeaked. She rubbed her wrist where the rope still bound her, though she seemed too sleepy to wonder about it.

Lucian had removed the other end from his waist and now held it, wondering where to put her so she would be safe.

Unwillingly, he held his hands out to her. She fell into his arms without a thought.

The brief contact sent a jolt of awareness through him, tantalizing him with sensations he ruthlessly suppressed.

He set her at arm's length before she noticed anything amiss. "I need to catch our dinner and start a fire." He began pulling out the necessary equipment from his saddlebag and tossed her a large cheesecloth. "Perhaps you could warm the bread when the fire is ready. The merchant's wife kindly packed us a bit of food for our journey."

Melissande drew her shawl more tightly around her. Scooping up the cheesecloth, she seemed to accept the chore.

"You will not continue to bind us together, then?" She looked faintly hopeful.

Hardening his heart, needing to protect her from her own impetuous nature, Lucian carried his end of the rope to a nearby tree and cinched it. She'd put herself in grave danger when she struck out on her own. He still could not believe his stupidity at not tying her up when they had lain yesterday. He had known he would slumber like the dead after two days without sleep while he observed the convent routine, searching for Melissande.

He would not indulge her comfort at the sake of her safety again. "I have much to do and cannot take you with me. You will be safe tied here."

"To a tree?" She lifted a disdainful brow at the idea.

"You have made it abundantly clear that I cannot trust you to remain with me, Mel. You leave me no choice."

The flexing of her delicate jaw hinted at the inner war she waged. "Roarke's wishes mean that much to you then, that you would kidnap a holy woman to please him? Are his desires so much more important than your own that you risk hellfire and damnation to give your spoiled brother what he wants?"

Her words, shot through with accusation and bitterness, were aimed to wound him. Everyone in his family had catered to Roarke, sometimes to the younger son's detriment. He had not turned into the most responsible of men, yet he had helped Lucian when he'd needed it most.

"I am willing to risk damnation because delivering you but scratches the surface of my debt to Roarke." He hitched a light crossbow over his shoulder, his eyes never leaving hers. It irritated him to explain himself to this woman, yet he owed her something for what she'd been through.

Roarke had found a way to protect their mother from the ugly truth that her eldest son had killed his foster father while learning the skills of knighthood from the country nobleman.

It hardly mattered that Lucian had been defending himself against one of Fitzhugh's legendary rages. Lucian couldn't help that the man's fury had been out of control. But he could have helped his own emotional reaction. He could have remained in control rather than allow his own anger to erupt.

Never again.

"The ruination of my life is repayment of your debt?" Lifted by the wind, her red hair fanned behind her in a righteous banner of indignation.

Lucian stared at her across the clearing, sorry she would come to despise him. Yet, as he felt the inevitable draw of her siren's body, the appeal of her vibrant spirit, he realized this was best. Her enmity would erect a much needed wall between them.

"The fulfillment of your childhood dream is what I sought, Mel," he admitted. "But even if you've come to equate that dream with your ruination, I cannot pretend I will not see it through." He turned to leave, eager to escape the censure in her eyes, the betrayal in her voice.

With a twinge of regret, he resigned himself to her hatred.

Melissande watched his retreating back in disbelief. Unable to tamp down the helplessness that rose like panic in her throat, she screamed at him as he left, calling him names no convent-bred woman should have known.

When it became clear he would not return to engage in a verbal sparring match, she stamped her foot in frustration.

She hated not being listened to.

Lucian's charming brother, Roarke, had ignored her no matter how she tried to capture his attention as a girl. Her parents had ignored her cries of refusal when they'd announced she would enter a convent. The nuns had ignored her pleas for release when she'd arrived.

Even Abbess Helen did not truly listen to her. As much as the elder woman seemed to care for Melissande, their relationship was not the sort where she could speak freely. Abbess Helen's position demanded that she be the teacher and Melissande be the student, the listener.

Perhaps that explained why she loved her children so much. They thrived on her stories and her attention. They listened.

Frustration made Melissande yearn to throw the cheese-cloth bundle in her hands, but she'd given in to enough childishness for one day.

She was trapped, and she wouldn't be leaving Lucian

anytime soon. For now she would make the best of a bad situation, and with any luck, the abbess would soon come to her aid.

Unwrapping the food, she felt a moment's pleasure at seeing a flint stone. She had not started a fire since girlhood, let alone prepared her own meal. That kind of work remained in the hands of a lower class of holy women who did not come from families as wealthy as the Deverells.

Scurrying about the clearing as far as her rope would allow, Melissande gathered kindling to start a fire, eager to try her hand at the task.

Oddly, a fond memory stole through her.

Plucking up the stone, she kneeled over the pile of wood and recalled the instructions of a long-ago voice.

You have to be patient with it, Mel…

Young Lucian Barret had taught her to make a fire on a fishing trip. Melissande had tackled the new skill with more enthusiasm than competence before throwing her hands up in disgust.

A small spark interrupted her recollections. Leaning over the dry sticks, Melissande fanned the spark with a soft breath.

Crack.

Snap.

The fire caught one twig after another, until the blaze burned merrily at her feet.

You did it!

Lucian's youthful voice, deep and rich even as a teenager, praised her in her memory. Patient as stone, Lucian had a way of encouraging her past her temper and soothing her prickly pride.

Funny that scene would come back to her now, so vivid she could almost touch it.

"You did it." The masculine voice rang through the

clearing, deeper and less animated than she remembered, but with the same words as the ghost of his youth.

Lucian stepped into the ring of firelight, rabbit in hand. The years had rendered him cold and distant where he used to be merely patient and reserved.

"You taught me well." Melissande rose to her feet.

Laying his weapon on the ground, he lifted a brow in silent contemplation. "I am surprised you recall."

Turning her head as he skewered the rabbit, she shrugged. "I've never had cause to light a blaze since our fishing expeditions."

"In ten years you've not needed to lay a fire?" With smooth efficiency, Lucian set the rabbit to cook and cleaned his hands with water from his wineskin.

"The work is rigorously divided at St. Ursula's." Melissande slid to the ground to wait for their meal while Lucian collected more wood. "Because of my noble ties, I was given more exalted chores than cooking and cleaning."

"I would think most women would be grateful." After propping a long log against a thick elm tree, Lucian lashed the two together with a short rope. The peaked wood made a framework to lay other sticks across.

"I was. That is, I am, grateful." Melissande gestured across the clearing. "I collected some long pieces over there."

Lucian peered through the dark behind her and started dragging over the other branches. "You certainly kept busy."

It wasn't exactly praise, yet Melissande warmed at his words. She made no reply, absorbed in the fluid grace of his movements.

"Your more exalted duties included supervising the abbey orphans?"

Melissande turned the rabbit, wondering if he sought to

make fun of her. "Do you not agree that nurturing children is one of God's most exalted tasks?"

"It is work I could never pretend to be equal to, Melissande. I am merely curious to learn if you had any other responsibilities."

Mollified, she returned to watching him complete the shelter. "I was only recently put in charge of the orphans. My other main task is translating manuscripts in the abbey scriptorium."

"Translation?" Lucian dusted his hands off and joined her at the fire. He sounded impressed, but Melissande was too busy sizing up the small sleeping quarters he seemed to be finished with.

"You're not done with that, are you?"

"I think it will be sufficiently warm." He turned back to look at it with a critical eye.

Melissande swallowed her embarrassment. "Aye, but not large enough for us both."

"You can't expect me to erect a keep for you each night on the journey home."

Leave it to Lucian to be utterly reasonable.

She took a deep breath and prepared to deal with him in an equally reasonable way. She had not spent ten years at a convent only to let her temper get the best of her. "I realize that. However, I am a novitiate, and I cannot conscience sleeping in such close proximity to a man."

"Neither can I conscience allowing either of us to catch our deaths because we're too self-righteous to sleep near one another."

Oh, how she envied his even tone, his facade of perfect sensibility. "I am sorry, Lucian, that my ideals lead you to believe I am self-righteous, but I will not have my reputation compromised by our sleeping arrangements."

"Trust me, Mel, your reputation will not be compromised. Roarke has complete faith in my ability to keep my hands off you.'' His tone made it sound as if he found the idea of touching her abhorrent.

She did not consider herself a vain woman, but it hurt to think the world viewed her as unattractive. Even more offended, Melissande fumed openly. ''I am not concerned with what your brother thinks of me, Lucian!'' Her voice rose to a perilous pitch. She would have to repent on her knees for this display, yet she could no sooner curb her anger than touch the sky. ''I only care about my reputation in the holy sisters' eyes. Do you think they will allow a fallen woman to care for the abbey orphans?''

Lucian edged closer. Gently imprisoning her arms in the vise of his hands, he demanded her attention.

Melissande went still. Not that she was scared, just... intimidated.

''You will have no cause to care for the abbey orphans again, because your arms will be full of your own children. You will not be going back, Melissande. Ever.'' Gray eyes burned into hers as surely as his touch heated her arms.

She could never be a mother, much as she might secretly long for such a fate. After all, what did she really know of mothering when she'd been torn from her own mother's side at a tender age?

''You are so sure that what you want will come to pass,'' she responded. ''Will you not at least consider the idea that I might refuse to wed your brother, and that he will gladly send an unwilling woman home?''

Lucian's grip on her tightened. She might have felt fear then, had not his expression softened at the same time. ''Wait until you see your home, Melissande. Have you not missed it?''

Home.

She had learned through the years it was better not to

recall the small Deverell property that had been as much a part of their family as she had. To mourn the loss of what she would never regain would have been foolhardy.

"Think on it, Mel." He moved closer, holding her gaze in his own. His voice lowered a notch, adjusting to persuade and seduce. "The soft slope of endless green hills. The cheerful gurgle of the brook you so loved to cross barefoot. Spring will be almost summer by the time we return."

His features glowed with the light of fond remembrance. Even the scar at his temple seemed to fade into the small wrinkles around his eyes as he smiled.

Her heart ached at the mental picture he created. Nostalgia almost choked her. It had nearly killed her to leave her close family as a child to take up residence with strangers. Her mother had begged her father to reconsider his decision to send their youngest to a convent, but in his haste to settle his youngest daughter his will prevailed. As it always had.

"And nary a snowcapped mountain in sight," Lucian continued, as if he sensed another one of her weaknesses.

Dear Lord, but she detested snow. A few bouts of lung sickness in the cold alpine winters had quickly cured any admiration she once had for the white gift of the mountains. Lucian eyed her expectantly.

"You miss it as much as I do," she observed.

His fingers released her at once.

"Nay." The word was harsh and cold. And an obvious lie.

He busied himself with removing the rabbit from the fire and dividing the portions equally between them. Strong, capable hands worked easily at the mundane task.

Melissande's belly rumbled, but she did not allow his diversion to distract her from her cause. She forced herself to eat several bites before asking the question that gnawed at her brain. "How long have you been away from home, Lucian?"

"Two years." He didn't even look up.

Wait. Curbing her impatience wasn't easy, but she suspected it would be necessary with him. She didn't want him to close the conversation altogether. "You've been in the Holy Lands all that time?"

"It is a misnomer to call that particular patch of land 'holy' anymore, Melissande." Lucian stared into the fire, lost in thought. "An untold number of men have been murdered there to secure that ground for one greedy ruler or another. I cannot imagine a place more profane."

She crossed herself. "How can you blaspheme God's purpose?" She knew that war gave men an excuse to indulge their bloodlust, but at least the purpose of the Crusades was noble.

"'Tis man's purpose to hold the land, not God's."

"Why would you go crusading if you don't believe in the effort?" She almost could not believe her ears. All the women of St. Ursula's devoutly supported the efforts to reclaim the Holy Land.

Abruptly he stood. Flinging the clean bones far into the woods, he effectively announced the end of the meal. "It is past time we should be abed."

All thought of foreign wars dissipated in the fear he wrought with a single pronouncement. Melissande sat rooted in place.

"We have a long ride ahead of us this week." He took out a pile of tightly folded linens from his bag and laid them out beneath the makeshift shelter. "It will be difficult enough for you as it is. I want you well rested."

The firelight, muted by the passing hours since they had stopped, flickered over him as he worked to straighten the blankets. Cast half in shadow, half in warm bronze light, he embodied the two contrasting aspects she could not reconcile—blasphemous heathen who would kidnap a would-be nun and patient childhood friend who would never harm her.

He stopped suddenly, as if reading her silent thoughts, and regarded her long and hard.

"I am sorry, Mel."

He closed the space between them with such purpose, she momentarily feared he would pick her up and toss her into the bed. But he walked right past her to the tree that held the other end of her rope. With quick efficiency, he untied it. "There is a creek not a stone's throw from here. You may ready yourself for sleep alone, but if you are not back shortly, I will have to retrieve you myself."

Requiring no more urging, she hurried out of the clearing toward the water. There was no sense trying to escape him now anyway. Much as she feared sleeping next to him, she wouldn't sacrifice herself to the wolves in her haste to depart.

Cautiously she picked her way through the dark, plagued by the knowledge that the nuns would never take her back if they knew she had spent so much time alone in a man's presence. Rather, they would take her back, but she would never be permitted to supervise the children again.

She scrubbed her face and hands, the icy water spurring her to work quickly.

Only one solution presented itself. She could not, under any circumstances, share such a small space with Lucian Barret.

Trudging carefully back toward the newly stoked fire, Melissande took deep breaths for courage as she thought how she would explain herself to him.

"Here, Melissande, you'd better take the inside." He

waited for her near the pile of logs he'd crafted into a shelter for their night's sleep.

"You are welcome to tie me to this tree again, Lucian, but I think it best for us to sleep further apart than that refuge allows." She halted on the other side of the blaze.

The old Lucian, the one she'd known as a child, would have at least listened to her. The new Lucian, the steely warrior who could kidnap her and keep her bound to him, crossed the camp in a blink and scooped her up in his arms. "We cannot afford to lose sleep to arguments, Melissande."

She had a brief impression of his body, that wall of rock, pressed against hers before he tossed her into the far corner of the moss-covered sanctuary.

"The fact is, you will freeze to death if I allow you to sleep unprotected from the mountain winds." He lifted one end of her rope and tied it about his waist, then lay beside her.

Melissande's heart thrummed in her ears. It wasn't right for him to be so close.

Pulling more blankets over her, he carefully tucked them all the way around her until she was wrapped in a woolen cocoon. He stared down at her without a hint of remorse for her distress. "I will not allow you to be harmed in any way, Angel."

The endearment hung between them, creating even more intimacy than their shared linens. She closed her eyes to shut out the kindness she saw on his face. His gentle care surprised her into compliance when she should have stood her ground.

She perceived the covers shift slightly and sensed Lucian relaxing beside her.

Releasing a breath she did not know she had been hold-

ing, Melissande allowed the warmth of their pallet to lull
her to sleep.

As she drifted between waking and dreaming, it occurred
to her she could not recall the last time she had felt so
protected.

Chapter Five

Upon awakening the next morning, Melissande enjoyed a moment of utter contentment before recalling her whereabouts. In that instant she appreciated the peace of being well-rested, the joy of breathing fresh mountain air while still wrapped in cozy blankets, and the knowledge of her complete safety.

Then the sounds of Lucian breaking camp penetrated her brain.

Sweet Heaven, how had she ended up in such a predicament?

Melissande remained still, needing a moment to gather her thoughts before she faced him again. The warm feelings still lingered, taunting her with the knowledge that she wasn't as removed from her worldly desires as she would have hoped.

Obviously she was not as self-reliant as she presumed, or she wouldn't have slept so blissfully at the notion of having a man beside her to protect her. She found the idea highly disturbing. Not in ten years had she slept soundly at the abbey, yet one night by Lucian Barret and she awoke completely refreshed.

She should have been busy worrying about her immortal

soul last night instead of resting contentedly in the presence of his strength.

"Come along, Melissande." Lucian called to her across the camp.

Perhaps if she feigned sleep, he would allow her to lie here a moment longer. She still had not planned her next move.

Suddenly he stood beside the shelter, leaning down over her. The nearness of his voice startled her. "If you want time to go the creek, you must arise. You've already slumbered too long."

As soon as she heard his boots depart, Melissande darted from the pallet toward the creek, the rope around her wrist dragging after her. She wouldn't be deprived of that moment of privacy. Wearing one of her blankets like a robe, she hastened through the trees to the water's edge.

The sun sat well above the horizon. Normally she had to awake for the day's first prayers in utter darkness. No wonder she'd arisen so rejuvenated today.

She washed her face and rinsed her teeth, then considered her options for escape. The further she strayed from St. Ursula's, the less hope she had of finding her way back alone.

But no matter how much she told herself to focus on a plan, the beauty of her surroundings kept intruding on her good intentions. Birds sang in the trees, a few hardy spring flowers fought valiantly for a bit of morning sunlight, and the creek burbled a happy rhythm as it made its way down the mountain.

Despite her circumstances, Melissande felt curiously alive. Patting her face dry with a corner of the blanket, she promised herself she would find a way to escape today. And this time, she would take the horse and let Lucian worry about finding his own way home. After all, he was a strong, grown man.

Very strong, and very grown in fact. There was something oddly appealing about the breadth of his shoulders, the uncommon height of his body.

Lucian regarded her with his shrewd gray gaze as she approached.

"I am ready to break the fast," she noted, trying to keep her voice light. Morning would have been the best time to escape, if only she hadn't slept so late.

Lucian pulled the blanket off her shoulders and quickly rolled it up. "Late risers must take their bread on horseback." He shoved the woolen roll into the saddlebag and pulled out a heavy crust of bread. "Hold this, and I will hoist you up."

"We cannot leave yet!" If they departed now, she would have no hope of slipping away until nightfall.

His arms fell to his sides. "And why not?"

He suspected something—that much was clear from the cynical lift of his brow and the too reasonable tone of his voice.

Melissande wished for a good lie to inspire her, but her mind concocted only feeble excuses. "Eating while riding makes me ill." Her cheeks burned. She felt as if their high color branded her a liar to all the world.

Lucian lifted the corner of his mouth in a pale shadow of a smile. "Your constitution has weakened considerably then. I believe I once watched you devour a whole batch of apple biscuits while seated upon that fat little pony of yours."

"William." Her heart wrenched at the memory of the sweet creature.

"Yes, William." He snorted. "What a sorry excuse for

horseflesh. How many biscuits did you slip the poor animal when no one was looking?''

''I'm sure I don't know what you mean.''

''Just as I'm sure I don't know what *you* mean when you say you cannot eat while riding.'' He reached for her and, before she could step back, hoisted her in the air and seated her atop the gray mare.

So much for her plan. She had just lost any hope of a daytime escape. She noticed, however, that Lucian had forgotten to tie them together. That would surely make it easier to slip away if she found an opportunity tonight.

He handed her the bread before vaulting onto the horse's back behind her. Melissande was too hungry to pout over having to eat while riding. Eagerly she took the bread and tore into one of the crusts.

''Do you know where we are?'' Melissande asked between bites. ''Or how far we will travel today?''

He remained silent so long she assumed he did not hear her.

''Lucian,'' she started more loudly, wondering if the years of war could have affected his hearing abilities, ''do you know how—''

''I heard you.'' He turned the mare down a steep grade.

''Surely it cannot tax your concentration too much to answer a simple question,'' she observed, hoping she could be as unflappable as Lucian today.

Watch kept over mouth and tongue keeps the watcher safe from disaster, she counseled herself in Abbess Helen's absence.

''Nay, it does not tax my concentration.'' As the horse picked its way down the sharp incline, Lucian's body pressed tightly against hers.

The solid breadth of his chest reminded her of his much

greater strength, tempted her with thoughts about his body she knew she shouldn't be entertaining.

Distracted by their intimate contact, Melissande almost overlooked the fact that he did not answer her. "Then why can you not satisfy my question?"

She waited a long moment for him to answer. As the horse swayed, Lucian's body brushed across hers, creating a wave of oddly pleasant sensation in her breasts and belly.

"I could answer you, Mel, but I won't." His words were disconcertingly close to her ear, heightening the shivery awareness that Lucian's touch had ignited.

She swallowed the last bit of bread, her mouth suddenly dry at the effect of his warm whisper. Struggling to appear unaffected, she cleared her throat. "And why not?"

"Because the only reason you wish to know our plans today is so that you may calculate a plan to run away from me."

Was she that transparent? Melissande opened her mouth to dispute the truth, but before she could speak, Lucian continued.

"I am astounded that a clever girl would continue to plot such a rash scheme, Melissande."

His stern words halted the musical dance of tingles down her spine. Which, she told herself, was definitely for the best.

"Leaving me now would be more than foolish, it would be downright dangerous. If you are so convinced Roarke will release you when he learns of your unwillingness to wed, why not bide your time with me until he returns you to the abbey?" He sounded reasonable, yet for the first time, Melissande wondered if Roarke really would let her go.

"I have thought of that," she admitted. It seemed silly to equivocate with him when he could practically read her mind. "But I am worried about my reputation if I am gone for that long. I fear I will not be put back in charge of the orphans under those circumstances."

She also feared marriage to a warrior who possessed the power to give her precious babes and the frightening ability to take them away again at his will. She would not mother children destined to be pawns in any man's elaborate schemes for power. Just as she had no wish to become part of a family that could be torn apart again.

The horse stumbled just then and Lucian's heavy arm snaked around her waist to steady her. Heat licked through her whole body.

"Your charges obviously adore you. The good sisters of St. Ursula's would be remiss if they did not put you where you would do the most good."

"Do you truly think so?" Her heart lifted. Maternal pride filled her. She turned around to see his face, wondering if he believed his own words.

"Absolutely." His gaze held hers, steady and unblinking.

He meant it.

"That is not to say I think you will be going back," he cautioned her. "I don't believe you are the kind of woman who is made for convent life. My guess is you will quickly remember what you used to love about England and find yourself happy to be home."

Melissande tried not to listen. She could never seriously contemplate life outside St. Ursula's. The orphans aside, she would not form a family with a power-hungry warrior who would have no concern for her wants.

"But if you should ever return to St. Ursula's," Lucian continued, "I have the utmost confidence the nuns will put you where you will do the most good. And that is with the children."

Warmed by the sentiment, she shifted in her seat to look up at him. Their gazes connected, locked, stole her breath.

She forgot all about their conversation and what she might have said to him. Lucian's nearby mouth captured all of her attention. Dangerous thoughts, yet so tempting.

Lucian's eyes strayed to her lips, a curious light in their gray depths. If she closed her eyes would he...

A noisy rustle in the trees jolted her from her sensual musing. A flash of red soared through the sea of evergreens surrounding them.

"Oh, look, Lucian! A bird!" A harbinger of warmer weather, she rejoiced at the return of the more brightly colored fowls—and the distraction from the absurd notion of kissing Lucian Barret.

She needed to redirect her thoughts. Fast.

Watching the bird until it flew out of sight, Melissande thought about what Lucian had said and sighed. "You are kind to compliment my abilities with the children, Lucian, but perhaps you do not understand the rigidity of convent life. The keeper of the future generation must have the most pristine record."

"You mean to tell me *you* had a pristine record at St. Ursula's?" The horse reached more level ground and Lucian allowed the mare to amble along at her own pace.

She couldn't stifle the laughter that rose in her throat. "Fortunately, Abbess Helen did not hold my earliest years at the convent against me."

"You were a child, Mel." He pointed high into the trees toward a fluttering patch of color. "There's another one."

She watched the red bird hop from limb to limb, surprised at the easy rapport she shared with Lucian today.

Perhaps she ought to wait until they reached England, then she could speak to Roarke directly. Much as she wanted to return to St. Ursula's, it seemed futile to fight Lucian and highly dangerous to escape.

She forced her thoughts back to their conversation. "Plenty of children go out into the world at tender ages. Most pages are younger than eight summers. Yet I childishly fought the nuns at every turn."

"You expect too much of yourself."

"So do you," she ventured, surprised to realize they shared that much in common.

"I need to expect much of you, lest you disappear whilst I sleep."

"Nay. I mean you demand much of yourself, as well."

He stiffened behind her. "I am not sure what you mean, Melissande." He slapped the reins lightly across the horse's back to gather speed. "But I suspect we have endured enough idle chatter for one day."

Quelling the urge to vent her frustration, Melissande wondered what nerve she had struck to make Lucian Barret retreat so fast. But she would sooner be struck by lightning than utter one more bit of ''idle chatter'' for him to denounce.

Sealing her lips, she settled in for the long ride.

Lucian couldn't make the mare go fast enough. With two people riding such rocky terrain, the horse could only cover a limited amount of ground in a day. Yet he needed the pound of hooves in his head to drown out Melissande's words. *You demand much of yourself.*

How had she seen so much, so fast?

The woman was more clever than he'd realized.

Lucian recalled her vibrant spirit from their youth. The fact that she adored spring birds and craned her neck to see every bit of nature did not surprise him at all.

He had been prepared for her loquacity. Melissande had

liked to talk as a girl and he could see that much hadn't changed.

But he did not recall such an insightful mind. Or such tempting lips, for that matter.

Apparently the years at St. Ursula's had changed her more than he realized.

As the terrain sped by in a blur of new green grass and melting mountain snow, Lucian wondered how he could keep his distance from her.

They headed west as the sun traveled its arc in the sky. The mountainous terrain slowly gave way to more gentle slopes and low hills. Lucian knew they could encounter other travelers this way, but their journey would be faster and easier.

Several leagues before the next trading village on their route, he spotted a church ruin in the distance. Though the sun was nearly set, the crumbling stone sat on a hilltop that caught the last of the fading rays.

He felt more than heard Melissande's swift intake of breath as she spotted the site. The rosy sunlight painted the ruins in majestic colors, resurrecting a more noble past for the faded little country chapel. Lucian could almost hear her mind at work.

Yet she refused to break the silence he had imposed. It had been thus all day long. She now sat, visibly yearning to see the ancient holy place yet too stubborn to tell him.

It was a bit out of the way, Lucian thought, but perhaps the ruins would keep her too busy to ask him provoking questions tonight.

Shifting his grip on the reins, he guided the mare up the hill.

"Oh, Lucian!"

Her sudden delighted gasp caught him off guard, but it

didn't begin to prepare him for the sincere look of gratitude she tossed him over her shoulder.

"Thank you." She smiled.

His heart caught in his chest.

The kindness in her eyes cast a light in his soul as fleeting and precious as the setting sun on the crumbling chapel wall. Then she turned back to the church and the light vanished as if it had never been. The only reminder that it had existed was the race of Lucian's heart, the horror in his conscience.

How could he view his brother's future wife with such fondness? The gentle sway of her body to the rhythm of the horse's walk became suddenly unbearable. The wind seemed to torment him by catching a strand of her vivid red hair and teasing it across his cheek.

Lucian felt certain the gates of hell swung even wider for him at that moment.

He yanked on the rein with little consideration for the dappled mare. "I'm walking." Vaulting from the horse's back as if demons chased at his heels, he rushed to put distance between him and Melissande.

"I'll walk, too," she offered, leaping awkwardly from their mount before he had a moment to protest. "It is a lovely evening."

For you, maybe.

Darkness settled like a thundercloud around Lucian. As much as he had always genuinely liked Melissande, he found he could not enjoy her company with this new strain of attraction mixed into his general admiration for her.

How in Hades would he suffer through the long trip back to England?

They reached the peak just as the last ray of light bathed the ruins in a final streak of pink. Melissande ran to stand in the center of the crumbling walls, as if eager to place herself at the heart of the light.

Lucian told himself to start unpacking the saddlebags, but his body ignored his brain's commands and he stood there staring at her.

"Hurry, Lucian!" she called, smiling and breathless. "You'll miss it!"

Turning toward him, Melissande held out her hand to invite him into the magical place of light she inhabited alone.

Her hair seemed to catch fire in the sun's farewell offering, as if she were touched by Heaven itself. His fiery stolen angel. It dawned upon him that she was utterly untouchable. Any marriage to his brother aside, Melissande had still declared herself devoted to her faith and her God.

As for him…his faith had died with Osbern Fitzhugh that fateful day two years ago. Lucian Barret was not just forgotten by God. He was—would always be—unforgiven.

Chapter Six

Gut instinct, honed from years in battle, warned him to remain safely outside the chapel. A man so lacking in honor as Lucian had no business enjoying a sunset with a noble-woman.

He had ignored Melissande all day, however, and guilt niggled him.

Leaving the mare to search for new grass, he stepped up onto the remains of the old stone church floor and joined Melissande. Through a moss-covered archway, they viewed the last tiny slip of a brilliant orange sun.

"I've never seen its equal," she whispered with low reverence, her smile beatific. "It is so very lovely."

"Don't they have sunsets at the convent?"

She sighed, oblivious to his sarcasm. "The enclosure walls are too high. Even if you manage to scramble to the top—" she smiled sheepishly "—the trees and mountains obscure the view."

He envisioned her, hellion that she'd been, climbing the sheer rock walls for a view of the world. He'd do well to remember that behind her mild manner, the hellion still lurked.

"You will see countless sunrises and sets when you re-

turn to England.'' Lucian held her arm just long enough
for her to step down from the platform of the stone floor.

Touching Melissande posed risks to his self-control that
he could never have foreseen.

He moved to sort through the supply bag, eager to sever
the unwanted intimacy of the chapel. He tossed her the
remaining food stores before disappearing to hunt for fire-
wood.

Melissande watched him go, wondering how she had offended him this time. She could not endure another evening
of silence after their total lack of conversation on the road
today. Even at the abbey she spoke her prayers aloud. With
Lucian, her pride demanded she not speak to him after he'd
chastised her.

How dare he! He had captured her for selfish reasons.
The least he could do was—

He had abducted her, and now was her chance to escape.

Although Melissande still wore the rope around her
wrist, she had not been tied to a tree or to Lucian or to any
other immovable object.

Her eyes strayed to the tired gray mare. It seemed cruel
to run the animal into the ground, but what choice did she
have?

After dropping the food stores on the ground, Melissande
made her way over to the horse. Debating which direction
to head, she prayed she could hoist herself up on the tall
mare's back.

''I am but a stone's throw from you Melissande,'' a familiar masculine voice called from the inky blackness surrounding the camp. ''You would be most unwise to try.''

By Ursula's sainted wimple. Would the man never relax
his guard? She stomped her foot in frustration, promptly
kicking a root and stubbing her toe.

Curse words bubbled in her brain but she did not give

them vent. *In the sin of the lips lies a disastrous trap,* she told herself.

"Are you all right?" Lucian's voice grew louder as he approached her from the shadows.

Just who she didn't want to see.

She hobbled on one foot, annoyed he had witnessed her tantrum and even more irritated that he decided he could talk to her *now*, when she verged on spitting mad. "I'm fine," she returned sharply, hobbling to take a seat on one of the flat stones scattered about the ruins.

"You are injured." He stepped into her vision, which was very close considering the vast darkness of the moonless night. "If you will not take care of yourself, Melissande, then I will care for you."

The urge to be contrary warred with the pain in her toe, but seeing the look of quiet insistence on Lucian's face, she mutinously stuck out her foot.

"Ten years in a convent has not managed to save you from your own temper, I see." He removed her slipper with more delicacy than she would have thought a hardened warrior capable. Warm fingers brushed over her thin stocking, causing chills to chase their way up her leg. He cradled her ankle in his lap.

"Not for lack of trying, I assure you." She rather hoped he would berate her for her temper—an argument would be infinitely preferable to this warm feeling his gentle caress inspired.

"You broke the nail and are bleeding right through your stocking." His thumb stroked its way over the pad of her foot and down the inside of her sole.

Did he even realize he touched her thus? In the dim light, she could only see that he studied her foot intently.

"Oh, dear." Surely she was a wicked woman to allow

him to touch her this way. "I'll see to it myself, thank you."

She attempted to pull away, but he held her fast.

"It would be easier for me to wrap." His hand strayed up to her ankle then hesitated.

The unfamiliar touch of a man's hand on a place so sensitive touched off a chain of little sparks from her toe to her thigh. All feeling narrowed to the one point where his fingers paused.

He glanced down at his hand where it brushed over her thin woolen hose. She saw the muscle of his jaw twitch and flex, as if he might be annoyed. Apparently there were no sinful sparks leaping through *him* at their slight contact.

"I'll get it," she insisted, pulling her foot from his lap and swiveling away from him.

He remained there, frozen, making Melissande more nervous with each passing breath. Did he think her a wanton that she would allow him to handle her so intimately? By the saints, he certainly knew she'd tried to protest.

"Perhaps that would be best," he muttered before striding back toward the horse.

Melissande fumbled with her stocking, her foot much colder now that Lucian had gone. Carefully she removed the broken nail and tore a square of her hose to wrap about her foot.

Makeshift bandage in place, Melissande realized Lucian had the fire going right beside the church ruins. He had already hauled over their linens and was rolling them out around her.

Warmth stole through her, having much more to do with the peculiar comfort she found in Lucian's presence than any blaze. She had not realized how lonely she was for human contact and companionship.

Not that Lucian afforded her much companionship, she thought, recalling their quiet day.

But he provided her with a sense of security she hadn't experienced since childhood. For all his gruff manner and resistance to conversation, Lucian had made it clear he would protect her at all costs. He wouldn't allow her to sleep in the cold and catch another case of lung fever. If she escaped, he would be close behind to rescue her from potential harm.

As much as he frustrated Melissande, she had to admit there was a certain amount of honor in the sentiment.

Strange to find such a noble quality in a mercenary knight.

Materializing before her, Lucian held out his arms. "You will be more comfortable over here." He nodded to the blanket closest to the fire.

He offered her his arm but she refused to accept it. His proximity confused her, unsettled her.

"I can manage." She pushed herself up with her arms to keep the weight off of her foot and settled herself on the pallet in front of the fire.

"You look a bit flushed, Melissande." He balled up an extra linen to prop her foot. "Are you sure you are well?"

Of course she wasn't well. Lucian had her thinking thoughts no proper convent-bred woman would ever dare to entertain.

"I'm fine." Except for the skin that still tingled where his fingers had grazed her ankle. "Thank you."

To distract herself from foolish thoughts, Melissande watched him dole out the remaining food, carefully dividing the meat and bread evenly.

"Perhaps we will come across a village tomorrow," she suggested, hoping she didn't sound overly interested.

Lucian looked around the fire for a moment, as if wondering if he should sit out on the ground rather than beside her on the blanket-covered chapel floor.

Melissande acknowledged it was kind of him to consider her sensibilities as a holy woman. Still, the nurturer in her wouldn't allow him to take his meal on the cold ground. She scooted over a little.

"Sit here, Lucian. I think it would be admissible considering the circumstances."

Despite his skeptical expression, he dropped down beside her. He seemed content to eat and stare with brooding eyes into the fire, but not Melissande.

"It must have been a beautiful chapel," she observed, enjoying the dance of firelight over the moss-covered rubble. Like the setting sun, the glow of the flames animated the cool stone and resurrected the divine spirit of the place.

He said nothing.

Perhaps she would have better luck if she formulated a direct question. "Do you think the architecture is native or—"

"Roman." He didn't even bother to look up from his bread.

Disappointed, Melissande sighed. "I don't remember your being so closemouthed, Lucian. Is it just around me that you don't want to talk, or are you like this with everyone these days?" Perhaps she meddled where she should not, but if she were to be in close company with this man for another sennight, she refused to be utterly ignored. She detested not being listened to.

"It is not just you, Mel." The resignation in his words belied the meager grin on his face. "Doesn't your good book tell you, 'In the sin of the lips lies a disastrous trap'?"

Fortunately the firelight would hide the rising color she felt in her cheeks. Abbess Helen had chastised her with that very proverb more times than she could count. Her indignation refused to be cowed by his cleverness. "You think I talk too much?"

"Absolutely."

Anger spurred her on. "Recall, sir, our spiritual teachings also tell us that 'The mouth of the upright is a life-giving fountain.'" She had never dared to try that retort on the abbess. It would have sounded too prideful. With Lucian, however, she did not care.

He pulled a small stick out of the dirt by his feet and tossed it into the flames. "Do not forget the rest of that one, Angel... 'but the mouth of the godless is a cover for violence.' I think that says it all quite nicely."

Could she have understood him properly? Either he was really insulting her or... "Are you suggesting that you don't talk much because you think you are godless?"

"You're a smart woman, Melissande. Make of it what you will." Pushing to his feet, Lucian packed away the empty cheesecloth and retrieved a new wineskin from his bag. He held it up for her to see. "Does the mouth of the upright wish to partake of a good Burgundy tonight? Or will sharing a skin with me profane the experience for you?"

She had never seen this Lucian before. Something cold and dark lurked in him—something far more dangerous than the facets she had seen thus far. Lifting her chin, she readied herself for another round of his strange verbal sparring.

"I enjoy a good wine."

Fire leaped in his gray gaze. With his dark hair and jagged scar, he looked like the devil himself. Tempting but dangerous, Lucian Barret was probably not a wise choice for a drinking companion, yet some rebellious spirit within her wouldn't let her say no to the challenge in his eyes.

"There's my girl." Returning with the wine, he sat a bit

closer to her than he had before. He smiled down at her with a mixture of pride and some other nameless emotion that forced her to scoot a little further down the blanket from him. "I wondered where the old devil-may-care Melissande had disappeared to."

Melissande accepted the wineskin from him and took a long drink. "She is tempered with a more practical spirit these days." The wine blazoned a trail down her throat and filled her with a delicious sense of abandon. She'd not taken more than the small sips used in communion in ten years.

He reached over her to retrieve the Burgundy. The brush of his arm against hers caused her skin to tighten and tingle right through her heavy gown.

"What you mean to say is that she has been tamed by the convent," Lucian replied dryly.

"Hardly!" She sat up straighter, surprised at Lucian's direct approach. Apparently when the man decided to talk, he didn't waste time dancing around a subject. "I have acquired a fair amount of wisdom in the last ten years, Lucian."

He looked out over the dark hills from their high vantage point. The wind caught his hair and rippled through the fabric of his loosened tunic, yet the man himself remained unmoved.

Melissande wondered if he would retreat into silence again now that she had disagreed with him, but a few moments later he passed her the wine and spoke again.

"I can see your new wisdom, Melissande. Though I'll warrant you've acquired it on your own in the scriptorium as opposed to on your knees in a drafty church." His tone was lighter now, as if he no longer sought to provoke her.

Pride filled her at his easy recognition of her learning. Yet her desire for humility forced her to argue. "I hope I have cultivated equal knowledge in both places." She turned her attention to the wineskin and drank deeply, welcoming its warmth. The fiery drink seemed to invade her bloodstream all at once and spin through her senses.

"You need not be so humble with me. I can see for myself what sorts of intelligence you have obtained."

As he turned to look at her, Melissande felt transparent. He did see.

Entirely too much, in fact. Those gray eyes probed the depths of her soul, recognizing her strengths and more numerous weaknesses.

"You have the advantage of me then." Caught off balance by his scrutiny, Melissande struggled for equilibrium. Too bad the wine had already robbed her of it.

He loomed so close, she could have touched him if she lifted her hand.

"And how is that, Angel?" A surge of emotion kindled in his gaze. He seemed closer still.

"You seem to understand me, yet I cannot fathom you." She cleared her throat, vainly trying to dismiss the heat that curled through her at his proximity. "I have no idea what sorts of intelligence you have gained since I last saw you, but I can tell you have been exposed to some unhappy circumstance."

He loomed no more.

Sinking away from her, Lucian closed his eyes and rubbed his temples with one hand.

She couldn't quit now. Not when she was so near to learning something about him. "Why are you so changed, Lucian?"

When he looked up again, his eyes were shuttered and dull, the devilish gleam she'd spied earlier had vanished.

"I will not dredge up my past to entertain you, Mel, no matter how curious you might be." The muscle of his jaw flexed with obvious irritation, but his eyes reflected a deep pain she knew was not of her making. "Do not ask me about it again if you wish to have any sort of communication between the two of us."

She nodded, recognizing this was not a good time to belabor the point. Whatever troubled Lucian to the point he thought he was godless must be addressed. She couldn't stand to see her old friend consumed by unhappiness, even if he was a warrior.

"Yet I find it rather difficult to fall asleep without talking," she finally ventured, hoping she did not push him too far.

He groaned in protest.

"How did you ever manage abbey life?" He shook his head with slow resignation.

"There was usually somebody praying somewhere at all hours of the day. The chant of it helped lull me to rest." *God forgive me for the slight untruth. I only want Lucian to talk to me.*

"Very well then." Surprisingly he sounded suddenly chipper. "I seem to recall you brought a book with you from the convent."

Oh, dear. This was not at all what she envisioned. "Yes— I thought you put it in your bags."

He grinned, the first smile of genuine pleasure she had seen from the somber Lucian Barret. "Then I shall read to you, and you can fall asleep to the sound of my voice."

Crossing the camp to retrieve the heavy, leather-bound volume, he looked far too pleased with himself.

She wouldn't learn anything about him this way.

"You are no doubt familiar with the work?" he called, yanking her one possession from his bag.

Two years familiar. "Aye. Homer and I know each other very well by now."

Waving the book above his head like a tournament prize,

he called, "Why don't you ready yourself for sleep while I choose a spot to start in here? There is some privacy on the other side of the chapel, I believe."

A moment to herself…maybe this could be the break she'd been looking for—

"And don't forget, I will come to get you myself if you are not back with all haste."

How could she forget? The brute also stood two feet from the horse as if to ensure she would not steal it.

Grumbling about the ill effects of being tied to a man, Melissande picked her way through the rubble to the deserted side of the church.

He did it again, she thought as she loosened her gown's lacings for easier sleep. He'd foiled her attempts to draw him out even a little bit about his past. She should have known better than to blurt out her questions with no semblance of subtlety.

Yet curiosity consumed her now. A mystery lurked around Lucian Barret, and she vowed to decipher it. Like one of her more complex manuscripts, Lucian's secrets begged her to unravel their hidden meaning.

Removing the plaits from her hair, she wound the strands into one long braid for the night and considered the man who had abducted her.

Although a soldier of God, he called himself godless. Although the eldest Barret son, he concerned himself with procuring a wife for his younger brother, as if Roarke were the heir. Although a patient, mild-tempered youth, Lucian had transformed into a hardened warrior who hungered for battle.

A definite mystery.

And as long as Melissande remained his captive, she considered it her duty as a religious woman to help him face his demons and recapture the heart he seemed to be lacking. Any God-fearing person would do the same for a childhood friend, she assured herself.

Certainly it wasn't just curiosity, although that particular character trait had brought the childhood Melissande one piece of mischief after another.

Maybe her interest had more to do with the glimpses she'd seen of Lucian's still generous spirit. She had to admit it had been rather kind of him to trek up to the chapel ruins to camp tonight just because he knew it would please her.

Unfortunately she suspected she would not accomplish much confronting Lucian in the guise of religious counselor. She might have a better chance of reaching him if she appealed to him as a friend. Secular logic would work more effectively with her self-proclaimed "godless" companion. He'd had made it very clear he did not hold the church in high esteem these days.

But could she set aside the convent teachings that had become such a part of her and simply talk to Lucian, woman to man? The idea held a note of danger, but she had to approach him in a way he could respect.

Gathering her courage about her like a protective shield, she picked her way through the crumbling ruin before she changed her mind. Could she do it?

Not giving herself a chance to reconsider, she stepped into the ring of firelight where Lucian sat thumbing through her book. Tonight, she would employ all her subtlety to extract a hint of Lucian's mysterious past.

Tonight, she would seek to recapture the camaraderie they'd known as children.

Lucian looked up and her heart pitched in unsteady rhythm. He had grown considerably in ten years. Why hadn't she noted his raw masculine appeal before now?

He did not have the face of a classically handsome man.

Rather, Lucian possessed a visage impossible to look away from. He fascinated her on some simple, elemental level.

The realization stole her breath.

Melissande saw him through new eyes—a woman's eyes. In the soft flow of firelight she absorbed every detail of Lucian's broad shoulders and muscular arms, his thick black hair that brushed the collar of his tunic.

She swallowed.

Hard.

Yet as their gazes met over the leaping fire, Melissande knew her instincts for approaching him were correct. If she hoped to understand him, the time to encourage conversation was now. Tonight. While he was sipping a good wine and already amenable to talk.

She closed her eyes against the dark appeal of the man and told herself that he was still the same person underneath it all—the same honorable young man—just as she was still the same girl inside.

And she missed him. Perhaps she missed her old self just as much.

Tonight, to learn the truth about Lucian, she would resurrect the bold and brazen Melissande.

Chapter Seven

Melissande Deverell could have tempted a saint with that fiery red hair and siren's body. When she stepped from the shadows, Lucian saw a ghost of her former self, the rash-and-reckless Melissande grown to a spirited woman.

Definitely a dangerous combination. How could a woman who looked like Melissande be a nun?

The Almighty must have a sense of humor.

Now, to top off the Lord's evening of fine jests, Lucian found he couldn't read Melissande's damn book.

"This is in Greek." He swiped the blasted volume through the air.

"Yes, most copies of Homer are—"

Lucian could see the exact moment realization dawned. The moment she recognized the flaw in his otherwise extensive education.

"It only makes sense, of course," he returned. "However, I cannot read Greek." The confession did not come easily to a man who had little left to pride himself on but his academic achievements.

She took the book from his hand and sat beside him, her unbound hair brushing over his arm. Her gentle, composed air warned him she would try to comfort him. He didn't think he could sit still through it.

Many failures weighted Lucian's shoulders, but intellectual flaws were not usually among them.

"No one can read every language," Melissande observed with studied nonchalance. She flipped through the pages to avoid eye contact.

Which was just as well. He might strangle her if he saw even a twinge of pity in her gaze.

"I draw the line at Sanskrit." She shuddered, her hair dancing an accompanying shimmy to her movements. "I cannot begin to interpret it, though I do a fair job of copying the letters."

A little of the weight lifted from Lucian's shoulders. She couldn't possibly know what a balm the words were to his spirit.

"I speak a passable Sanskrit." He couldn't have held that admission back if he tried. It seemed important that she not think him completely uncultured.

Admiration lit her brown eyes even more than the leaping blaze at their feet. "Truly?" She clapped her hands in delight. "I wish you could see some of the books at the abbey, Lucian. The illustrations look so interesting, but I cannot comprehend the text that goes along with them." Her brow furrowed in frustration. "Can you imagine how vexing it is to spend months copying a manuscript you cannot interpret?"

"I have a fair idea." Lucian tapped the giant Greek volume in her hand.

"At least you do not have to stare at these pages, day after day, knowing you are destined not to understand them." Her face clouded, her voice hinting at well-guarded bitterness. "It is a cruel torment to mindlessly copy books without being able to ponder their ideas as you work."

He found himself curious about who would force her to do a job she clearly resented. It was the only remotely negative sentiment she'd uttered about her beloved abbey.

"You have no choice in the matter of what books to copy?"

"Sister Eleanor chooses what I shall copy as a matter of whether she is pleased with me or not. When she is most spiteful, she gives me Sanskrit, but sometimes—" She crossed herself in obvious horror at her own words. "Father, forgive me."

Poor Melissande. Although she had always been a touch temperamental, Lucian had never met a more good-intentioned soul. Surely she never did anything so wrong as to deserve a job she detested.

He took an instant dislike to Sister Eleanor. "Melissande, you need no forgiveness to speak the truth."

She wrung her hands together. "It is wicked of me to call her spiteful."

"She sounds spiteful to me."

Melissande cast him a scathing glance.

At least she didn't look so guilty anymore. But it couldn't hurt to rile her a bit more to be sure. "Besides, I could call you temperamental and you wouldn't think *me* wicked."

"Temperamental?" Indignation straightened her shoulders and lifted her chin.

"Since you have a temper to match that flaming red hair, I don't feel like I need to ask forgiveness for pointing out the obvious."

"Ooohh!" She clenched her delicate fingers into a fist. The fire in her brown eyes leaped and sparked.

Lucian knew her youthful counterpart would have slugged him.

All too soon, she calmed herself, however, and adopted

the practicality that seemed so at odds with everything he remembered about her.

"Well, it may be true that I have my fair share of temper, but it is unkind to point out people's failings." She smoothed the leather cover of Homer, then straightened her skirts. The busy flutter of her hands suggested she was not as resigned to quiet acceptance as her words intimated.

"That is why I prayed for forgiveness for pointing out Sister Eleanor's shortcoming. Surely she does not mean to be spiteful."

Some demon pushed him to spar with her. Some downtrodden part of his own pitiful soul longed to see her at her most feisty. "Like hell she doesn't."

Her fist flew at him from the far side of her body. He saw it coming—expected it—but he made no move to stop it. Curiosity made him wonder what kind of punch she could muster after all these years.

With a sound "smack," her knuckles connected with his upper arm. He couldn't help but feel proud at how much muscle she managed to leverage into that punch.

He grinned.

In fact, a strange sensation washed over him that he hadn't experienced in years. He let his head fall forward with the weight of it.

Laughter.

"Are you all right?" Gingerly she touched his arm where she'd just pummeled him. "Lucian?"

He could no longer keep it in. As her questing fingers ran up his shoulder, the laughter bubbled up from a long neglected place in his heart.

"Lucian?" She did not sound so concerned this time. Irritation mingled with the last vestiges of her worry. "Are you laughing?"

Good Lord, she was a prize. Propping his elbows on his

knees, he held his head in his hands to keep from falling over as good humor assaulted him.

"How dare you!" She now shoved at his shoulder, full of righteous anger. "If you think that was a paltry attempt at a punch, Lucian Barret, let me assure you, I can do better."

He laughed harder. "I don't doubt it, Angel." Reaching across her body, he plucked up her hand and lowered his voice to a conspiratorial whisper. "Too bad you didn't try it out on Sister Eleanor."

She stared at him for so long, Lucian thought she might get offended all over again.

Then, like the sun venturing out after a long rainy spell, Melissande giggled.

And giggled.

"You're horrid!" She jabbed him with her elbow. Once. Twice. Three times, before collapsing in giddy mirth against his shoulder.

Something warm unfurled in Lucian at the unthinking friendliness of her gesture. Something tender and precious and completely misplaced clutched at his sorry excuse for a heart.

Oh, God.

He froze, but Melissande didn't seem to notice amidst her laughter. She held her belly in joyous abandon, head thrown back and eyes closed.

Her pose was far too replete, too satisfied, too… sensuous.

"Melissande." What had he been thinking, baiting her like that? He knew better than to resurrect the woman of his dreams.

Didn't he?

"Melissande." He half shouted at her now, unable to

bear the torture of her sweet body against his for even a split second more.

She righted herself immediately, resuming the contrite look that he'd sought to banish only moments before.

Damn.

Thinking fast, he sought his mind for a diversion, a way of putting some space between them without invoking the rule of silence he'd forced upon her today. "Perhaps you could read to me tonight, in light of my lack of Greek?"

The dubious look in her wary brown eyes told him she sensed some ulterior motive on his part. Yet her naïveté prevented her from seeing his real inner struggle.

His body was still warm where she'd touched him, a burning imprint of her vibrancy against the stark backdrop of his cold existence.

"Certainly." Dutifully she opened the book and Lucian had a brief impression of her at the abbey two days ago when she'd read to the children. She had laughed and frolicked then, too.

No wonder she loved the children with such devotion. They answered the suppressed longings of her heart, giving her a place to bestow all that vividness and life she had to offer.

"We might as well start at the beginning." She smoothed a page of parchment with reverent fingers while Lucian's heartbeat slowed. "Perhaps we can read as we ride tomorrow."

"If you like." Perfect. It would save him from infernal conversation that only led him into revealing more of himself than Melissande should know.

She launched into the *Odyssey,* translating the text easily as she read.

As she wove the tale of the Greek hero Odysseus, Melissande wondered at Lucian's peculiar behavior tonight.

Obviously he did not want to forge any sort of friendship with her, else he would not have pushed her away after teasing her into such merriment. Like a well-defended keep, Lucian erected stolid borders around himself to discourage any infiltration.

Still, he sat near her as she read, warming her far more than the lively blaze by their feet. He could not be all that displeased with her if he was willing to sit idly by and listen to her read.

The stars winked in the heavens, rendering the perfect setting for a story. The cool night air above them and cold stone floor below them provided a pleasing contrast to the crackling fire that burned alongside the crumbling stones where they rested.

Melissande relaxed into her role as storyteller, welcoming the chance to indulge in a well-loved pastime.

Was it vanity to enjoy the sound of one's own voice? She sincerely hoped not as reading out loud ranked as one of her dearest pleasures. The trip of Homer's gorgeous images off her tongue thrilled her anew.

Lucian interrupted her early in her tale. "You see how constant and faithful Penelope is?"

Jerked out of the story, Melissande blinked to clear her thoughts and lowered the book. "Faithful, indeed, to wait twenty years for her husband to return from war."

"Yet your heart is so fickle you forgot all about the man you claimed to love in a mere ten years."

Did he mean to tease her, or did he condemn her? Annoyed, Melissande lifted her book again. "Shall I continue?"

He leaned back on the blanket and propped himself on an elbow to listen. "By all means, lady. You are a natural-born troubadour."

The compliment tickled her to her toes. Deep into the

night, Melissande read. As the fire waned and cooled, Lucian tossed her a blanket to wrap herself in, but not once did he suggest they put the book away.

Lost in the magic of the narrative, Melissande found herself adopting voices for the characters and theatrics for the gestures. When the hero Odysseus landed on yet another ancient island, she acted out the part of Nausikaa, the foreign princess who fell madly in love with the wandering Greek and begged him to remain by her side for all time.

Though he refused, gallant Odysseus departed with the chivalrous sentiment, "All my days until I die, may I invoke you as I would a goddess, Princess, to whom I owe my life."

"Melissande?" Lucian's whisper halted her before she began the next stage of the poetic journey.

"It is beautiful, isn't it?" She loved the romance of the tale, the obvious love between Odysseus and Penelope no matter how much time they spent apart. Yet despite Odysseus' love for his wife, he took care to be gentle with Nausikaa's feelings as he left her.

"You can hardly see the page anymore, Mel." He pointed to the dwindling embers and her close proximity to the tiny flame that remained. "You will fall into the hot ashes if we don't admit defeat and go to sleep."

Reluctantly she closed the book. "But it is a beautiful story, is it not?"

He pulled the volume from her hands and wrapped it in a portion of his woolen blanket. The care with which he handled her prized possession touched her.

"I am surprised Sister Eleanor allows you to read something so pagan." He sifted through the pile of linens around Melissande.

A grin pulled at her lips. "She doesn't realize how fluent in Greek I am."

His wandering hand brushed against her leg in his quest to find something among the wool coverings. Unnerved by the sudden contact, she jumped. "Can I help you find what you're looking for?"

He held up the forgotten rope that trailed from her wrist. "I already found it."

She experienced a moment's hurt that he didn't trust her in the least, although she knew that made no sense. He shouldn't trust her. Melissande would leave him if he gave her half a chance.

No matter how she told herself she understood Lucian's reasoning, the reminder of being forced to travel to England with him robbed the night of its sense of shared adventure.

After cinching the knot at his waist, he met her gaze. They had been sitting close together before, but now that the rope connected them, their bodies were so close they almost brushed against one another.

"I have no choice." Earnest gray eyes dulled in the fading light, Lucian's voice held a note of empathy. "I cannot allow you to come to harm, Melissande, and it is infinitely dangerous for a woman to travel the French countryside alone at night."

He didn't understand. Would never understand. Stung by the realization that they would never recreate the friendship they once shared, Melissande shook her head. "And you must understand that I, too, have no choice. I could no sooner forget my young charges at the abbey than I could give up my own children. No woman would give up her babes without a fight."

"They are being well taken care of, Mel. You know that."

Her heart ached at the thought of her children being well cared for but never loved. "But the person they have come to depend on most has abandoned them. And I am sorry,

Lucian, but I do not consider myself replaceable in their eyes. None of the other sisters will love them so completely as I do.''

Lucian leaned forward until naught but a hand span separated them. ''And you know why that is, Angel?''

She might have offered some reasons, but she knew he did not seriously wish for her to answer him. Besides that, she found it difficult to formulate a thought when his face hovered so close to hers.

''It is because you were not meant to be a nun.'' Though his words rang with mild frustration, he softened them with a light sweep of his hand across her cheek. ''You were meant to be a mother.''

Melissande's soul-deep shudder answered his touch. The hardened palms of his hand fascinated her. The delicate brush of his heavy fingers at her temple caused her flesh to leap with tingling awareness.

''You care for those children with your whole heart because you were fated to be a mother and bear little imps of your own.''

Her womb contracted in hungry acknowledgment of his words. How could he see the depths of her heart, her most carefully guarded secret, when he had known her but two days since their shared childhood? But no matter how much she yearned for motherhood in her heart, in her mind she acknowledged it could never, ever be. She had been torn from her own mother's side unwillingly because her father had wanted her to serve his own political ends. Bad enough she'd had to leave her own mother. How would she endure having a child taken from her to serve a husband's ends?

Still, she didn't even think of denying Lucian's claim. No matter that it could never be, she could not have disputed the fact.

Looking up into his eyes, she saw Lucian about to retreat. Instead of learning his innermost secrets tonight, he had somehow divined hers.

In the course of an evening, he had stirred the deepest hungers of her soul and now he planned to just roll over and go to sleep without so much as a "Sorry to force you to confront the biggest sorrows of your life, Mel." Just who did he think he was?

Unwilling to weigh the risks to her actions, Melissande drifted closer to Lucian's warmth, his strength. Strange that she would seek comfort from the very man who had unsettled her in the first place. But he had instigated this intimacy and she was not ready for it to end.

A moment's doubt reproached her when Lucian's eyes widened and his huge warrior's frame stiffened to stone. Was her proximity so unappealing? No matter—the wild tangle of emotions Lucian had dared to call forth would not be quelled by any fear of rejection.

She longed for the healing comfort of human contact, needed to assuage the gaping emptiness in her heart.

With trembling fingers, Melissande reached to stroke his face the same way he had skimmed hers. Some inner demon urged her roving touch down to the contours of his mouth, straying on the fullness of his lower lip.

His flesh was warm and surprisingly soft. Perhaps she had discovered the only part of this man that wasn't hewn of rock. Perhaps he was not incapable of tenderness, after all. Surely such a pliant mouth knew how to speak gently— to spout words that would soothe her heart rather than break it with too much insight.

No doubt such a mouth could kiss a woman gently, as well…

For one breath-stealing moment, Melissande envisioned Lucian's lips upon hers, his mouth tasting her with the same delicate care he used when drinking his fine Burgundy.

Heat flooded her cheeks, her limbs. Whether from embarrassment or from desire for that kiss, Melissande couldn't be sure. She glanced up at Lucian, half wondering if he would be able to divine her thoughts now as well as he had earlier. Would he be able to see her hunger for his touch?

His gray eyes glittered almost black in the fading firelight. As their gazes connected, his seemed to absorb hers, and Melissande could feel herself being pulled in by his watchful stare.

Then his eyes narrowed a fraction, jarring her from her sensual thoughts.

What was she doing? Her heart thumped the walls of her chest so hard she thought it might cause the very ground to rumble beneath its rhythm. She had no right, no business, touching Lucian Barret.

Later she would be ashamed by this brazenness. The wildness in her faded under the press of guilt and recrimination, so she moved to lower her hand.

Her fingers had barely left his lips when Lucian braced her forearm in an ironlike grip. He held her there, hand in midair. She wondered at the restrained power she felt in his grasp and assessed the mix of emotions on his face.

Anger. That was there in full measure. Was he angry because she'd touched him or because she'd stopped?

What fascinated her more was the other emotion she saw in his eyes—something hot and restless and akin to hunger that made her feel edgy and languid with heat at the same time.

Or maybe she merely absorbed the heat that emanated from him. Tense and palpable, the waves of warmth rolled off him and around her, drawing her forward in spite of the threat of impending storm in his eyes.

"Angel." He whispered it with husky reverence.

The strange tangle of emotions in her belly twisted and tightened even more hopelessly.

Then his mouth lowered to hers, just as it had in her wayward daydreams, and she forgot to be frightened or intimidated. He grazed his mouth across hers with infinite gentleness, as if she were the most fragile of creatures.

Sparks shimmered behind her eyelids as her breath caught in her throat.

Oh, my.

She slid her wrist free of his loosened grip and placed her hand on his shoulder. In the warmth of the fire, Lucian had loosened his hauberk, leaving naught but his tunic to cover his chest. Melissande slid her fingers across the soft linen, tracing over the wealth of muscles surrounding his shoulder.

She wanted to explore those muscles, to trail her fingers over every hard plane and nuance, but she could not concentrate on the effort while he kissed her, while his thigh pressed against her own.

Sensation enveloped her, dazzled her, fed her hunger for touch and fueled it at the same time. She could only think about pressing closer, and closer still.

A slow melting effused her limbs.

Her mouth opened in a joyous little sigh at the sensory heaven of it all, and Lucian lost no time deepening his kiss.

A flood of heat swept through her, pooling in the womb whose emptiness had started this whole delicious journey.

The scent of him, only half realized until now, filled her nostrils with hints of campfire and leather.

"Lucian." She moaned the name with all the new longing of her awakened body, yet the moment she uttered it, he seemed to regain his senses.

He froze, his arms turning to wooden weights around her and his lips leaving hers to the rapidly chilling night air.

Frustration churned through her.

"Lucian?" She wanted to drag him back to her, though she knew it was already too late. Her body thrummed with sensations both terrifying and glorious. How could he leave her?

"My God."

More damning than the more vitriolic curses she had heard from him, the oath confirmed her fears that Lucian regretted the kiss.

Regretted touching her.

In the sin of the lips lies a disastrous trap... The proverb took on a whole new meaning now.

"I'm sorry," she murmured, wishing she had not called forth her former self on an idiotic mission to win Lucian's confidences tonight. If she had maintained her hard-won reserve and the air of piousness she ought to project, none of this would have happened.

Instead she had simply been herself.

With stiff movements, he removed the blankets from his body and placed them over her in a ritual she now recognized as some sort of self-imposed penance. "It is not your fault, Melissande. Good night."

The clink of his sword settling along with him against the cold stone floor echoed in the night long after the sound itself.

With it, Melissande's recriminations reverberated in her mind, disparaging her for ever resurrecting the girl of her youth. She folded her hands to pray, then beseeched God to send Abbess Helen to her—soon.

The sooner Melissande escaped the enigmatic pull of Lucian Barret, the better.

Chapter Eight

Lying on his back in the chilly air of the decaying chapel, Lucian counted stars until they faded. The roof of the church ruin had long ago fallen to crumbled bits on the ground, leaving him plenty of space to study the heavens.

Watching the gold-fingered dawn claw its way across the sky, he could not decide if he welcomed the new day.

He had not slept all night. Each deep breath Melissande took reminded him of the liberties he had taken with his brother's intended wife.

Two years ago, after Osbern Fitzhugh had died of a sword wound inflicted by Lucian's hand, Lucian did not think he could sink any lower.

Last night proved him wrong. To add to his sins of pride and violence, now he must add the grievous moral wrong of lusting after his brother's future bride.

And Lucian had more reasons than most men to honor his brother. Hell, he owed Roarke a debt he could never repay. Roarke had lied to their mother about the circumstances of Fitzhugh's death to protect her from the ugly truth. Roarke had shouldered Lucian's responsibilities as heir when Lucian relinquished his claim to the title.

Thank God their birth father had not lived to see the day

his eldest son would raise arms to a Fitzhugh. The families had fostered one another's sons since the reign of William the Conqueror.

Although the arrival of the new day marked his chance to depart the church ruins full of taunting memories, Lucian could not be certain he relished facing Melissande this morning any more than he'd enjoyed the torment of sleeping beside her last night.

And it had been torment.

He'd had an easier time dodging Saracen blades than he'd had shutting out the memory of Melissande's body pressed to his own, her generous curves straining closer to him with every breath. Hell, it was all he could do even now to keep his hands off her while she slept a few feet away.

As the glimmer of dawn brightened, Lucian struggled to come up with a plan to address the events of the previous night.

Melissande's kiss.

Try as he might, he knew he would never forget her questing touch, the softness of her fingertips as she stroked them over his mouth.

What had she been thinking? No, damn it. He knew what she'd been thinking. He just still couldn't believe she'd been thinking it. About *him*.

For all her attempts to be reserved and her quest to return to the convent, Melissande still possessed the brazenness he remembered in her as a girl. In fact, all evening he had seen her, not as a nun, but a woman.

Lucian imagined what it would be like to wed a vibrant spirit like Melissande Deverell. She would fill a man's days with intelligent discussion and excerpts from the *Odyssey*, and she would fill his nights…

Of course he had no right to imagine that scenario at all.

Imagining, however briefly, had only led him to act on his dreams and to accept the kiss her tentative touches had seemed to invite.

No more.

The kiss would remain in the forgotten ruins of the churchyard, and he and Melissande would never speak of it. Perhaps the encounter merely revealed to her that she was not meant for the convent.

The sooner he delivered her to Roarke, however, the better.

"Melissande." He used his most authoritative voice, thinking if she saw no hint of friendliness in him today, she would not broach the subject of what transpired between them. Heaven knew, Melissande loved to talk. "Wake up."

He did not linger over her. A glimpse of red hair springing free of its wayward braid was enough to inspire inappropriate thoughts. Instead, he stalked about the camp, packing the flint and scattering the ashes from the fire while she rose.

Sometime during the night, he had untied her. As wide awake as he had been, he would not have missed any attempt to escape.

If she noticed, she did not comment, but disappeared around the back of the chapel to prepare herself for the day. Lucian moved to the nest of blankets she'd vacated, hoping to roll them quickly and to pack so they could be under way.

He did not count on the scent of her in the still warm linens. He breathed in the lingering perfume of her clean hair and the dried flowers that must have been packed around the merchant wife's clothing.

Disgusted with himself, he dropped the blankets and started rolling them into tight bundles for the saddlebag, hoping Melissande would keep her thoughts to herself today. He could barely tolerate his own recriminations. He didn't think he could face hers, too.

Melissande watched Lucian from the cover of a crumbled rock wall as he attacked the bed linens with a vengeance.

Combing her fingers through her hair, she wondered how best to broach the subject of their kiss with him. They needed to discuss what happened and to clear the air so it did not hover over them like a rain cloud.

Besides, she needed reassurance that their stolen embraces didn't mean anything. If she examined the events of the evening too carefully, Melissande feared what she might discover—that she really was not meant for the convent, that ten years of her life had not taught her a whit of practicality or quiet reserve.

Judging from Lucian's fierce scowl, however, a discussion with him would not be easy.

Washing her face with the water Lucian gave her, she considered their shared kiss and the night she'd spent at his side. Once again she'd slept better than she had in years, even with the weight of her sins on her shoulders.

Something about Lucian's presence comforted her on the most fundamental level. He gave her a sense of protection, security, she had not known at the abbey. At St. Ursula's she fended for herself. Here, she knew Lucian would fend for her, too.

Braiding her hair more tightly, she fought the softening of her heart toward a warmongering knight. The kiss had been an honest mistake—the result of her tortured feelings at Lucian's learning her deep desire to have a baby. Melissande had not known what to do with the wealth of unhappiness his insightful words had caused and she had turned to him for some measure of solace.

The fact that it had led to a kiss was a mistake, and certainly the fault of her inexperience with men.

It would never happen again.

Mind made up and hair neatly plaited, Melissande marched from behind the church ruins as Lucian finished the packing. The more this festered, the more worried and guilt-ridden she would be about it. If only he would talk to her…

"Lucian, I've been thinking—"

The cold look on his face stopped her midsentence. Distant eyes flashed her a clear warning. "Not today, Melissande. Not now."

They stared at each other a long moment, taking each other's measure. No match for a man of his quiet intensity, Melissande looked away first, uncomfortable under his scrutiny.

"Fine." Her cheeks burned as her embarrassment grew. "But you only make it worse by pretending it didn't happen."

"We'll stop in a village today to trade for two horses and supplies. I expect you to stay close to me and to keep quiet for your own safety. Understand?" Lucian tied the bags to the mare's saddle, his movements quick and precise.

So much for fostering a friendship between them.

"I've been trained to be obedient for ten years, Lucian, I wouldn't think of giving you any trouble." She flashed a bright smile, unwilling to let him silence her again.

His wary look told her he didn't believe her for a moment, and Melissande couldn't have been more delighted. She had forgotten the fun of teasing and laughing. His playful ribbing the night before had reminded her how soul-lifting such merriment could be.

Before their enjoyment of the evening went too far.

Watching Lucian fling one leg over the dappled gray's back, Melissande admired his fluid grace and strength. She felt that easy power for herself when he hoisted her up in front of him.

The brief touch brought to mind a wealth of memories from the fireside encounter—his arms wrapped around her, the soft brush of his fingers on her cheek...

Melissande guessed Lucian remembered the same things, for he yanked his hands back as if burned.

Giving up her habit had been a big mistake. As they began their trek toward the village, Melissande realized she should have fought Lucian on that count. Without that uncomfortable barrier between her and the rest of the world, Melissande felt less like a novitiate and more like an ordinary young woman.

As the morning breeze captured and teased a strand of stray hair over her cheek, Melissande also regretted the loss of her wimple. She had not gone out without her hair covered since childhood. While she didn't exactly mourn the stifling garment, she had to admit a wimple helped keep her in a more somber and reflective state of mind.

There were other, less obvious changes wrought in a mere two days. She no longer woke for matins and lauds, the prayer times between midnight and dawn. Feeling more rested probably called forth her inherent tendencies to make mischief. Melissande never realized how much bleaker life seemed when she was exhausted.

"I have removed the rope," Lucian announced amidst her cataloging of her new faults. "But I plan to resurrect it after we visit the village and get a second horse."

How comforting. "You think I'll run off with your horse?"

"You'd be gone in a heartbeat." His words rumbled against her back as much as she heard them with her ears. "I just don't want you to waste your morning plotting an escape that has no chance of happening."

"Most considerate of you, Lucian." She paused a moment, surprised for the first time at how easily she used his familiar name. "Or I suppose it is 'my lord' by now, isn't it? Your father must have already given you some title or another."

"My father is dead these five years."

"I'm sorry—"

"He died peacefully. There is nothing to be sorry for."

"That means you are the earl?" How could he be off kidnapping women from their convents with such weighty responsibilities to consider?

"I've given over that honor to my brother." He retreated into the rock wall she remembered from the day he stole her away.

"What?" She pivoted in her seat to look at him. Searching his face, she saw no clue, no telltale reason for this unheard of gift. "You just handed over an earldom to your brother?"

"Aye." His jaw set to granite. His lips compressed into a thin, hard line that mirrored the colorless scar at his temple.

"You would make a wonderful earl," she protested, horrified he would relinquish something that meant so much to him. "You had grand plans for your family lands. I remember—"

"They are my lands no more. Any plans I might have had for them died—" His gaze leveled with hers in a clear warning not to pry. "Roarke is handling the responsibilities very well and with my eternal gratitude."

"But—"

"So you see, Melissande, you'll be wedding the earl, after all." Covering her lips with one finger, he silently pleaded for her to drop the subject.

Her heart caught in her throat at a fleeting image of marrying Lucian Barret.

"I will not be wedding anyone." She turned around to stare straight ahead. Or maybe to chase the vision of herself with Lucian from her mind. "And I resent your implication that I would concern myself with marriage for rank and privilege."

"What other reason is there to tie the matrimonial knot?"

How could he be so obtuse? Obviously the years had stamped out any tender feeling in his heart. "Being a nun, I'm sure I wouldn't know."

"You are not a nun," he promptly reminded her, steering the horse toward the small village in the distance.

Melissande gave up talking to him. For now.

Obviously his mood ran to grossly contrary today and she had no desire to bring his wrath upon her head.

The sun had risen to its full height, warming the day to a degree Melissande had never enjoyed in the alpine mountains before.

"We are truly in the lowlands now, aren't we?" She looked around with satisfaction, forgetting her decision not to speak to him.

"The rest of the trip will be easier. We will move much faster on separate animals."

In no time she'd be standing before Roarke Barret, explaining why she couldn't marry him and why she must return to the convent.

Then she would face being censured by the convent community and blamed for something that wasn't her fault. She knew too well how St. Ursula's politics could demand the most unfair punishments.

Once a young girl had been dismissed from the abbey because it had been discovered that a boy who adored her had been tossing notes and little trinkets like flower chains over the wall to the object of his affection. Although the girl had done nothing to encourage such behavior, she had paid dearly for the boy's actions.

Melissande's heart had ached when she learned the girl's family could not afford to take her back after her convent dismissal and she had been cast out on her own.

Melissande prayed, long and vehemently, that Abbess Helen and her army would come for her soon. The more time she spent away from the abbey, the greater the chance that her fellow sisters would think she had been up to mischief of some sort.

Dear God, the longer she spent away from the abbey the greater the chance she *would* get into mischief.

Witness last night's kiss.

Caught in thought, Melissande scarcely noticed their arrival in the tiny trading town.

"We can trade horses here," Lucian announced, reining in beside a small stable. "If you stray from my side so much as a hair's breath, we will leave immediately atop that poor broken-down mare together."

She itched to retaliate in some way, but could not afford a childish indulgence. *A mild answer turns away wrath, sharp words stir up anger,* she recalled, remembering one of the abbess's favorite proverbs.

"As you wish." She fell from the horse into his arms, righting herself quickly to ward off the inevitable twinge of awareness his touch provoked.

He raised a brow, but did not question her professed obedience. Instead he pulled her along behind him toward the back of the stable, looking utterly unaffected by their brief contact.

After haggling with the stable master, Lucian procured two horses for their journey home for a few coins and the trade of the gray mare. Relieved to be excused from the intimacy of sitting in front of Lucian for another day, Melissande looked forward to riding her own mount.

She visited with the new horses, one chestnut and one black, while Lucian bartered for food supplies.

Disappointed that Lucian would tie the reins from her horse to his own, Melissande considered explaining to him that she would not try to escape him again, but thought she would be wasting her breath.

Now that they were so far from St. Ursula's, it would be foolhardy to strike out on her own. Besides, she had faith that Abbess Helen would receive Melissande's message soon and come to rescue her.

Of course, she could not tell Lucian that. It might help the abbess if Lucian were surprised by her contingent's arrival.

She stroked the black filly's nose, hoping Lucian would come to no harm for abducting her. As much as she had been inconvenienced and frightened, she would not want him punished for something he thought she would ultimately appreciate.

He was different from most warriors she had met. His enjoyment of the *Odyssey* hinted at a scholarly temperament at odds with her bloodthirsty image of knights.

The man read Sanskrit, for St. Ursula's sake. There was more to Lucian Barret than killing and destruction.

"We are ready," he announced, stealing up behind her with a sack of food for the journey. He withdrew two strips of beef and two biscuits before securing the sacks to his saddle. "We dine on the road, Melissande." His grin wrinkled the scar on his temple, the pale line practically disappearing in his good humor. "I hope you shall not be too ill to eat and ride at the same time."

Wrenching her portions out of his hand, she stabbed a defiant foot into the filly's stirrup and in the process lifted her knee much higher than she ought. "I'm sure I'll manage somehow."

His gaze narrowed to the short length of leg her action bared and remained there as he boosted her up. "I just hope I will," he muttered, turning to the chestnut mare.

Both horses were quick and light, bred for swiftness and distance. Melissande thrilled to the feel of the wind on her face as they barreled out of town at twice the speed they had ambled into it.

Lucian had indeed tied her reins to his saddle, but her lack of control over the filly hardly tainted her rush of joy at the steady drumming of horse hooves beneath her.

Such a simple pleasure...and one she had gone without for so long.

For leagues they raced over the hills, the towering Alps an impressive backdrop to the east. The spring air swept by them, warmer and heavier than the cool mountain breezes Melissande had shivered through for a decade.

The sun hovered low on the horizon before Lucian slowed their pace. The horses grew tired, and Melissande's legs ached from the unaccustomed activity, but she blessed the day nevertheless.

Her hair had long come loose from its braid. During the wild ride she had gladly let it whip in the wind behind her. Now a tangled mass of curls tumbled over her shoulders in a sensuous fall that tickled her neck and warmed the bare portion of her shoulders.

Life without a wimple had its merits.

She followed Lucian to a copse of trees, watching his back sway in the saddle, his body silhouetted in the amber light of dusk. Unbidden images of their last sunset sprang to her mind, along with the events of the night that followed.

Memories of their kiss had teased at the corners of her mind all day. For Lucian, who had no doubt experienced his fair share of kissing, the event might not have made such an impression. Yet Melissande recalled every heated nuance, every touch and taste they had shared.

Realizing for the first time why the convent preferred virginal members, Melissande could see how the memory of a man's arms could distract a woman from more lofty concerns. She had only experienced so much as a kiss and she found it difficult to concentrate.

Imagine if their shared caresses had led to more.

By the time they stopped, Melissande could not look Lucian in the eye for fear of betraying her musings. Astonished at the vividness of the mental pictures she created, a blush crept up her neck and heated her cheeks when he approached her.

She distracted herself by trying to recite a psalm, but when his hands snaked around her waist to assist her from the filly, Melissande knew she had no hope of distracting herself.

Ever observant, Lucian ducked under her lowered chin to see the expression on her face. "Are you unwell?"

Her heart raced as if he could read her mind. Foolish, perhaps, but Melissande had never been able to lie or to hide her feelings with much success. "I am fine," she mumbled, jerking from his grasp. "Just a little winded… and my foot is a little sore from where I hurt it yesterday."

He looked skeptical, but bent forward to examine her foot.

As he did, a loud swooshing sound streaked past her head.

Even ten years in a convent did not make a woman forget the sounds of death and destruction. The sound of men and battle.

An arrow stuck in the tree where, only moments before, Lucian had stood beside her.

"My God—"

Before she could utter a prayer, Lucian yanked her down to the ground beside him, where he fell to his belly. "Be still."

Fear thudded through her at the watchful, predatory expression on Lucian's face. He peered out into the falling twilight, utterly still and dangerous.

"What was—" she hissed, only to be shushed with his fingers to her lips.

"Arrow," he whispered, his eyes never straying from his smooth visual sweep of the surrounding terrain.

The evidence still stuck ominously in the tree behind them. Short black feathers had been cropped and dampened to give the weapon just the right speed and distance.

And if Lucian had not bent to check the foot injury she'd lied about, he would be dead beside her right now.

Instead of daydreaming about Lucian's embrace, she should have been remembering that his way of life represented everything she abhorred. While Melissande had dedicated her life to God, Lucian had dedicated his to war.

He might be an old friend, but Lucian Barret was also ruthless and dangerous, a trained killer. And no matter how sweetly he kissed her, he was—and would always be—a warrior.

Chapter Nine

Lucian watched Melissande's face go ten shades more pale, then cursed Roarke for getting them into this mess. Why the hell couldn't his brother have married a nice girl from Northumbria and have done with it?

Instead he'd sent Lucian on a fool's mission to retrieve a woman he'd probably tire of in two year's time. Fickle, spoiled Roarke had always been able to charm their mother, winning his own way since he was a babe.

Of course, fickleness aside, Lucian owed him. But, Christ, this had been a lot to ask.

If anything happened to Melissande because of Roarke's sudden hunger for a convent-bred wife, Lucian would personally kill him.

It wouldn't be the first time he had raised arms against a loved one.

Damn.

"I don't see anyone," Melissande whispered, edging closer to him in a rustle of leaves and sticks.

He gritted his teeth in a fresh wave of frustration. Couldn't the woman even be quiet in a life-and-death situation?

At the same time, he grudgingly admitted her incessant

chatter was part of her charm. Her cheery demeanor and vibrant outlook made brooding difficult, even for Lucian.

Gently he lifted his fingers and placed them over her lips. His irritation with her grew in direct proportion to the desire that flared in reaction to her soft mouth.

His heart hammered against the ground beneath them, partly in ill-timed longing, mostly in genuine fear.

He had joined the Crusades two years ago on a mission of penance, not caring whether he lived or died. But now that he served as Melissande Deverell's guardian in a dangerous world, he could not afford to let anything happen to himself.

Without his protection, God only knew what might happen to such an innocent.

Her lips twitched beneath his touch. He glanced at her, not surprised to see her wide-eyed and gesturing in clear supplication to speak.

Fortunately she honored the command of his glare, but not without a definite internal struggle. By now he knew she detested being quiet.

Soon a deceptive calm settled over the outcropping of trees, encouraging him to investigate with caution. Signaling to Melissande to stay put, he crept forward through the brush, waiting and watching for the slightest movement.

A sudden pounding of hooves and flutter of birds scattering sent him diving back to the ground to lie over Melissande, the noise startling him into protective mode.

Hand on his sword, ready for trouble, he listened to the horse's hooves recede to the south, unwilling to believe the real threat had departed.

Refusing to move, he waited, every instinct on alert.

After a long, quiet moment, an elbow caught him in the gut from underneath.

"Can we get up now, please?" Her slight wriggle beneath him shifted his focus from fear to lust faster than a Moor's blade.

Their bodies stretched on the ground in one fluid line, his sealed over hers in a manner that called to mind the most primal of procreation positions.

Only the veil of her hair and a few layers of clothes separated their skin.

Heedless of any threat but the one a certain red-haired woman posed, Lucian couldn't scramble to his feet fast enough.

"Of course." Blood pounded in waves through his body, restricting the flow of thoughts to his brain. He stared down at her prone form in the underbrush. *Damn.* What the hell was the matter with him?

Extending a marginally steady hand to Melissande, he helped her to her feet. He dropped her fingers as soon as she regained her balance.

"What do you think that was about?" Her voice trembled through the question, her complexion startlingly pallid as she stared at the arrow protruding from the tree near their heads.

Lucian gave himself a mental shake, willing himself to forget the impression of lying above her. He studied the red marks and black feathers on the instrument of war until a small amount of concentration returned. "It is well shot," he noted, his mind slowly beginning to emerge from the fog of lust. "My guess is an assassin. Perhaps someone sent by the abbess to reclaim you."

"Abbess Helen would never allow one of her men to kill you without so much as speaking to you." She looked unsettled by the suggestion. Indignant even.

He shrugged, wondering if she could be as naive about her convent sisters as she seemed about the rest of human nature. "I cannot think of anyone else who would know we are together."

Her eyes narrowed to shrewd slits. "Unless it is someone who seeks only you."

One name came to mind at her words.

Damon Fitzhugh.

Perhaps Osbern Fitzhugh's true son had finally learned of his father's death and had come to seek revenge.

Of all the timing…Lucian had prayed Damon would find him in the Holy Lands and end the torment of his guilt there. But after two years he had seen no sign of the English knight in the ranks of Crusaders.

"Lucian?"

Lucian had witnessed bloody battle after bloody battle, but always he emerged, healthy and whole except for his heart and soul. And now, when he could no longer afford to indulge his guilty conscience, when he was charged with the most important mission of his life, his former friend-turned-enemy had come to extract vengeance.

It makes no sense.

"What makes no sense?" Melissande asked, her color slightly returned.

Had he spoken his thoughts out loud? "It is nothing." He strode to the tree and yanked the arrow from its lodging with both hands.

"Apparently it is something," she insisted. "Do you have an idea who did this?"

Examining the device carefully, he ignored her. His head still swam with worries he had not foreseen.

If Damon Fitzhugh had finally decided to seek revenge, wouldn't he have done it with his family colors to honor his father? Noblemen did not *hope* their enemies knew who attacked them. They emblazoned their banners, shields and arrows with their colors to announce to the world their identity. To do so was a matter of family pride.

A commodity the Fitzhughs had never lacked.

"No, I don't know who did this," he told her, relieved he could be honest about this much. "If you don't think it is an emissary for the abbess, then I have no idea who would want to kill me."

The suspicion in her eyes seemed to fade as he met and held her gaze.

She trusted him.

The knowledge stung him with his unworthiness.

"But for a moment you thought you had an idea," she wheedled, pinning him with the intensity of her stare.

How did a sheltered woman see so much?

"That has nothing to do with you." Lucian moved toward the horses with determined steps, hoping he could successfully put her off the scent for once. "What does concern you is our new route."

Melissande's breath caught and hitched in her throat as Lucian led her horse over. "What new route?"

His resolve wavered at the thought of touching her again. Her unbound hair draped over her shoulders like a russet robe, both regal and wanton.

"We go back into the mountains." Lunging for her waist in an effort to get it over with, Lucian unwittingly threaded his hands through the veil of hair that surrounded her. Skeins of the silky strands brushed his palms where he held her.

"To St. Ursula's?" Her voice held a gleeful note of possibility.

He strode to his own mount, loathe to squash her hopes again. "Nay. We will merely follow the alpine route through France until we are much further north."

They needed time to escape into the rocky passes that

separated the mountains from the hills where it would be easier to elude an enemy. Lucian hoped the sun would not sink too soon.

"It is even colder as you go north," Melissande returned sullenly. He could almost detect the shiver in her voice.

"Better cold than dead," Lucian observed, unwilling to debate their path.

Dark shadows lengthened before them while daylight slipped behind them.

"So I've tried to tell myself on many a frosty eve," Melissande mumbled, braiding her hair again as they plodded toward the shelter of the Alps.

Lucian hated the thought of backtracking to the mountains, but it took him by surprise that Melissande did, too.

Normally he would let the matter drop. Now, however, after Melissande's fright and knowing she would have to ride for many more leagues, Lucian thought it couldn't hurt to distract her with her favorite pastime—talking. "You have not enjoyed the Alpine views St. Ursula's provides?"

They journeyed slowly up the rocky inclines leading back into the mountains. Cool air descended upon them, as much from the encroaching twilight as the slight rise in elevation.

"The abbey setting is lovely." Her dismal sigh said otherwise. "In fact, I rather appreciate the remoteness of the place, the utter quiet that pervades. The never-ending winters are what depress me. Sometimes it seems like we'll never see the sun again."

As recently as two days ago, Lucian would have used that knowledge to press his brother's suit and to encourage her to stay in England.

Not now.

Her blatant honesty exposed a facet of Melissande he

had only guessed at—her deeply hidden misgivings about convent life.

He stared over at her in the growing dark, her pale skin the only part of her that remained visible. Seeing that creamy white skin in the ominous mountain shadows reminded Lucian of her delicate nature. He cursed his brother again.

"Perhaps you have forgotten English weather in your long absence, Mel. The winters are bleak there, too."

Trudging over rock and loose stones, the horses's hooves clattered a dissonant rhythm against the silence.

"I guess," she admitted slowly. "But at least in my father's home, we were permitted to build many a merry blaze to keep us in good health and good cheer." Her voice lowered with nostalgia. "'Twas not considered hedonistic to roast your toes all evening while we told stories and shared cups of warm wine."

A pleasing domestic image of Melissande stole through his mind. For a moment he envisioned himself seated beside her, tipping a cup to her smiling lips...

"The sisters do not get together in the eve to share companionship around a fire?" Lucian had never visited a convent or monastery before. There were many along the land route to the Holy Lands, but he had avoided them like the plague for fear he would further displease God by disgracing their hallowed halls.

She snorted. "Much of our lifestyle has to do with self-denial. We are not allowed to indulge in many things the rest of the world would find pleasurable."

As if hearing disloyalty in her words, she quickly amended them.

"That's not to say we don't find happiness in many of our good works. For example, my joy in my children and their care. But we do not pursue pleasure for pleasure's sake." She looked over at him as their horses brushed close to each other through a narrow pass. "In other words, no companionship around a great blaze to chase away winter's chill at St. Ursula's."

His leg scraped against hers while the animals squeezed between rocky walls. The memory of her body crushed beneath his came roaring back to torment him.

He needed to shut out that particular incident for his own sanity. He needed to keep his mind too busy to remember.

He needed to talk.

Melissande's cherished hobby suddenly became more enticing.

"So what would you do to pass the evenings at the abbey?" By continually speaking of her years at St. Ursula's, his lust-filled body would eventually get the message, right? Melissande Deverell was forbidden to him.

"During the days I worked with the children, but only with the understanding that I could not slack off in my duties to Sister Eleanor."

The dark grew so thick their conversation took on a more intimate flavor, like sharing pillow confidences with a lover in the deep hours of the night.

Keep talking!

"So you worked for Sister Eleanor at night?"

"I had to report to the scriptorium after meals, and could leave only when the prayer bells tolled for matins at midnight. I had to observe the vespers and compline prayer alone at my desk."

Her voice so lacked emotion that Lucian struggled to gather a sense of how she felt about it. Was she bitter at the way the convent drove her to extra labor? Or was she as accepting as she sounded?

"Sounds lonely," he observed, squinting to see through the darkness for a place to make a safe camp.

"That part I did not mind." Lucian heard the smile in her words. "But the scriptorium is notoriously cold. And that part I truly detes—did not like."

Who would? The woman worked herself to exhaustion so she might have a few hours to play mother to a bunch of orphans. Lucian began to compile a clearer image of her blissful life at St. Ursula's.

Melissande and her vibrant spirit didn't go down without a fight. And she had struggled for years to convince herself she genuinely liked being a novitiate so she could retain some sense of happiness in a world turned upside down for her.

She probably would have run into his arms the day he'd abducted her if it hadn't been for the children. They were her lifeline. The one aspect of her existence where she still found real joy.

Well, maybe she wouldn't have run to him, he amended. She did seem to disparage the knighthood and its members.

"Don't misunderstand me," she blurted into the dark. "I may have had an ongoing battle with Sister Eleanor, but the other sisters were wonderful to me."

Should he believe her? He began to get the sense that Melissande deceived herself into thinking she was happy even when she was not.

"Abbess Helen has been like a mother to me since she arrived," she continued, stifling a yawn. "Kind and gentle…a steadfast guiding force for me. Did I mention she's grooming me to be the next abbess?"

Lucian stilled.

"No. You did not." A pretty big omission if you asked him.

"That may be why Sister Eleanor feels threatened by me." She yawned again, distorting her words in her tired stretch. "I think *she* would like to be the next abbess."

The revelation had several repercussions for Lucian. If Melissande was being prepared for the abbess position one day, her absence would be all the more fretted over and investigated. Mayhap the unknown shooter today had really been a member of the abbess's army, despite Melissande's protests to the contrary.

Second, Melissande obviously had a potent enemy in Sister Eleanor, no matter how much she wanted to ignore it. If this Sister Eleanor came from a powerful family, perhaps she could have sent one of her kin to ensure that her troublemaking nemesis never returned to St. Ursula's to take the top slot away from her.

"Lucian, can we stop soon?" Her voice sounded faraway, though she still rode close beside him, her mount tied securely to his.

He scoured the landscape with his eyes, looking for a reasonably secure place to camp.

"Soon, Mel." He wished they could stop, too. How could it have grown so cold so fast? Even the air felt thinner with their increasing altitude.

Something frigid tickled his nose while he hoped with all his heart he spoke the truth.

"Oh, no." Melissande's despairing wail drew him from his thoughts, alerting him to another tickle at his nose, then his forehead.

A haze of white glistened in the light of a crescent moon as tiny flakes danced down from the sky with growing force, blanketing them in a veil of frosty crystals.

Lucian grinned for a moment, caught up in the beauty of the luminescent shower.

"Only in the Alps," Melissande moaned, her voice hitching on a suppressed cough. "Snow in May."

Chapter Ten

A glad heart is excellent medicine, a depressed spirit wastes the bones away. Proverbs 17:22. Or was it 17:23?

Either way, the point remained the same to Melissande. Don't spread doom and gloom by complaining, no matter how bone-cold and tired you feel.

And, Lord, she was cold and tired. How long had they ridden since their hidden attacker had shot at them? Three hours? Four?

Snow piled over them so quickly now that Melissande didn't even bother brushing it from her shoulders and arms. The blanket Lucian had retrieved for her had long since become saturated with the cold, wet flakes.

Still, they trudged on. Snaking through narrow mountain passes, they climbed back into the Alps and into the frigid weather she had never liked.

If she didn't get warm and dry soon, she would end up with another case of lung fever. After the first time she'd been stricken with it, the illness seemed ever easier to catch. A night in the wilderness exposed to this sort of weather practically sealed her fate.

She refused to succumb to the lung fever that had threatened her life not a year ago. With no one but Lucian to care for her, she couldn't afford to get sick.

Annoyed with the gloomy thoughts she seemed powerless to staunch, Melissande ventured a comment to her long-silent riding companion. "Will we ride through the night? I do not mean to pester you, only to quench my curiosity."

Perhaps she sounded as pathetic as she felt, for Lucian immediately pulled his horse to a halt and turned on her. "You are unwell?"

She attempted to straighten under his glare. "A bit tired, perhaps."

He wiped a frustrated hand through his hair. "It is almost dawn, Melissande, I am not surprised."

Dawn? No wonder she could hardly see straight. "I only meant to make conversation, Lucian, not to irritate you. I find it exceedingly dull to ride for so many hours without conversing."

"I thought you were sleeping." His glare eased somewhat.

"On horseback?" She had trouble settling down in her convent bed each night. How would one ever fall asleep on a horse?

"It's been done, believe me." He looked tired, too. She hadn't seen it at first when he had scowled at her, but now the lines of concern and exhaustion were apparent around his eyes.

Melissande blamed Roarke for his thoughtless treatment of Lucian and made a mental note to speak to him about it if she lived through their journey to England. "Well, not by me. I cannot fathom a more uncomfortable way to slumber."

Lucian maneuvered his horse a few steps backward and held his arms out to her. "Come here."

The invitation sent a tremor through her. His embrace tempted her, but falling into his lap seemed like a declaration of weakness. She lowered her gaze to hide her longing.

"I will be fine here, thank you."

"Nonsense." He plucked her off the black mare with no hesitation, hauling her across his body like a child's rag doll. A grin twitched at his lips, a pleasing change from his customary solemn expression. "You have slept successfully in my arms before."

The blush started in her toes and heated her body thoroughly on its way to her cheeks. She did not think she could utter a rejoinder even if she might have formulated one in her embarrassment.

True enough, she had slumbered like a babe in his arms after the day she had tried to escape him. The sleep she had missed during her long trek to Linette's house she had made up for while curled against Lucian Barret.

She heard a rumble in his chest that might have been good humor as he kicked his horse into motion and led her mare to follow behind them. Settled neatly with her cheek flush to his heart, Melissande warned herself about the impropriety of dozing off while held in a man's arms.

"We will ride until I find a real shelter, Melissande. Something with walls and a roof and a place for a fire."

Several hours later, with Melissande sound asleep on his lap, Lucian realized what folly his quest had become.

Daylight granted him visibility for many miles now, but the sight of undisturbed white snow over the landscape only depressed him. No sign of anything with four walls for as far as the eye could see.

Weary as he was, Lucian didn't mind the journey for himself. The exertion suited his endless quest for penance.

But Melissande…

He hated every step of the wretched trip through the mountains for her sake, especially when he thought of how much she'd been through these past few days.

She was more delicate than he recalled. Perhaps her vibrant spirit had fooled him into thinking she was stronger than she was. At first Lucian had been surprised at the frightening cough racking her body in her sleep, as it seemed unlikely to him that one cold spell could wreak such havoc with her body.

Then, as he went over the past few days in his mind, he realized how worn out she must have been before the snow storm—how her utter exhaustion might leave her defenseless against the chill winds.

She seemed warmer now that she was in his arms, but her sodden blanket and clothes couldn't be helping the cough that had come more and more frequently in the last few hours.

Cursed mountains.

Over and over, he wondered if he could have avoided backtracking into the treacherous Alps. Each time, the answer was no.

A killer stalked them. Lucian didn't know who or why, but someone had come damn close to killing him last night, and he couldn't risk injury to himself for Melissande's sake. The girl would surely die without his protection.

He'd never had so much reason to live.

But no matter how much he assured himself of that truth, the fact that she grew more pale by the hour twisted his gut with guilt. If Roarke hadn't asked Lucian to steal her in the first place…

Caught up in the need to blame Melissande's condition on someone, Lucian didn't hear the travelers' approach until they were naught but one hundred paces before him.

Four men plodded toward them on horseback, carefully

picking their way over the treacherous mountain road. After conversing with them for a few minutes, Lucian learned they were not far from a small trading town, a village with a real live inn to house passing pilgrims and nobles.

Thank God.

In his haste to traverse the remaining leagues, Lucian did not spend much time thinking about his unwitting reaction of thanking God, but he noticed it nevertheless.

Odd he should thank God for anything when he had closed all communication with Him two years ago.

He reined in the horse and her eyelids flew open, her gaze bright with fever. "Lucian!" A smattering of freckles stood out in stark relief against her too pale skin. "Where are we?"

"An inn." Gently he sidled out from underneath her and dropped to the ground. When he helped her off the horse, her strange pallor unnerved him. Even her vivid red hair seemed a shade more dim.

"Well done," she announced, smiling feebly up at him.

Lucian tossed coins to everyone he passed on their way, hoping the groomsmen and stable boys would take the hint and care for the horseflesh. Even the innkeeper hastened to do Lucian's bidding, hurrying up the stairs ahead of them to open a door.

"'Tis my best room, sir—um, my lord." The man stumbled over his words as well as his feet as he scampered back to let Lucian enter. "Will you be needing anything else?"

"My wife is ill," Lucian announced, lying her gently on the pallet in spite of Melissande's obvious protest to the words and the intimacy. "We will take our meals here. Bring us something from supper last night, a hot bath and a fire for the grate."

Bowing himself out the door, the innkeeper left them alone.

Melissande elbowed herself to a sitting position. "How dare you share a room with me and allow that little man to assume we are wed!" Her voice sounded scratchy and strained.

He might have been amused at her misplaced indignation if she hadn't looked ready to pass out. Searching through his bag for the wine, he hoped she would lie back down without his having to help her. He did not like the feeling of possessiveness that stole over him whenever he took her in his arms. "You are ill, Mel. I cannot leave you. And if you were not ill, I would not give you your own chamber because you would try to escape me."

"I will not stand for it, Lucian, I—"

She slumped onto the linens suddenly, clutching her chest as she struggled for breath.

"Sweet Jesus, Mel." He dropped everything to race to her side. "Are you all right?" Easing her to recline completely on the bed, he watched a small wash of color fill her cheeks once again.

Nodding, she relaxed enough to let him reposition her. "It is wrong to share a room." More a croak than a sentence, her words fell on deaf ears.

"You damn well know better." How could she be so stubborn about something so insignificant? "Use your God-given sense, will you? Who would protect you from lustful knights if you are in the next room over? Who is going to take care of you if you're down the hall? The innkeeper?"

As if the mention of the man drew him from the air, the innkeeper appeared at the door with a parade of food, water and wood. Four youths, probably his sons and daughters, bustled about the room to enact Lucian's orders. "The tub is on its way up, sir,'' the innkeeper volunteered. ''Is there anything else?''

''Is there a reputable physician in town?''

''The local midwife has some knowledge of herbs.'' The man smiled with ingratiating affability.

''Send for her.'' Lucian waved the tub into the room and tossed out another round of coins before turning back to Melissande.

Only when he heard the door close behind the last of the servants did he reach to touch a tentative hand to Melissande's soaked green gown.

The heavy fabric clung to her pale skin, molding itself into every contour and curve of her body, a body he had no right to see.

His hand hovered in midair.

The hell with his rights. If Roarke wanted her alive when they returned home, he would damn well have to forgive the fact that his brother had to play nurse to her on the way.

With more force than he intended, his fingers attacked the toggles down the front of the gown.

Her scream rent the air as she shot off the rope mattress. ''Lucian Barret!''

Color suffused her cheeks now. Her breathing heavy and unnatural, Lucian was hard-pressed to keep his wayward eyes from straying to the hint of cleavage he had exposed.

''What are you doing?'' Breathless and blushing, she pulled the edges of her kirtle together.

Wasn't it obvious? ''I thought you were sleeping.''

''So you use that as an excuse to—'' Her brows furrowed in consternation. Voice dropping to a whisper she continued, ''Undress me?''

The mental image the words conjured rendered him speechless. But damn it, he hadn't meant to leer at her. She looked ready to collapse. He just wanted to get her warm and dry.

He stood, edgy and restless. "Since you are awake, you are certainly capable of undressing yourself." It took a monumental effort, but he moved his feet toward the door, away from her soon-to-be-naked body. "I expect you will address the matter in my absence."

Congratulating himself on his willpower, Lucian shut the door between them and waited, trying not to imagine her movements on the other side of the thin wall.

How would he ever hand her over to Roarke?

As much as he owed his brother for handling everything after Fitzhugh's death, it galled Lucian to think of giving Melissande to a man who would never fully appreciate her.

Roarke merely wanted a wife whose body was untainted, whose children would be his beyond a doubt. When Roarke recently recalled little Melissande Deverell, the adoring shadow of his youth, there had been no quenching his curiosity about how she'd turned out. He'd wanted only her.

But Roarke had paid her no mind when they were children, and Lucian suspected his brother would not understand or appreciate her now, either.

Lucian, on the other hand, had been fascinated with her even as a child. The girl had more grit than most boys twice her age. And smart...he'd only had to show her something once for Melissande to catch on.

Despite the wall of reserve the convent instilled in her, Melissande would never lose her backbone or her intelligence. Hell, as much as it scared him, Lucian thought she might be smarter than him.

Hoping he'd allowed enough time to elapse, Lucian rapped on the door once and let himself back in.

And there she sat.

Right where he left her, still draped in sodden clothing.

Obviously the woman was not as smart as he'd thought earlier.

Melissande didn't miss the thunderous expression on Lucian's face, but without permission from God Himself, there was no way she would remove one stitch of her clothing while he shared her room.

"Perhaps you were confused about the reason I left the chamber," he began, speaking very softly.

"Nay." Weary and sick, Melissande lacked the energy to argue with him. Surely he understood her dilemma.

"Then why are you turning blue in a dress that is no longer fit to wear?" A tic in his eye gave away his growing ire. The scar next to it pulsed in time with the tic.

Melissande shivered. Did he think she *wanted* to freeze to death? "I have no other garments to wear."

She could see him swallow. Her own mouth felt dry.

"I will procure clothing," he announced, his voice low and deep. "Stay here."

He returned in no time and tossed a ball of women's garments in the door. Barking at her to hurry, he left her alone once again.

She needed no further urging. The lung fever did not respond well to wet clothes. Melissande knew the familiar tightening in her chest, the inevitable sting of her own breath in her throat.

Please God, deliver me, she prayed. *Allow me to return to the children.*

The ill-fitting maid's clothes were a welcome change. She donned the stiff cotton kirtle and worn woolen tunic before sliding into bed, heedless of doing so much as plucking her own clothes off the floor.

Weary to the bone, she feared sliding into sleep and not waking up.

Maybe Lucian will talk to me...

A sharp rap at the door preceded his return.

She noticed he had changed garments, as well, though his tunic and braies were obviously his own. He would have a hard time finding a man anywhere close to his size.

Following him around the chamber with her eyes, she watched as he hung her discarded clothing by the fire to dry.

Sleep beckoned, but she refused to give in to it in case death awaited her there. With an illness as severe as lung fever, Abbess Helen said, one never knew.

"Would you like supper now?" Lucian asked, brows furrowed.

Her belly rumbled in response and she nodded, realizing she had not eaten since yesterday at noon.

She could not sit up to take food, but he did not seem inconvenienced. He simply cut her portion into bite sizes and fed her from his fingers while she lay on her side.

Not for the first time, the sense of being utterly cared for flowed over her. She had been independent for so long, had fought to define herself on her own terms at the convent. But just now, it filled her with contentment to allow someone else to care for her. Lucian—the world-weary warrior who already shouldered burdens beyond her ken—appeared strong enough for both of them.

There was more to being a knight than killing, it seemed.

"Lucian." The word slipped out, no more than a sigh, when she had eaten her fill.

"Hmm?"

"Thank you."

She sensed his stillness, his discomfort with her appreciation even with her eyes closed. But she was too tired and too weak to concern herself with his rigid humility.

If she really were to die before she ever regained consciousness, she wanted him to know how much she appreciated his solicitous concern for her. She pried her eyes open again.

"It is nothing," he scoffed, wiping crumbs from his tunic. On a normal day the gruffness of the words would have intimidated her into silence.

But this night seemed too important for her to back down now. She might not be fortunate enough to battle the lung fever this time. Perhaps she would never have another chance to speak to him.

"It is not nothing," she protested, hoping in spite of her exhaustion that she spoke out loud as she thought the words. "These few days have been enlightening for me. You have made me remember much of myself that I sought to forget, fragments of my character that shouldn't be suppressed." Part of her realized she could never confide such disloyal thoughts against the convent unless she was only half-conscious. But another part of her screamed that she had never thought so clearly. "You've made me feel whole again."

Did he answer her or was she dreaming this whole conversation? She definitely heard his eating knife chewing into the cutting board with overzealous swipes.

Lucian did not know how to accept her gratitude.

It bothered her to think she might never know why, but for some reason, the man considered himself unloved by God.

Godless.

Please don't let me die now. I could help him.

"Lucian?"

His presence filled the room around her, even if he retreated from the intimacy of her words.

An urgency filled her as she fought to remain awake a little bit longer—a driving need to deliver an important message to Lucian Barret.

She could not tiptoe around his surly mood today. She needed to tell him.

"God loves you."

Distinctly she heard a garbled moan, as if her words pierced him with the bite of the arrow that missed his head yesterday.

Strangely, Melissande realized she still had more to say. The burning need to confide something to Lucian had not been quenched by her avowal that he was loved by God.

Another rebellious thought niggled her fevered brain, taunting her with a threat to leap from her lips if she opened her mouth.

Hadn't she conquered her wayward tongue long ago? Surely she wouldn't be so foolish as to say the ridiculous words that floated around in her head.

In the sin of the lips…

But what did it matter if she said it, when she would probably never wake up?

"And so do I."

Chapter Eleven

For the next sennight, Lucian poured all his time and effort into his paltry attempts to heal Melissande, knowing if he allowed himself so much as a moment to relax, her haunting words would torment his soul and claw at his insides.

And so do I…

Lucian scrubbed the cool cloth over Melissande's forehead, willing away the lure of her final fevered sentiment.

Foolish girl. She had been so exhausted, she had obviously forgotten the context of their discussion. Although the comment that preceded "And so do I" had been that God loved him, ridiculously implying Melissande loved Lucian, too, her illness must have rendered her mind a muddle of disjointed thoughts.

He repeated the internal diatribe to himself for at least the hundredth time since she'd slipped from consciousness, reassuring himself that a nun would never fall in love with a man. She must have been speaking in the spiritual sense.

The other option presented too tempting a scenario, a dream long abandoned of wife, home and family. He didn't deserve such tender sentiments, certainly not from someone as pure as Melissande.

He rinsed the cloth and scrubbed, careful not to lower

the sheet that covered her any more than necessary. For her sake as much as his own, he had hired one of the innkeeper's daughters to cool the rest of his patient.

She looked no better today. Her breathing continued to deteriorate until it became so shallow and raspy that Lucian had started feeding her warm water with honey at regular intervals to ease the sharpness of her inhalations.

It wasn't much, but he recalled the home remedy from his childhood and put it to good use. Certainly the midwife who came to visit couldn't offer anything more substantial.

Useless woman.

Lucian left Melissande's bedside to retrieve heated water from the cauldron above the grate. Pouring a fresh cup of water and honey, he considered the worthlessness of half the midwives in the world.

Some were highly capable, no doubt, but he'd never had any luck with them personally. The healer who had been sought to cure Fitzhugh, in fact, had actually given Lucian false hope that his foster father would recover. When Osbern died, the midwife had left without a trace.

Good thing. In his newly discovered penchant for violence, he might have killed her.

God loves you...

Slamming the cup onto the crude wooden table near her mattress, Lucian cursed her proclamation. What the hell did she know anyhow?

He shouted for the innkeeper's daughter, Tamara, and handed over his nursing duties to the girl. Damned if he was helping anyway.

Raking a restless hand through his hair, he spared one more look toward the bed where Melissande lay. Her cheeks were pale and lifeless, her hair a quenched fire of dull auburn.

After instructing Tamara to send for him immediately if

there was any change, he headed for the inn's common room. Ignoring the two other patrons, a scruffy pair of Franciscan friars, Lucian called for a pitcher of ale.

Downing two full horns in quick succession, Lucian waited for some sign of the mind-numbing effect the brew could give.

Nothing.

He stopped counting after four, powerless to resist the temptation to get drunk.

Away from Melissande's side, Lucian could only think of her.

No matter how much ale he consumed, her face swam in his vision—sometimes alight with laughter, sometimes pale with illness or…death.

Shouting for another pitcher, he willed the ache in his chest to go away. The thought of Melissande dead squeezed his insides like a page's petrified grip on his first real blade.

A part of Lucian recognized her death would be the ultimate punishment for his past sin, the punishment he had sought these past two years. Now that the supreme pain of it faced him, however, he did not run to embrace this penance the way he gladly shouldered his others.

This he could not bear.

Melissande was too pure of heart and gentle of soul to die so young. It struck him as hideously unfair that God allowed Lucian the Murderer to walk the earth, strong as the west wind and healthy as a weed, while an angel would perish without so much as a friend to comfort her.

A pang of guilt nipped him. He shouldn't be indulging himself in drink, he should be near her in case she needed him.

What if she wanted to talk before she died?

A hoarse bark of laughter escaped him when he realized he would give his sword arm to hear her incessant chatter.

And in his drunkenness, he did something he hadn't done in years.

God, grant Melissande her life and I shall listen to her prattle morning, noon and night.

Unthinkingly, the prayer slipped out into the common room with the volume only the inebriated use.

He had prayed.

Jesus.

Lucian cursed, as if to negate the invocation he uttered as naturally as his own breath.

Slumping against the rough wooden trestle, Lucian buried his head in the crook of his arm, wishing like hell he had ignored Roarke's request and left Melissande at St. Ursula's where she would still be healthy and happy.

At the abbey, she would have devout women to bend their heads in supplication for her. Here, in the middle of the deserted Alps, she had naught but Lucian's drunken bargains with the God he had alienated years ago.

Lucian knew his sorry excuse for a prayer would not be heard.

A movement from across the common room caught his eye, and Lucian peered up from his ale to see the Franciscans engaged in animated conversation.

Holy men.

Not ten paces from Lucian sat two men that God would listen to. Men whose invocations for Melissande might be answered.

Lucian's gut roiled at the thought of approaching them. In light of his sins, he didn't have any business speaking to men of the cloth.

Yet he owed it to Melissande to swallow his fears and approach them. She had given him so much in the few days they had been together. Her laughter and vivaciousness served as a balm to his spirit, bringing light to an existence that had grown unbearably dark.

Melissande deserved their benedictions.

"Good Brothers, I…" His shout trailed off. What could he say? He wanted them to pray for a nun he'd kidnapped?

The men turned as one, their pleasant expressions clouding with concern as they stared at him.

Lucian faltered, unsure of himself. His head spun with the effort to talk.

"My son?" A man's deep voice suddenly hovered above Lucian's head.

The endearment, a phrase also favored by Osbern Fitzhugh for all the young men he fostered, stilled Lucian. Slowly he lifted his chin.

One of the Franciscans, the older of the two, leaned over him. "Are you all right?"

"Fine." Lucian massaged his temple, turning away from the monk.

Not easily offended, the friar took a seat beside him on the bench. "I heard you call out for your Savior earlier." Good humor threaded through the Franciscan's voice. "A man does not often do so except in times of great distress."

Lucian studied the stranger's salt-and-pepper beard, closely groomed and clean. Though his clothes were coarse and humble, they were not dirty.

There had been a time in Lucian's life when he would have been fascinated to talk to a wandering Franciscan monk about how it felt to forsake home and fortune to follow God's call. Although Lucian had always known he was not destined for the church, he had been nevertheless intrigued with its scope and power and its poor Franciscan brethren who ignored all the fancy trappings to walk the more simple path of Jesus.

Not anymore. If not for Melissande, Lucian would never have called out to this man.

The monk thrust his hand forward in greeting. "Brother William."

With a curt nod, Lucian acknowledged the name without giving his own. The monk's earnestness, his honesty, was apparent in wise green eyes. Lucian wondered what Brother William saw in his. Gathering his courage, he took a deep breath. "I— My friend is ill."

"Perhaps she would benefit from a Christian blessing, my friend."

"What?" How did this man know Lucian spoke of a woman? He held the friar's gaze, daring him to explain how he knew about Melissande. Could William be associated with St. Ursula's?

"Her poor health is the talk of the innkeeper's family," he returned easily. "I wonder if I might bestow my blessing upon her?"

Of course Melissande would want Brother William's blessing. The best Lucian could offer was a drunken invocation that probably amounted to blasphemy in God's eyes.

"Please." Lucian could not begin to express his gratitude for the offer and for Brother William's insightfulness to extend it. "She rests abovestairs."

Pushing back the trestle bench, Lucian rose and led the man out of the common room. Knowing what awaited him in the sick chamber, he moved slowly, fearing Melissande's waxy complexion and unnatural stillness would be worse than when he left.

He hated the long nights of hoping for a raspy breath to know at least she still breathed. He hated knowing that his actions had done this to her. And, dear God, but he hated his brother for demanding Melissande as if she was his cursed prize.

''She's in here.'' Lucian gestured toward the door, thinking how trusting the friar seemed to accompany a stranger to a sickroom, not bothering to ask if Melissande suffered from something contagious.

Brother William nodded and stepped in front of Lucian, finding courage where Lucian hadn't, and opened the door.

Lucian avoided the sight of Melissande for a long moment, watching William's face as the holy man surveyed the patient.

''She is uncommonly beautiful,'' William remarked, his voice appropriately dispassionate but sincere.

Lucian looked to the bed, hoping to see some resurrection of the woman he knew. But she lay there as deathly ill as before.

''You should see her when she is well.''

A stupid thing to say, Lucian supposed. What did her beauty matter at a time like this? Or any time, for that matter?

Perhaps he merely craved the sight of her fully animated again, her infectious laughter bright enough to lighten even his most somber of moods.

''She is your wife?''

The question startled him. Guilt pinched him. ''Nay.''

''She should be.'' The preacher swung from the bed to meet Lucian's gaze.

''She is promised to my brother.''

''Does he know of your regard for her?'' Brother William lifted a shaggy gray eyebrow and fixed Lucian with a catlike green stare.

Lucian seethed, refusing to be saddled with a sin he had not committed. His conscience already overflowed with those he had. ''I have not touched her, Brother.''

Fortunately, Brother William seemed content to let the matter pass, returning his attention to Melissande. "As God wills, my son. I hope you are prepared to claim her if the need should arise."

Trepidation shook Lucian's hand as he pressed it to his forehead. The monk would never suggest such a thing if he knew the sins of Lucian's past. The very idea of marriage to Melissande...

"It won't."

Brother William held his palm to Melissande's temple. "A little fresh air would serve her well so long as you keep her warm. A bit of sun on her face might help."

Unorthodox, maybe, but Lucian would try anything at this point. Before he could thank the friar for his advice, the man launched into prayer, his powerful voice filling the room.

"You shall wander the barren desert, but you shall not die of thirst..."

Lucian knew he should slip from the room and leave Brother William to work a miracle and heal Melissande, but he found his feet would not move. Entranced by the music of the priest's words, he stood there, his hungry spirit fighting for the bit of nourishment the humble Franciscan's words might provide.

"You shall see the face of God and live..."

Tears burned behind Lucian's eyes for the longing the prayer evoked. He would not see the face of God and live. Melissande would. Even if she died this moment, her place in Heaven couldn't be more obvious.

Because of Lucian's rash actions of two years ago, a hand raised against the kindly man who fostered him, he would ever be denied God's comfort. Still, in his selfishness, he yearned that she would not die and seek her heavenly seat just yet.

He needed her, damn it.

He could not bring himself to say the prayer again, now that the ale seemed to have worn off a bit, but he added a hearty amen to Brother William's words.

For what purpose, he could not be certain, but as sure as knew his own name, Lucian knew he needed Melissande to come back to him, healthy and whole.

Her goodness and purity, her inquisitive nature and irrepressible chatter, represented the one thing Lucian had not felt since God had forsaken him.

Hope.

From somewhere far off in the distance, Melissande heard Lucian Barret's deep voice say "Amen."

Did she dream it?

The voice and the word seemed incongruous and yet utterly right together.

Her dreams had been so vivid and frightening. She felt a danger looming over Lucian but she was powerless to help him. A faceless stranger sought to kill him in some of the dreams or else Lucian sought to punish himself for some sin of his past, but turmoil constantly swirled around him.

Hearing him speak that one word of praise and thanksgiving to God heartened her. If he could still say "Amen" with such a depth of feeling, surely all was not lost. Maybe he would see past the self-inflicted penance he wore like a badge of dishonor and find the strength to reclaim his life.

Her lungs burned with the effort of breathing and she longed to be at rest. Yet the curiosity that had plagued her all her life was piqued now.

Was Lucian ready to share a bit of himself with her? Could he forgive himself for his past and return home to take his rightful place as lord of the Barret lands? Could he give up his warrior's world of killing and destruction? His steadfast refusal to participate in life?

Melissande had to find out. Not only that, but she needed to help him. Burning breath after burning breath, she dragged air into her lungs, determined to make certain Lucian Barret did not slip any further astray.

Days and nights passed before the breathing eased. The effort to battle the latest bout with lung fever had been difficult, but one morning Melissande awoke and sensed she'd won.

The room about her was strange and yet familiar. She knew the smells and the sounds of the place, having floated in and out of consciousness for who knew how long.

But she did not recognize the sight of it. Small and crude, the narrow chamber resembled her tiny quarters at the convent, but for the hot grate that kept the space at a reasonable temperature.

The real difference stemmed from Lucian Barret's presence. His tall, muscular body filled the chamber with efficient movements as he hummed over the cauldron on the grate.

She must have made a noise of some sort, for he suddenly dropped his spoon and whirled around to face her.

Then he grinned.

Not the small nod to humor her that he'd given in the past, but a full smile that made Melissande's heart stop.

"You are awake," he announced with foolish obviousness, closing the distance between them.

Suddenly aware of her lack of clothing beneath the sheets and the total disarray of her hair, Melissande held up her hand to halt him. "I must dress first."

He stepped closer. "You may require some help."

Surely he jested. She clutched the linens closer to her

body, keenly uncomfortable with her nakedness near him. "Certainly not! I will manage if I can just—"

"Don't be ridiculous." Lucian turned on his heel. "Tamara will assist you."

Light-headed from the effort of moving, Melissande rubbed her temple. "Oh. Tamara. Of course." How foolish she had been to think he would try to help her dress.

After shouting into the corridor, Lucian ushered a young woman into the room whom Melissande did not know.

"Oh, my lady! You are well again," the girl enthused. "Lord be praised, but I did not think you would make it."

The girl seemed to know her. "Tamara?"

"Yes, my lady." Tamara turned to wave away Lucian.

Melissande swallowed her surprise when the hulking warrior meekly ducked out the door.

"I need some help, please." It embarrassed her to have to ask. As a novitiate she had been taught to keep her body private from all eyes, even her own. But she could not afford modesty now.

Tamara did not seem to suffer from such humility. She chatted aimlessly about various visitors at the inn and the kind attentiveness of Lord Barret and the warmer weather that followed the snowstorm all the while helping Melissande into the green dress the merchant's wife had given her.

"Lucian has been attentive to me?" Curiosity drove the question right off her tongue.

"*Oui!* I've never seen a man so solicitous of his wife before." She nodded her head with sagacity beyond her years. "And we get plenty of married couples at the inn. Half of 'em don't care about each other at all."

Melissande wanted to know more, specifically about Lucian, but before she could think of a way to redirect the woman, Tamara reached for a wooden comb and began untangling her patient's hair.

A sharp rap sounded at the door, sending Tamara off the bed. "He is returned, my lady. Call if you need me."

Lucian walked into the chamber, thanking Tamara as she hurried around him. Then he turned to Melissande. "You are prepared to greet me now?" His words somber and quiet, he lacked the broad grin of before.

Melissande found herself wishing for it back. "Yes." She felt awkward around him suddenly. Unsure of herself with a man who had taken care of her the whole time she'd been ill. "How long have I been indisposed?"

"Almost three weeks." He had reached the bed and stood with both legs pressed against it, staring down at her. "I thought you'd never recover."

"It is not such a long time, actually. The first year I had it, I suffered for almost two months." What a miserable winter that had been. Sister Eleanor was so aggravated about the work Melissande missed, she assigned Sanskrit to her helper for nearly a year.

"You've had this before?" Lucian frowned.

"Several times. After you contract it once, you are all the more disposed to sickness."

His brow furrowed. A casual observer might interpret the severe expression on his face as anger, but Melissande realized she knew him well enough to recognize concern. Maybe fear for her.

"What causes it?"

"Exposure to the cold weather, it seems." She yawned, surprised at how weak she felt after the effort of dressing and conversing.

"And you did not confide this bit of information to me?" His voice definitely sounded angry. Perhaps she'd been wrong about thinking he was only fearful for her health.

"I didn't see a reason to mention it when we had little choice between facing the cold weather or confronting a killer." She strove to keep the defensive tone from her words with little success.

Lucian threw his hands in the air before they slammed down against his thighs again. "If I had known I could have made sure you kept the damn snow off your blanket. Or offered you more blankets. Or any number of things." He pinned her with a steely look of cold fury. "You could have died from this, Mel. You need to take better care of yourself."

Waves of anger emanated from him. Melissande inched further into her pillows, too exhausted to confront him just now. Why was he so angry? It was her health, not his.

"I have been taught not to complain, Lucian. It never occurred to me to discuss my health weaknesses with you."

He sank to the bed beside her, his hip grazing her thigh. Although she told herself she was too tired to move, part of her acknowledged she remained still just to feel his solid presence next to her.

"Melissande." He addressed her slowly, thoughtfully, as if speaking to a child. "How long ago did you first contract this illness?"

She calculated the years in her mind. "Seven years ago."

Like a mountain eclipsing the landscape, he rose from her bed to stand before her, inhabiting every bit of her vision. "And they did not send you home?"

"St. Ursula's *is* my home."

"How could they conscience keeping a child in the alpine mountains who was susceptible to a deadly illness exacerbated by cold weather?" He tipped her chin up to look at him, compelling Melissande to open her sleepy eyes.

The rough texture of his sword-wielding hand seeped into her skin, flooding her with his warmth and a sense of being healed. She wondered how it would feel to close her eyes and lean into that strong palm. "The world is dead to those inside the abbey, Lucian. We handle our own affairs."

He drew his mouth into a pale semblance of a smile. "Not any more you don't, Melissande. We are getting the hell out of the Alps and never looking back."

She started to contradict him, but he placed a forbidding finger over her lips. If she hadn't been so tired from the weeks of battling the fever, she would have been more forceful about arguing the point.

Today, she let him have his say. In fact, she allowed herself a lazy fantasy of what it would be like to stay with Lucian. What if he were not taking her to England to wed Roarke, but to marry *him?*

Her heart leaped at the strong temptation the image presented—succumbing to Lucian's kisses as his wife, growing round with his babe, healing the darkness that lurked inside of him.

The vision dissipated as quickly as it had arisen when Melissande imagined Lucian teaching their son how to wield a sword, how to be stoic. She would never raise a warrior or breed another generation of brutal men cut off from their emotions. Her mother hadn't been able to keep her family together no matter how much she'd pleaded with her husband. What made Melissande think she could ever create a genuine partnership with a man, and a warrior at that?

"I don't care what trouble you give Roarke or how much you try to wrangle your way out of a marriage," he warned, shooting her a level glare. "I'm telling you here and now that once you get to England you are staying there for good."

Pivoting on his heel, he stomped across the planked floor and out the door.

She sighed, regretting her lack of strength. When she recovered, she would tell him in no uncertain terms that she would be headed back to France in less than six weeks.

Melissande yawned and reclined on the mattress, wondering briefly what Roarke Barret would be like as a grown man. She hadn't allowed herself to think of the man, choosing to hope she'd never have to face him. But given Lucian's determination to deliver her to England, perhaps now was the time to remember Roarke. He was probably as manipulative as he had been as a child.

Although she hadn't recognized his behavior for what it was until years later, Melissande knew he had taken advantage of her infatuation with him, sending her on small errands for him, cajoling her to pilfer fresh muffins from the kitchen when he was hungry, or coaxing her into catching his portion of the fresh fish Lady Barret sometimes demanded from him. Roarke had always been so different from the rest of his family, a smooth-talking charmer among his blunt, hard-working kin.

Even if he turned out to be a prince among men, Melissande would not marry him. First of all because he would be a knight by now, the same as Lucian. Second, her commitment to St. Ursula's—and God, she amended—was much more important to her than wedding an earl who didn't deserve his older brother's lands.

Besides, three powerful forces drew her back to St. Ursula's, the three reasons she kept her sanity in the abbey despite the Sanskrit and lung fever and Sister Eleanor.

Three precious children held a part of her heart, and she would never give them up for either of the Barret men, no matter how sorely dreams of the elder Barret might tempt her.

Chapter Twelve

After a torturous three weeks at Melissande's side, aiding her through her convalescence, Lucian thanked the Fates when she seemed well enough to ride again. Stealing through the lodging in the predawn hours, he made the necessary preparations for their trip and left another sack of coins for Tamara and her family.

For the initial week of her recovery, it had been easy to care for her. She had been so fatigued from the fever that she slept much of the time, waking only to eat and to read from the *Odyssey* for an hour or two in the evening. But after several days, she had started her campaign to return to St. Ursula's.

Foolish woman.

He walked away the first time she introduced the topic, but as soon as he shut the door between them, he recalled the vow he'd made while she'd hovered near death.

God, grant Melissande her life and I shall listen to her prattle morning, noon and night.

Unwilling to break such an oath, he had returned to her and was promptly rewarded with Melissande's numerous attempts to bargain for her freedom. Not that he would ever consider granting it while a killer might follow in their footsteps. Lucian had made inquiries among other travelers who visited the inn, but had learned naught of their pursuer.

Following a quick stop at the stable to alert the groom they were leaving, Lucian made his way to the tiny room he shared with Melissande.

Their close quarters had become the most compelling reason to get Melissande on the road home. Once she started to regain her health and vitality, Lucian could not concentrate around her.

His hand hesitated on the latch to where she slept. Just knowing she was within the chamber, sleeping peacefully, utterly vulnerable, wreaked havoc with his mind and body.

Gritting his teeth for strength, he turned the handle, determined to protect her from any threat. Including himself.

She had bathed last night. The room still held the fragrant smell of the bath soap Tamara had found for her. As he eased closer to the bed, careful not to wake her yet, Lucian realized her hair radiated the floral scent from where it lay strewn over her pillow in a deep red fan.

As if a vise squeezed his chest, Lucian struggled for a full breath as he stared at her. He squelched the urge to fall to his knees and to worship her with his hands, his mouth…

Was the pain that clenched his chest his lust or his guilt? Seized equally by both, Lucian wondered how grave an error it would be to skim his palm over her cheek and through the skeins of pillow-warmed hair.

He lingered beside her for a long moment, knowing this would be the closest he ever came to fulfilling the misplaced longing he felt for her.

As if she sensed his presence, she turned toward him in sleep, curling on her side at the edge of the narrow pallet. Her blanket edged further down her body, revealing another tantalizing inch of her skin and confirming his guess that she was indeed naked beneath the covers.

The knowledge spurred his hunger for her, edging the clamor of his desires to the forefront of his mind and effectively nudging away the guilt for a moment.

Now settled on her side, Melissande draped one arm across her body to rest beside her head, so close to where his thigh grazed the bedding.

Sinking to his knees, he lifted a tentative hand over her, absorbing her warmth and essence before his skin ever connected with her flesh. Slowly, gently, he let his fingers fall onto her shoulder and curve around the softness of her bare arm.

Heaven.

Her skin was smooth and fragrant and far too inviting. Not for all the world would he nudge aside her blanket another inch to unveil the lush breasts he knew resided there. But that didn't mean he couldn't think about it. Dream about it. Long for it with all his heart and soul.

She sighed, startling him for a moment with the fear that she had awakened. Instead she settled more deeply into her pillow, a satisfied smile rounding her lips at the corners.

Pure torture.

What scared him more than his own lust for Melissande was the fact that she seemed to return it. Her tentative touches in the chapel, the way she'd returned his kiss, the way she smiled at him in her sleep...all suggested she might share his desire.

Of course, she was too young and sheltered to know better.

But for Lucian, the realization that he could lower that blanket and wake her with languorous kisses to her breasts drove him to the brink of insanity.

How could he ever let her go? How the hell could he turn her over to Roarke after having lost his heart to her for the second time in his life?

Melissande had won him long ago. Her spirit, her wit, her quick intelligence had impressed him when he was little more than a boy. And now...now he was more impressed than ever, but he had become a man so unworthy of her that his growing regard would only offend her if she knew the depth of his sins.

As much as his gut twisted at the notion of Melissande in the arms of another man, it was far better than imagining her suffering from a fatal case of lung fever in a nunnery with no one who loved her by her side.

"Melissande." His voice sounded husky and full of unspoken emotion. He cleared his throat and rose to his feet. "Melissande."

Her eyelashes fluttered over her cheeks with the delicate sweep of a butterfly's wing. "Lucian?"

The desire to answer her call was so fundamental, so deeply rooted in his being, that he wondered how and when she had worked her way into the empty places inside him. "We leave this morn," he told her, incapable of gentling the brusqueness in his tone. "Rise and dress and meet me below."

Well, that's a fine way to wake up, Melissande thought miserably, unable to jump out of bed no matter what the high-and-mighty Lucian Barret willed.

Rubbing a lazy palm across her eyes, she remembered the wonderful dream she'd been having where Lucian...

Dear God, she'd been dreaming something totally inappropriate about him. Her face flushed even though she was in the room alone.

What sort of spell had the man cast upon her to inspire such wanton thoughts? In her dream, Lucian had been kneeling beside her bed, running his fingers over her body and it had felt so real and so delicious that Melissande found it difficult to brush away the lingering desire the imagined touch had wrought.

One thing was certain. She would not allow herself to sleep naked again. Although she'd adopted the habit in her weeks of convalescing as a way to conserve on laundry for the already overworked Tamara, obviously sleeping without a night rail encouraged shameless thoughts.

Shameless delicious thoughts that would plague her all day.

Hurrying to dress, she chastised herself. As a novitiate, her thoughts should be directed toward the spiritual and not toward the flesh.

Crossing herself two times for good measure, she prayed for guidance through her current predicament. As much as she knew it was sinful for her to think of Lucian, or any man, in that manner, she admitted to herself that it was not the first time a blatantly lascivious thought had crossed her mind where he was concerned.

Thank heaven they were finally escaping the intimacy of the chamber. She scrambled out the door still plaiting her recalcitrant hair, eager to put the last month behind her.

Her step faltered when she spied him already atop his horse, tying the lead rope for her mare.

His hair blended into his black hauberk, cloaking him in darkness from head to toe. The scar stood out in stark relief on his temple this morning, his every feature as stern and defined as a marble statue.

Even under the layered fabric of his tunic and hauberk, the play of muscle in his arms was apparent as he worked.

Her vision of him as a warrior returned. For the past fortnight she had deceived herself into thinking of him more as her friend, sometimes even as more than a friend when she thought of their shared kiss…

"Good morning," she called.

He stilled, then straightened, staring at her with the distance of a stranger.

"Lucian?"

As if awakening at her call, he broke his gaze and vaulted down to assist her onto her mount. "Sorry," he mumbled, wrapping both hands about her waist to lift her.

A bolt of awareness shot through her at his touch, singeing her nerves and calling to mind the dream she'd been having about him only moments before. Warmth pooled in her belly and effused her limbs, enhancing the feeling of weightlessness as he held her suspended in the air above him.

His gaze locked with hers, distant no longer.

She stared down at him, drawn by the heated promise in his eyes. His mouth was within kissing distance, taunting her with memories of the last time their lips had touched. The result had given rise to a flurry of sensual dreams she hadn't escaped from even at the heights of her illness.

Would he settle his mouth over hers again?

Melissande closed her eyes. Hoping.

Yet as his name escaped her lips in a breathless sigh, she found herself settled firmly onto her horse's back, the distance between them restored.

Had she dreamed the exchange?

Her heart beat so furiously she was obliged to take shallow breaths of the crisp morning air.

Mayhap she was just being fanciful. No matter that they'd shared one stolen kiss those many weeks ago. Lucian was far too honorable a man to harbor romantic feelings for the woman he regarded as his brother's intended bride. Or a would-be nun, for that matter.

Their kiss in the chapel had probably been an accident he regretted—a misstep brought on by Melissande's brazen touches and bold manner.

Annoyed with her traitorous longings, Melissande forced herself to repeat every proverb she could recall before delving into conversation with Lucian. She didn't deserve to indulge in talk until she served some sort of penance for her worldly wants.

Somewhere between the Sayings of Lemuel and the Sayings of Agur, she realized Lucian called to her from his horse. She forced herself to use the smooth, modulated tones of her convent voice. "Yes?"

"You are uncommonly quiet today. Do you not feel well enough to travel?" Swivelled backward to face her, Lucian regarded her with concern.

"I am giving your ears a rest." Summoning a smile, she wondered if she could dispense with her penance early and talk to him. Appealing as it sounded, probably not.

"Please do not. You've had me worried." He turned back around to guide them through a thicket of close trees. "Besides, I've become rather accustomed to you."

Lucian wanted to hear her talk? The temptation proved too much to bear. Perhaps she could finish the penance after lunch.

"Actually, I do have a proposition…"

As Lucian listened to her musical voice fill the clearing, he wished he could afford to focus more attention on her. Technically he was *listening* as she discussed her reasons for wishing to go back to St. Ursula's. His brain, however, did not really comprehend the finer points of her arguments. Right now, Lucian needed to heed the gnawing fear in his gut that they were being followed.

All morning—whenever he hadn't been envisioning Melissande cocooned in the bed coverings as he'd seen her earlier—Lucian had been tormented with a sense that someone stalked behind them, waiting to take a shot at him while he was most vulnerable. The mountain terrain seemed ominously quiet, as if danger lurked nearby and every creature great and small was aware of it except for Lucian. He couldn't say what made the hair on the back of his neck prickle, but he could not deny his warrior instincts.

Melissande's voice soothed his raw nerves and maybe served a higher purpose if they were being followed. The stalker would think his quarry engaged in conversation, hence more vulnerable to attack.

Far from distracted, Lucian was strung so tight he'd snap if the breeze so much as blew across him the wrong way. He would not let himself or, more accurately, he would not let Melissande be unprotected for even an instant. He had to draw out the enemy while the element of surprise was on Lucian's side.

Melissande's words covered his silence, allowing him to brood over the identity of the person who followed them. Perhaps the too-quiet pursuer was simply a fellow traveler, but Lucian knew on a gut level that it must be the shooter from the lowlands who forced them back up into the mountains. With all the time Melissande had been ill, their unwanted guest certainly had time to track them.

With the methodical cunning instilled by war, Lucian formulated a plan for removing the threat. The time had come to act.

After scouting the landscape for safe shelters, he drew her horse beside his and turned in the saddle to face her, keeping his voice as low as possible. ''You need to ride on without me, Mel, to that bend in the trail. There is a predator behind us—''

Before her head could swivel around, Lucian threw one arm out to intercept her chin in his hand and kissed her, hard. Under the guise of nuzzling her neck—strictly for the benefit of whomever watched them—Lucian whispered against her softly scented skin, "Do not look back. We must be discreet."

"What is it?" Her heart pounded wildly under his lips. He forced himself to ignore the sensual draw of that rapid pulse and to concentrate on the threat at hand.

"Not what...who. If I let you go, will you ride straight ahead, no looking back?" He didn't want to let her go.

Melissande nodded and Lucian pulled away, regretting the terror he saw in her innocent eyes. She'd not seen violence as a child, and heaven knew she hadn't seen it in the convent. What would she think if she knew Lucian planned to dispatch whoever lurked behind them?

"I will drop down in a moment, but you must allow my horse to stay in front of you, as if I were still riding. Then take cover on the other side of those rocks." He had no choice but to send her forward, much as he hated the thought of her being alone in this wild terrain for even a moment.

"What will you do?" she whispered, her brow furrowed in displeasure and worry. He could see she struggled not to deluge him with questions, thoughts. He knew her natural inclination would be to talk over every option available.

Lucian also knew they didn't have time for that.

"Eliminate the threat." He double checked the knot on the lead rope between horses. "Stay there until I come for you, and we shall be safely on our way." For a moment he considered what would happen to her if he didn't make it back to her.

That course of action was unthinkable. He wouldn't allow it to happen.

"Lucian—" She worried her lower lip, for once unsure what to say.

"There is no time, Mel. I will be there." He allowed his

gaze to linger over her, hoping he conveyed a confidence that would reassure her.

She stared back at him, wide-eyed and frightened, and nodded. "All will be well."

The gift of her trust hit him like chain mail being tossed over his body, cloaking him with invincibility as he went to face an unknown enemy.

Secure in his plan, Lucian slid silently to the ground. To her credit, she did not even glance down as she rode by his hiding place, though the stony set of her jaw told him she was none too happy with the plan.

Damn.

He clenched his fingers about the hilt of his sword, waiting for the horse and rider that followed many paces behind them. He had not so much seen their presence this morning as he had felt it, but he trusted his instincts implicitly.

Melissande arrived safely at the curve in the trail and the rock outcropping at about the time Lucian heard a horse in the distance. Her faith in him overwhelmed him, humbled him, strengthened him to honor the magnitude of her trust.

He would not disappoint her.

With the patience of a man long accustomed to stealth, he waited. The trees obscured the face of the oncoming knight, a man who rode armed to the teeth.

The newcomer seemed to lack Lucian's size and—

Lucian's grip on his sword faltered as the man's face came into view.

Peter Chadsworth.

A fellow knight. A fellow Englishman. A fellow foster son under the tutelage of Osbern Fitzhugh.

Dear God. Half of him wanted to whoop with joy at the sight of an old friend. His smarter half knew this could be no happy reunion.

If Peter Chadsworth followed him through the woods

without identifying himself, chances were the man meant to do him harm.

Before he could dissect the matter any further, Peter's mount passed Lucian's chest, near enough to touch. After the head of the horse, Lucian raised his sword and knocked the rider neatly from his saddle. The blow reverberated with satisfying force up Lucian's arms.

Amid much cursing and spitting, Chadsworth rose. Honorable knight that he was, Lucian allowed him to.

"Bastard!" The fallen man lifted his weapon, prepared to defend himself. Encumbered by the quiver of arrows that rode high on his back, now crooked from his tumble, Chadsworth didn't stand a chance in hell of winning a ground battle against Lucian.

No matter. If his former friend meant to kill him, the man posed a threat to Melissande. And that, Lucian would not suffer.

He unleashed a series of blows to set Chadsworth on his heels. Lucian held him at sword point, not ready to kill him but determined to extract some answers.

"Why do you follow me?"

Peter ran shaking fingers over a flesh wound on his thigh. "As if you didn't know." His injury did not keep the venom from his voice. "Murderer."

The word sliced through Lucian with more force than any blade.

"Ah." Lucian supposed he should not be surprised. All of Osbern Fitzhugh's fostered knights had been fond of him. But Peter Chadsworth had been one of the more mild-tempered of the bunch and, truth be told, one of the more simpleminded. Lucian would not have anticipated such a level of vengeance in one so innately kind. "You seek revenge on Osbern's behalf?"

"And for his son." The downed man's hand clenched on air, as if seeking his sword nearby.

"Damon Fitzhugh needs your help in claiming vengeance?" Lucian emitted a short bark of laughter before he kicked Chadsworth's weapon farther away.

"He did not ask for help. I give it out of loyalty to him." For the first time, he looked less sure of himself.

"You would steal his right to kill me?"

Chadsworth was more of a dolt than Lucian realized, though dangerous enough to have nearly killed him once before with his lethal crossbow aim.

"He wants you dead," the man shouted. "He repeats it like a litany every night before we sleep, every morning when we awake."

"You have been at war with him?"

"Aye." He closed his eyes for a long moment, perhaps recalling the same horrors Lucian did when he thought of the Crusades.

"Yet he no longer travels with you?"

"He conducts business on behalf of the king." Chadsworth announced his news with the pride of a younger brother. "He returns to England by harvest time."

Lucian nodded. He still had a few months then.

In the meantime he did not think he could kill young Chadsworth. Instinct told him the man's plan to seek revenge had been completely of his own, simpleminded making. He looked up to Damon like a worshipful squire reveres a knight.

A throbbing commenced in his temple. He would learn no more from this man, yet he could not kill him. Lucian knew he would curse himself to hell and back if he let the man go, and thereby allowed one of the dolt's misguided arrows to hurt Melissande.

Perhaps the risk would not be so great if he could ensure himself a substantial distance over a wounded enemy.

He braced himself. Then squeezed the shaft of his sword as he hefted it.

"God go with you, Peter." Striking a blow with the blunt side of the sword to the younger man's head, Lucian hit him hard enough to keep him senseless for an hour or two, but not hard enough to do permanent damage.

With any luck, Chadsworth would be so groggy and confused upon awakening, he would lose more time finding his horse and hauling his sorry carcass over the animal's back again. And now that Lucian knew of the man's intentions, he could be that much more alert to danger. Assuming Chadsworth would be foolish enough to continue his quest now that he realized young Fitzhugh would not thank him.

"My God." The startled gasp was too horrified to have come from Lucian's jaded conscience.

He turned to see Melissande a few feet away, taking in the scene with stunned eyes in an ashen face.

"What are you doing?" Lucian barked, more harshly than he'd intended. How could she have left the safety of the shelter he had directed her to? A few moments earlier and she could have gotten caught in the middle of swordplay. She could have been injured or—

"How could you do this?" Tears pooled and spilled down her cheeks as she looked upon the fallen figure of Peter Chadsworth.

She stepped toward the body, but Lucian grabbed her, unwilling to let her discover the man was still alive. "Leave him be, Mel."

Her hand flew to her mouth, maybe to muffle a sob or to quell the queasiness some people experienced at the sight of blood. The skin on her arms felt chill and clammy to his touch. Her words were barely a whisper. "How could you do this?"

He would not put her mind at ease by telling her the man would wake up in the afternoon.

No, it would be easier to distance himself from Melissande if she finally viewed him as the man he had become.

A killer.

As he hardened his heart and lifted his gaze to her condemning one, Lucian knew that, at last, she saw him all too clearly.

Chapter Thirteen

After they rode away from the dead man in the deserted forest, Melissande wasn't surprised that Lucian checked and rechecked the rope that tied their horses together.

If given half a chance, she would leave him now without a backward glance.

How could she have so misjudged him? How could she so grievously misread his character to the point of half falling in love with a cold-hearted killer?

In fact, it had been her deep regard for Lucian that made her betray his wish that she remain safely ensconced in her rocky hideaway while he fought the enemy.

Try as she might, she could not force herself to sit quietly with the horses knowing Lucian might meet his death in a quest to protect her. She had slipped down the mountain, heavy stick in tow, to tip the odds in Lucian's favor and offer whatever help she could.

She had been so relieved to discover Lucian already a victor in his battle. His opponent lay bleeding and beaten on the ground, while Lucian stood over him without a scratch. Before she could make her presence known, however, she'd watched in horror as Lucian raised his sword above his head and killed the man—a defenseless man—with one foul swoop of the blade.

Melissande would have understood if Lucian had struck the blow in combat. But the smaller man Lucian attacked had already been defeated. Lucian's actions broke a basic rule of battle, and an even bigger moral rule.

For hours she shed tears over the young man Lucian brutalized. And, though she did not ask, she knew the person Lucian killed could not have posed any real threat to them on the alpine road. The baby-faced knight looked scarcely out of his squire years, hardly a match for a warrior as well-favored as Lucian Barret.

When they camped that night, Melissande stood unmoving while Lucian tied the rope to her wrists and attached the other end to his waist. She did not protest or comment, and she doubted she would ever find the need to speak to him again.

The silence would surely drive him mad.

He fought daily with the urge to tell her he had not killed Peter Chadsworth. When she looked at him with those wide brown eyes full of disillusionment, he wanted nothing so much as to restore her faith in him.

As they made their way toward the French coast, however, rapidly closing the distance to the Barret lands, Lucian knew he did not deserve her faith or the gift of her conversation. Although Melissande misread Peter Chadsworth's injuries, she had not misread Lucian's character.

"Will we cross the channel tonight?" she called from behind him, startling him with her first attempt at speech in days.

"Not unless you really want to." He would be willing to change his plans to please her. And he couldn't blame her for wanting to end the journey with him as soon as possible. "It is almost dark."

"Nay." She shook her head, her red braids dancing across the green fabric of her tunic as she looked north toward England. "I am not ready to return yet."

Her willingness to linger with him pleased him immeasurably.

"I thought we would seek shelter at the monastery on the hill." He pointed toward an imposing structure overlooking the sea, scarcely able to believe she had broken the sennight of silence.

Following his gaze, she wrinkled her nose. "I hear monks do not look fondly on sheltering women. I would prefer to sleep under the stars again."

"As would I." He steered their horses toward a thatch of trees some distance from the water. "We can camp over there."

She nodded, apparently satisfied, and said no more, leaving him to ponder her words and new demeanor. She seemed more somber somehow, as if the days of quiet reflection had matured her, or maybe saddened her.

Either way, Lucian mourned the change. As much as he knew he should rejoice at her willingness, even eagerness, to distance herself from him, he wished for a reassuring glimpse of her former vital self.

Would Roarke be able to resurrect that vivacious spirit Lucian missed? The thought made him burn with envy. When had he become so possessive of Melissande?

Battling the jealousy that took him by surprise, Lucian untied the lead rope between horses and approached Melissande to retie it between their wrists. The act had become a nightly ritual between them.

Usually she offered him her wrists and turned her face

away as he knotted the rope. Tonight she extended her hand and stared at him boldly, as if defying him to restrain her.

The last rays of sun lit Melissande from behind like a golden halo. The challenge in her dark eyes unnerved him. "It seems we are bound together, whether I will it or nay." Her voice whispered through him, making him recall all the reasons she was far more dangerous to him than he could ever be to her.

He forced a smile to mask the heaviness in his heart. "You shall be well rid of me soon, Melissande. Your captivity ends on the other side of the sea." He smoothed his fingers over her bared wrist, wishing he did not have to compel her to remain at his side.

Her skin was petal-soft and creamy, pale and delicate in contrast to his sun-worn hands. He wondered how that small patch of exposed flesh would feel against his lips, how it would taste on his tongue.

The pulse in her neck fluttered and jumped, as if reading his mind.

"But we will not idle in England for long." She made no move to extricate herself from his touch. "You will accompany me back to St. Ursula's, and we shall be together then. Would you still feel the need to bind me to you then?"

Yes.

"No." He needed to just tie the rope and have done with it. He definitely needed to step away from her and the warmth emanating from her. "I will not escort you, Melissande."

Even if Roarke asked him to do such a thing, Lucian would refuse. He'd have to.

She stared at him a long moment, then shook her head slowly. She stepped closer. "I will not allow anyone else to accompany me."

Lucian's world tilted on its axis. Perhaps his brain did not function properly when she stood so near. "You don't trust me, remember?" Hadn't he proven to her he was a knight with no honor? "You *can't* trust me."

A determined light flashed in her eyes, her delicate jaw set. Stubborn woman. What would it take to convince her?

Forestalling further debate, Lucian made one last attempt to scare her off.

"Do you have any idea how much I want you right now, Melissande? How much I've wanted you every day since that ill-advised kiss in the chapel ruins?"

Her shocked expression told him she hadn't the slightest notion.

He forged ahead ruthlessly to inform her.

"I watch you while you are sleeping and imagine myself lying beside you. In my mind's eye, I am beneath the covers with you, pinning your body to mine with my hands, tasting the curve of your neck with my mouth."

Her eyes were still wide with surprise, but her breath grew shallow at his words. Did the notion of sharing her covers with him hold a certain appeal? As much as the idea tantalized him, he couldn't allow his shock methods to decline into something she found fascinating.

He couldn't risk moving any closer to her. Forget physical intimidation. He was the one intimidated enough he had no choice but to remain as still as stone. One inch closer to Melissande and his control would combust into flames, turning to ashes at his feet.

"But I wouldn't quit there, Mel."

She licked her lips, propelling him closer to igniting with her wickedly innocent mouth.

"Every night I dream of covering your body with mine, spreading your thighs…" Why hadn't she stopped him?

Where was her sense of maidenly outrage? "And entering you. Claiming you. Making you mine alone."

Her furrowed brow suggested she puzzled over this rather than being horrified.

And in the meantime, he was so wound up with wanting her now he didn't dare to breathe the air for fear of catching the scent of dried flowers, the scent of Melissande.

"Do you have any idea how untrustworthy this makes me when you belong to my own brother, Melissande?" He ground out the last words between clenched teeth. "Don't ever make the mistake of trusting me."

She trembled slightly.

Good.

That's exactly what he wanted. What he needed from her. Her friendship was far too dangerous to them both.

But despite the tremble, she met his gaze levelly. "Perhaps that's exactly why I do trust you."

Lucian stifled a curse.

"You've never acted on those feelings," Melissande continued, watching him as carefully as a mouse eyes a nearby hawk. "And you do not allow your warrior status to make you feel entitled to anything you want. I admire that."

Lucian was stunned. Speechless.

"I've considered the matter of the forest road carefully, and I've realized I trust you anyway." She lifted her free hand to lay it gently across his chest. "Explain to me what happened with that man who followed us." Hope flared in her eyes, a testament to her faith in him.

Oh, God.

He couldn't let this happen, couldn't allow her to concoct a fanciful vision of him that he could never live up to.

The delicate brush of her palm on his chest heated his blood and fired his imagination. Perhaps there was another way to scare her off, to ensure she kept a safe distance between them for the rest of the journey.

Not bothering to weigh the merits of his scheme, he leaned forward, savoring the way her eyes widened a fraction. Her faint floral scent drifted to his nose, stirring his senses and fanning the hunger that had stalked him for weeks.

He kissed her. Hard.

His lips fell upon hers with more force than he'd intended, yet Melissande tilted her head back to accommodate him. Her pulse pounded through her veins at her wrist, where he still held her captive.

There was no finesse, no teasing exploration. He cupped the back of her head to steady her and plundered her mouth with blatantly provocative sweeps of his tongue.

His mind screamed a protest, asking him what the hell he was thinking to kiss her this way. Had he really meant to scare her off? Or was he merely exploiting the moment for a chance to taste her?

Her small moan robbed him of the ability to figure it out.

He dragged her against him, their bodies aligning in a sensuous connection, thigh to thigh, hip to hip, his chest to her high, rounded breasts. Her dress molded to his legs in the breeze, tendrils of her hair wound around his shoulders to stroke him with red silk.

Why didn't he offend her sensibilities with his coarseness? His impudence?

Refusing to retreat until he'd succeeded, Lucian trailed his hands up her arms, over her shoulders to slide down the green-velvet bodice of her gown.

Melissande gasped, he could feel it right through her kiss. Yet she did not pull away.

Blood whooshed through his veins in heated tidal waves, resounding in his ears like the crashing surf. Too bad he couldn't stop himself. Not yet. Only Melissande could stop this insanity.

He was surprised to feel his hands shake just a little as he reached for the ties on her bodice. He'd wanted this so much, dreamed about her for so long. With slow precision, he gauged the knot with his fingertips. He wasn't about to break the best kiss of his life to examine how to best untie her gown.

Somewhere beneath the deafening pound of his heart, he heard Melissande's voice as if far away.

"Wait."

He released her immediately; her body, her gown's ties, all traces of green velvet. But the memory of how she'd felt in his arms—he wouldn't ever let go of that.

He pulled away in time to see her eyelids force themselves open with lazy effort. She blinked back at him, the fire in her eyes barely banked.

Her lips were still swollen from his kiss, yet her brow furrowed in confusion.

"You weren't kissing me because you wanted to just now, were you?"

He couldn't mistake the censure in her tone.

"Trust me, I wanted to." That much was always true.

"But you didn't kiss me to indulge some personal passion for me, did you?" Her arms folded over her chest, as if to shut herself away from him as much as possible. "You want to scare me away more than anything."

How could he deny the truth?

She tipped her chin at him. "Haven't you figured out by now that's the wrong tack to take with me?" Her eyes glittered, locking head-on with his. "Next time you try a trick like that you might be surprised who scares who."

His jaw probably hit the ground. Lucian was too busy staring at her in disbelief to notice.

Had the convent-bred Melissande truly just baited him with sensual threats?

His blood pounded with an unqualified yes.

With considerable effort he peeled his gaze from Melissande as she moved around the camp, focusing instead on the rope that had fallen unbidden to the ground in their kiss. He picked it up and let it dangle from his fingers, knowing he could not bring himself to tie it around her.

Not after all that had passed between them.

Instead he found himself envisioning other, more pleasurable ways of tying her to him. He imagined her ensnaring him in her long skeins of red hair, tying her to him with a lover's silken threads. He imagined tying Melissande to him as his wife, slipping the bond of marriage around her finger instead of the bond of captivity about her slender arm.

Tossing the rope aside, he admonished himself for dangerous daydreams.

Father, forgive me.

Still awkward with his renewed habit of heavenly supplication, Lucian had succumbed to the realization that he desperately needed prayer in his life. If he was to deliver Melissande to Roarke with her virtue intact, he required all the divine intercession he could muster.

"Are you all right?" Melissande straightened her clothing and stared at him with gentle concern.

"Fine." He willed his breathing to a more even pace. He had to put a stop to this, to put space between them if she wasn't going to do it for them.

He stalked toward the saddlebags, urging away the raw sensual hunger in his body. He discovered the flint among the other supplies and pulled out the stones. "Would you care to light the fire?"

She shrugged, but held her hands out and Lucian tossed her the tools.

They worked in silence to prepare the dwindling rations, and Lucian wondered what she was thinking. She didn't say much, even when they ate their meal.

"Perhaps we can finish the *Odyssey*?" He needed something to distract him from Melissande.

"I don't think so." She shook her head, loosening her already precariously tied braid a bit more.

"How fortunate you are to read Greek." He wouldn't normally use her generous spirit to manipulate her, but he wanted to know how Odysseus fared in his adventures at sea. And he had to shift the focus of his thoughts away from Melissande. "You have the luxury of plucking up your book and satisfying your curiosity anytime you choose."

"The ending is awfully romantic. I really don't think—" Melissande bit her lip in indecision.

"Understood." The last thing he needed was another night of firelight and *amour* with this woman.

The *Odyssey* ended romantically? Absently, Lucian drew figures in the sand with a short stick, wishing Odysseus had a more realistic fate. One more akin to Lucian's.

"Odysseus was a great warrior," he observed.

"I guess."

Lucian saw an opportunity to push her away and he took it. "That means he was forced to kill people on occasion."

He sensed her stiffen beside him.

But he could not relent. "There are times a man must defend himself."

"It does not seem like defense to hit a man who has already been downed." Her tone did not seem to censure, merely question.

"Sometimes a man fights to protect more than just himself. A warrior's whole purpose is to protect. Sometimes he protects lands or ideals...or in this case, a person.''

He glanced over at her, seeking an expression to gauge the impact of his words. Sensing his stare, she lifted her chin, fixing him with the fathomless depths of her dark eyes.

''You felt you were protecting me?'' The disbelief in her words warred with the shades of empathy her gaze projected.

''He sought to kill me, Mel. He would have killed me in the lowlands had I not bent down at the moment he released his crossbow.'' He picked up her hand and squeezed it between his palms, as if he could further impress his thoughts upon her. ''Next time he would not have missed. And where would you be if I died out here, Melissande?''

Slowly shaking her head, she did not agree with him. ''The Church teaches me—''

''I know what the Church teaches you.'' He moved to his knees and planted himself in front of her, blocking her view of the fire, the forest, everything but him. ''Are you aware that at the same time they're preaching 'turn the other cheek' to you, they're telling me to take up their cause in the Holy Lands and kill for it?''

''The Crusades save Christianity from the infidel—''

''The Crusades steal land from people as noble and kind as you or I, Melissande, yet I have fought for the ideals because...'' How did he arrive here? He had meant only to remind her that he would forever be a warrior. That it came with the territory of knighthood to kill. Oddly, he had succeeded only in circling back to the one death he had not meant to cause.

''Why, Lucian?'' She reached to touch his face. Her delicate fingers smoothed over his cheek in a gesture of reassurance, acceptance. "Why would you go into a battle you did not believe in?"

His efforts to defend the knighthood suddenly rang hollowly in his ears. He was a fraud to pretend he hadn't killed without reason. No amount of postulating and theorizing about the nature of battle would relieve the guilt in his murderous soul.

He had been a fool to try.

"My foster father believed in the Crusades with all his heart." The words burned in his throat as they eased past his lips for the first time. The time had come to confess his sins and to set Melissande Deverell safely away from him once and for all.

And, Lucian realized, to a certain extent, his recent return to prayer had unearthed a deep desire for absolution he had not known he possessed. Melissande could not, would not, provide that absolution, but she could serve as his confessor. It was because of her, after all, that he had taken the first step toward God again.

"You mean, Lord Fitzhugh?"

Of course she knew him. Osbern's property neighbored her lands as much as Barret Keep. Lucian withdrew his hand from hers, unwilling to feel her pull away in horror when he confided in her. "Aye. He found the Church a year or two after you left England."

Melissande laughed without mirth. "I should say that was a good thing. No one was in more need of religion than Lord Fitzhugh."

"Why do you say that?" His head whipped up. Everyone at home idolized the man since his death. Lucian couldn't resist hearing an opinion of him that might not be so sainted.

She shrugged. "I thought that was a common sentiment.

Even as a child, I recognized the man's ferocious temper. Especially after a few rounds of ale.''

"He stopped drinking after he started going to church." Lucian rose and dusted off his knees before seating himself by her side again. Her observation gave him no comfort.

"Did he stop flying into rages over nothing?"

"For the most part." Except when the conversation turned to the Crusades. "Anyway, I joined the wars because of him." Revealing his sins would be more difficult than he thought. Would she be frightened of him when she learned of his deed? He didn't want to scare her, only to open her eyes to who he was.

She leaned forward, closing the distance between them a bit more. Her eyes sparked with curiosity. Lucian thought it ironic that he finally had drawn her out of her week-long silence only to dump his most closely held secret on her narrow shoulders.

"He became like a father to you after yours died, I imagine." Her sharp mind wrapped around the facts and used them to further the story.

"I tried to please him, but ultimately, I couldn't." Lucian admired her intelligence even as he dreaded the conclusion of her efforts.

"You went to the wars because he wanted you to!" She looked indignant on his behalf. "What more did he expect?"

"Nay. I went to the wars because it was my foster father's dying wish." The image of his last conversation with Osbern Fitzhugh flashed through Lucian's mind.

Sympathy softened her features. Her hand reached for his, but Lucian gently captured hers and set it back in her lap. "There is more." He lifted his eyes to hers. "And it is ugly."

"I'm listening." She frowned. Worry creased her forehead.

How unusual for him to be talking and her to be silent. Lucian wondered if it would be their last conversation. He stared into the fire, trying to forget he had an audience for his tale.

"We had argued repeatedly about the wars. Osbern wanted me to go, spurred me on with flattery that I was the most accomplished knight he had ever trained. His son, Damon, had already left to take up the cause. So had several men whom Osbern fostered along with me. It disappointed Fitzhugh daily that I remained in England, craven and unworthy."

From the corner of his eye he could see Melissande shaking her head. He guessed she would oppose his harsh words, but he could not allow her to interrupt for fear he would not be able to finish his account.

"One day Fitzhugh broached the topic while we were in the practice field—Osbern, Roarke and I." He had to show her why his brother's loyalty was so important to him, why he owed Roarke so much that he would steal her away from the convent. "He flew into one of the rages you remember."

Melissande gasped and Lucian imagined her facile mind had already worked through the rest of the story. But he could not stop now. He needed to tell the tale as much for his sake as for hers. It had lived silently in him for so long, cutting him to pieces again and again…

"I meant only to protect myself from his blows." He turned to her then, wishing he could convince her—himself—that he had not meant to harm the man. "I had my practice shield raised against him, but it did not seem enough. I—" The words cost him. The burning in his throat grew to flaming heat, but he forced the rest of the story past his lips. "I raised my sword against an old man. I, in my prime and completely rational, my opponent nothing but a failing old man in a wild frenzy.

"I killed him, Melissande." Lucian still asked himself how the hell it could have happened. How could the wound to Fitzhugh's arm been life-threatening, delivering his death in naught but a few days' time?

"You—" She faltered. "You raised your sword against him to protect yourself and—"

"Do not make excuses for it. It is common knowledge in Northumbria that I murdered Osbern Fitzhugh."

She blanched and Lucian knew he should have told her this much sooner—before they'd ever kissed. It appalled him to think that he had darkened her lips—so pure and innocent—with his lust.

The memory must appall her twice as much.

"You could not have had much choice...."

He could hear in her voice how desperately she wanted to believe it. Almost as much as he wanted to.

"I had a choice, Mel, and I chose poorly. My instincts for violence cost a man his life. My own brother labeled me a murderer, though he was quick to protect me."

"Roarke saw it." The resignation in her voice reflected the fact that his black deed was beginning to sink in. She could no longer find a way to justify his action.

"Yes. And even though he knew what happened, he helped hide the fact from Mother." Did she understand the magnitude of that act in his eyes? "'Tis why I owe Roarke the world, and why I went so far as to abduct you."

"I am repayment." She sounded unnaturally calm.

"Yes."

Her silence unnerved him, yet he feared if he looked at her he would see hatred in her eyes. He did not know how to handle this quiet Melissande. What was she thinking?

Was she terrified of the violent streak he had unveiled to her?

Gritting his teeth, Lucian turned toward her, knowing the condemnation he would find but needing to see her face.

Worse than outrage, he found pity in her gaze, tears streaking a river down both cheeks. "You have fallen so far."

Regret lodged in his throat, choking him. He imagined she looked at him as an angel would peer down upon mere mortals, sorry for their failings but powerless to change their sinful nature.

"It is not too late for forgiveness, though, Lucian. God loves you." Her pronouncement was choked through her tears before she turned away to hang her head in her hands.

Void of comfort, her words echoed in the air behind her, recalling the declaration that had once followed that sentiment.

And so do I.

This time, silence remained in the aftermath of her words. Although Lucian had succeeded in pushing her away, success came at the expense of the heart he thought he'd lost long ago.

Chapter Fourteen

The English landscape blurred around Melissande as her horse tore through the countryside. Lucian had maintained a relentless course, hell-bent to unload his captive at Barret Keep.

Although her body had grown numb to the days on horseback and nights of camping outdoors after the weeks on the road, Melissande's heart ached with a pain all too real. No matter how far they traveled from France, she could not forget Lucian's confession.

She watched him race over the hills ahead of her. He had retreated to his old self since then.

Silent. Distant.

The return to his former ways made her realize how much he had changed to please her while they were in the Alps. He had talked to her, even though he found such idle chatter uncomfortable. He had listened avidly to her relate the *Odyssey* to him, asking her for more when they went for too long without consulting the book.

No sign of this Lucian remained. Once again he was a man with a mission, a warrior knight intent only on her reunion with his brother.

Lucian reined in abruptly, leading them eastward toward

a small stream they'd been following all morning. Melissande caught a glimpse of his stern profile, his chiseled features.

Would he ever make peace with himself? Or would he forever feel responsible for everyone around him?

She should have offered him more comfort when he'd admitted the sin of his past. The abbess would have found just the right thing to say, dispensed the wisdom of a proverb, and helped Lucian find a way to forgive himself. But Melissande had wept freely, like the child she sometimes feared she still was. She had far too little opportunity to act on her own instincts in her life. At the convent, decisions had been made for her. So much so, that now she found it difficult to trust her own judgment.

And no doubt, this time, she had made a poor choice in not saying more to Lucian about his foster father.

They ate another afternoon meal in silence while Melissande sought the nerve to apologize. Lucian's aspect could be more intimidating than Sister Eleanor's when he was angry.

Still, she refused to play the child any longer. Gathering her courage, she cleared her throat to speak, determined to offer him what comfort she could.

Lucian bolted from his place on the grass before she had the chance. "I'm washing up," he announced, motioning to the creek nearby as he started to back away from her. "You are welcome to do the same."

Melissande nodded, but he was already striding across the clearing that looked vaguely familiar. Did they near Barret lands so that he must take time to bathe now?

Or did he simply wish to escape conversing with her?

She looked with longing at the sparkling brook, wishing she could dangle her toes in the coolness, until she spied Lucian shedding his tunic.

The vision of his muscular back imprinted itself in her memory, the way his body tapered down from broad shoulders to narrow hips...Lucian's strength had been apparent fully clothed. It was all the more obvious when stripped of his tunic. The thought niggled Melissande's conscience when she considered the time and effort he had channeled into learning his skills as a warrior, only to have her preach to him that he should turn the other cheek.

Lucian spoke truly when he said the Church called men to fight for its ideals. How could she abhor what he did when it was sanctioned by the same church to which she had dedicated her life?

Driven by guilt at her quick condemnation of him, Melissande's feet shuffled hesitantly toward the brook. The man would not have cast off all his clothing when he had specifically told her she could come to the creek with him...would he?

She sidled closer, still mulling over Lucian's past.

Osbern Fitzhugh had been a good man with a big heart until he indulged in too much ale. Melissande had seen him lose control on two separate occasions during her childhood. Why didn't the rest of Northumbria recall the man had a violent temper?

The splashing of water called her back to reality and Melissande peered down to the creek's edge.

He stood, still half-clothed, his face and hair dripping from a dousing. Her breath caught in her throat at the sight of his bare chest, perhaps even more impressive than his naked back.

She might have lost her nerve to approach him, and would have turned back, had not a twig cracked beneath some subtle movement of her foot.

His head whipped around to confront her and she glimpsed the trained warrior in the tense lines of his body.

Relaxing as he spied the source of the noise, Lucian resumed dressing in the shady cover of the surrounding copse of trees.

"I am finished." He ambled over to her while slipping the tunic over his head. "You may have the creek to yourself." The fine linen clung to his wet arms. A bead of water rolled over the scar at his temple and down his cheek.

Melissande fought the urge to reach out to capture the drop with her finger. Lost in contemplation of his masculine form, she startled as he walked right by her, no doubt returning to the horses.

"Wait." She reached out to hold him back, her palm connecting with the solid expanse of his chest. "I would speak with you a moment."

He said nothing, but he waited.

The coolness of his damp body filtered through the thin linen of his tunic. She thought she should let go of him, but found she couldn't will her fingers to remove themselves. The solid strength of him fueled her courage to explain herself.

"I am afraid you took offense at my flood of tears the other night—" she hesitated, wishing she did not have to remind him of something so painful "—when you told me about Lord Fitzhugh."

His jaw set in a stony line. Still, he did not move, nor did he try to extract her hand from its intimate resting place against his heart.

"Perhaps you thought I cried in condemnation of you, but I assure you my tears only reflected the sorrow I saw in your eyes and felt as you felt. 'Tis obvious to me it was an accident. I am surprised and saddened that you cannot see it that way."

The sun shone brightly on the horses and fields beyond them, but here by the water, they were sheltered by the forgiving shade of thick trees. The darkness made confidences seems easier to share, touches simpler to offer.

"I know you would never do anything to purposely harm Lord Fitzhugh." Melissande stepped closer to him, plucking up one of his hands in her free one.

"He died in wretched pain, bewailing my cowardice to the heavens as he went." Lucian peered down at their clasped hands as if that kind of touch was utterly new to him.

"Probably delirious from blood loss." Why did it seem so logical to her while the rest of his friends and family chose to believe the worst of a good man like Lucian? "An infection may have set in his wound."

"A midwife gave him medicine to prevent infection." Lucian shook his head stubbornly. "She arrived almost immediately."

"Since when is a midwife infallible?"

"I still raised my sword and stung the fatal blow."

Melissande spied the years of self-blame and remorse in his eyes. "You raised your sword to defend yourself, Lucian! You expect yourself to have absolute control at every moment, but you are only human. No doubt you were reacting to one of Fitzhugh's fits of rage without clearly thinking through the possible consequences. And who could think intelligibly when they are being attacked by a madman?"

He tipped up her chin as if to study her more intently. With clear gray eyes, he peered down at her.

"You believe in me."

His words were not a question but a dawning realization. He squeezed her fingers in a tightening, urgent fist.

"Yes."

She would have complained on her fingers' behalf when

he suddenly released her palm and pulled her fully against him, his eyes never leaving hers.

Melissande stilled. Her body crushed to his, a delicious, fevered warmth spread through her. Thinking became impossible. In the short space of an embrace, her world had narrowed to she and Lucian—a place where feelings and the senses took precedent over logic and reason.

"Lucian..." Her words faded into a kiss when his lips fell on hers in hungry demand.

In the sin of the lips lies a disastrous trap... The proverb circled through Melissande's mind, but the desire to return Lucian's kiss overwhelmed her. Would it hurt to quench the thirst for him that had been growing in her for weeks, no matter how much she tried to deny it?

Perhaps one embrace would satisfy her curiosity, ease the longing. She would return to the convent soon, after she expressed her wishes to Roarke. Melissande would never again know the feel of a man's touch.

She parted her lips in silent encouragement and was rewarded with Lucian's groan and a deepening of their kiss.

Creek water seeped from his garments into hers, suffusing her bodice with his sultry heat.

"No one has ever believed in me," he whispered between trailed kisses down her neck. When he reached the barrier of her gown, he raised his head, cupping her face in his hands. "Why you?" He fixed her with a glare that was part demand, part desperate need for affirmation.

Melissande ignored the demand and answered the need. "I've known you to be an honorable protector and a good person."

He dragged his palm down her unraveling hair and over her breasts through the clinging fabric of the green gown. "You call this honorable?"

His touch ignited the last bit of restraint she might have

called upon, torching her resistance to ashes in the space of a blink. Desire kicked through her, oblivious to Lucian's sense of honor.

She refused to analyze the consequences of her actions. Shades of her former bold and brazen self roared back to life with a vengeance. She craved passion.

And she would have it.

She laid trembling hands along the squared planes of Lucian's scarred face and tilted his chin toward her.

"I know who you are, Lucian, and I believe in you."

"Angel." He sighed the word with quiet reverence and drew his fingers down the curves of her hips. "If no one else ever believes me, it is enough that you do."

She might have answered him, but the friction of his palms brushing about her waist and down her thighs jumbled her thoughts. Shivery sensations fluttered the length of her spine and through unsteady legs.

Gray eyes bore into hers with dark longing, yet Melissande could see indecision in the furrow of his brow, feel his hesitation as his hands stopped their quest.

She could not bear it if he did not continue to hold her. What would a few stolen moments hurt before they returned to civilization and left their memories of one another behind forever?

Tracing a light path up his chest with her fingertip, she admired the strength of the man, wishing her touch could banish his constraint as his touch had expelled hers.

Still she was surprised to hear herself whisper to him. "I need you, Lucian."

With a curse and a growl, he curved a hand around the back of one thigh and hauled her leg from the ground to wrap it around his body.

Melissande gasped at the intimacy. The leather of his braies skimmed the velvet of her dress, creating a sensuous slide of fabric around her legs and between her thighs. Waves of pleasure radiated from the places their bodies connected. The damp warmth of his body sealed them together, locking them in a steamy embrace.

The scent of sun-warmed leather, spring grasses and the clear stream behind them surrounded her, vibrant smells absent from her life in the convent. She couldn't absorb sensations fast enough, hungry for pleasures she'd been denying far too long.

Lucian brought his mouth down on hers, his kiss as out of control as she felt. She squeezed his shoulders, needing him to balance herself in the onslaught of new awareness she'd half imagined for weeks.

She rocked her hips against him, eager for more of the tantalizing tremor that pulsed through her at his touch. His answering groan sent shivers racing through her, infusing her with a heightened sense of her own feminine power.

He wanted her—wanted this—as much as she did.

Fire took hold of her belly, her legs. She couldn't fool herself into thinking she would be satisfied with a few stolen moments any longer. Curiosity and desire demanded to discover where this tantalizing trail would lead.

She ventured one palm beneath his tunic to smooth over the muscles of his chest.

"Angel...Mel..." Lucian's whispered words wound through her thoughts, his voice hoarse and anguished.

She pressed kisses to his corded neck, the soft fur exposed by the open ties of his tunic.

The needy flames consuming her were too strong to fathom retreat now. Whatever secrets Lucian's body harbored, Melissande was determined to extract them.

"Please," she whispered, not knowing what she asked for but certain Lucian would.

Lucian lowered her body to the pine-needle-covered

ground, murmuring words of encouragement, promises that he would protect her.

Had she ever doubted it?

Although somewhere in her brain, a small voice entreated her to use caution, Melissande trusted Lucian more than she trusted herself. Not only would he never hurt her, he knew how to give her body the most pleasure it had ever experienced.

With each new kiss, each caress, she found increasing fulfillment. And with each touch, the stakes raised for the next one, leading her to believe a shimmering goal of pleasure awaited her at the end of this sensual journey.

With clever hands, Lucian untied laces and released garters until she lay half naked beneath him.

She waited for his caress to resume, the moist heat of his mouth to possess her body again.

Nothing.

Melissande propped an eye open to find him staring at her, his gaze absorbing every detail of her bared body.

No one else had ever seen her body since her childhood, though Sister Eleanor had often chastened Melissande for her less than spare figure.

Curving a hand around one of her breasts, Lucian traced its shape. ''To think you hid this body under a nun's habit.''

The reverent brush of his hand and open admiration erased a decade's worth of Sister Eleanor's disparaging comments.

Eager to feel his strength upon her once again, she tugged him down to resume their kiss.

Only now his gentle explorations were unencumbered by clothing. His lips did not have to hesitate at a neckline. They journeyed down her breasts, the rough texture of his unshaven chin grazing over her tender skin moments before the flick of his tongue eased the burning path.

Immersed in the scent and feel of him, Melissande allowed no thought to mar her pleasure in his touch. His mouth moved to tease and to taste the crests of one breast, and she moaned with the pure joy of it.

"Lucian…" Sighing his name, reveling in the way it sounded, she twisted her frustrated fingers in his tunic. She wanted to feel more of him, to experience the texture of his body without barrier.

Barely removing his lips from her skin, he worked the tunic over his head and flung it aside.

Equally tempted to look as to feel, Melissande settled for a quick peek at the lightly curled hair on his chest that narrowed into a thin line and disappeared into his braies.

He was beautiful. Despite the numerous scars his bare body revealed, his body was perfect in Melissande's eyes. Hardened by battle, honed with practice, his warrior form epitomized the tenacious spirit of Lucian Barret.

And the danger.

But he had shown her he did not kill without remorse. His choice to go to war was dictated by penance, not by bloodlust.

Melissande wrapped one leg around him to bring him even closer, needing to reassure herself that Lucian could be as tender as he could be dangerous.

She hungered to possess some small part of him, the tender and the dangerous, the scholar and warrior.

His fingers traced a pattern up her inner thigh, his nails grazing her delicate flesh. A curious tension spread through her body and heated her skin, converging in an overwhelming ache between her legs.

She wrapped her hand around the reassuring strength of

his arm, waiting for the touch she craved, hoping it would somehow relieve the knot twisting inside her.

When his fingers met the juncture of her thighs, Melissande cried out, scoring his back with her nails. Pleasure knifed through her with a keen edge.

Capturing her cries with his mouth, Lucian kissed her, all the while manipulating the most secret part of her. He whispered to her as he touched her, words both sweet and seductive, as he lulled her nearer to some shimmering destination of pleasure.

The knot inside Melissande tightened and grew. Her mouth watered for the fulfillment he could bring. A fevered flush spread through her body, until at last, one finger slid inside her.

She screamed her response to the heavens, waves of heat breaking over her body again and again, until she was naught but heartbeat and trembling flesh.

With each pound of blood through her veins, she rejoiced at the wonder and joy of Lucian. She had no idea the relations between man and woman would be so utterly fulfilling.

His head pillowed by her breasts, his breath warmed her body in the aftermath of their lovemaking. Melissande ran idle fingers through his hair, wondering how her convent sisters could have complained of the burden of marriage when this was the sort of pleasure it brought.

At the same time, Melissande recalled she was not married.

What had she done?

She gazed down at her exposed body entwined with Lucian's near-nakedness. They would have no choice but to wed now.

They had obviously committed the ultimate act of intimacy. Melissande knew from whisperings she overheard at the convent that once a woman's body was pierced by a man, she had lost her innocence forever.

Could Lucian see it? Would a stranger be able to look at her and know she had just been initiated into womanhood?

Lucian raised himself over her, looking far less sated than she felt. Hunger flared in his eyes as he leaned down to kiss her. His body seemed to come alive against her as he moved, nudging her thigh and belly in the strangest manner.

"Lucian?" she began tentatively, hating to spoil the wonder of what they just shared, but desperate to clarify what this new turn in their relationship meant. She cupped his face in her palm, needing him to look at her. "We are not even married."

He released her as if her body was suddenly poisonous, rolling off her to lay by her side some feet away.

Melissande mourned the loss of his touch although she still felt as if a glow must be apparent all around her.

She hated to end their time together here, but knew a church should sanctify their union. In her heart, she was certain Lucian felt the same way.

"You understand, don't you—" she ventured.

"Of course," he shot back, the words surprisingly sharp for how intimate they had just been.

Melissande reached for her clothing, trying not to sound as stung as she felt. "I just think—"

"I know." He wiped a weary hand across his brow. "It is fortunate one of us came to our senses." This time he softened his words, his voice sounding as tortured as she felt.

It was not in his nature to talk things over to the degree that Melissande liked to. She should be accustomed to his uncommunicative ways.

He sounded sincere enough, anyway, and Melissande thought he must understand the need for him to wed her at once. Now that they had been intimate, there was no choice.

She watched him dress, wondering if he felt the same glow through his body that she experienced. It didn't seem that lovemaking could possibly yield as much pleasure for a man as for a woman.

"I am ready," she said finally, surprised how eager she suddenly felt to get back on the horses and find a place to wed Lucian.

She thought she would never marry or have children—

An abrupt pang stung her heart at the thought of the abbey orphans. Once she married Lucian, she could never go back to them.

A baby of her own would be a blessing. Indeed she had nurtured a secret dream for one all her life, yet even a child of her flesh and blood could not erase the memory of the three she already loved.

Trudging through the small wooded area, Melissande watched their dear faces swim through her memory. What if she could still help them? Write to them, watch over them from afar? Indeed, she would pen them a missive immediately to ease their minds, and maybe Lucian would permit her to send them each a fund to start their lives away from the abbey when they grew to adulthood.

Or…what if she could adopt the children herself?

Her mind bounded forward with the possibilities as she followed Lucian from the copse of trees. He walked so quickly that she was encouraged he was as eager as she to speak their vows and return to their former occupation.

A flush of pleasure stole through her, followed quickly by old fears and doubts. Was she even capable of being a good mother to those children? In the convent, there had been others to help her raise them, other women for the children to love. But she would be on her own with them if she could convince Lucian to bring them to England. Would the upheaval in their lives only upset them?

Heaven knew she had been beside herself when her parents had turned her life upside down to bring her to the abbey. She'd had so little experience being mothered herself, what if she couldn't perform the task well? She couldn't bear the breakup of another family. Not after the loss of her own at a tender age.

They faced each other for a moment when they reached the horses. Lucian's expression creased in worry. And although Melissande still felt the resonant joy of their lovemaking, she knew her face must reflect her fears.

His hands shook ever so slightly as he lifted Melissande onto her mount. He deposited her there with unnecessary hurry, as far as she was concerned.

Something seemed wrong. Even if he was unhappy about their thwarted passion, he should still care for her solicitously. Especially after what just transpired between them.

"We must hurry to make Barret Keep by nightfall," he called over his shoulder, not even sparing a backward glance in her direction.

"We will still go to your brother's?" Melissande had rather hoped they would find a chapel and spend the night at an inn. It struck her as awkward to go to the home where Roarke resided. No doubt he would be angry to find Lucian had wed the woman he wanted to marry.

"Where else would we go?" He kicked his horse into motion, apparently unconcerned over her response.

Maybe he was right. She understood why he would want to be surrounded by family for a wedding. With any luck, he would not be so surly by the time they reached the end of their journey.

Despite the worries churning through her mind, her body

still hummed from the pleasure Lucian had owed with his lips and hands. What would it be like to indulge in such passion night after night?

Melissande had not allowed herself to think about marriage in years. Even when Lucian abducted her to wed Roarke, she had not considered it for a moment. Returning to the safety of the convent and the duty of helping the children were more important to her than passion.

But now it seemed she no longer had a choice. She and Lucian had shared the intimacy of husband and wife. They must wed. Would Lucian wield all the power in their marriage the way her father had always been able to overrule her mother? She remembered too well that it had been her father's decision to send her to the abbey despite her mother's objections. And of course, he had his way in the end. She couldn't abide the idea of being overruled. Ignored.

At least in the convent she had learned methods for obtaining her own way on occasion. Perhaps with Lucian, she would not be so fortunate. Her mind reeled with adjustments to her life's new plans in light of the afternoon's events.

In fact, she thought so hard and so much, she didn't even realize they had entered Barret lands until Lucian shouted to her that the keep was in sight.

Odd, his voice still sounded remote these hours later. Perhaps Lucian was merely nervous at the prospect of confronting his brother with the news of their nuptials.

Roarke was sure to be mad.

As they drew up to the main courtyard, Melissande's heart filled with nostalgia. She had so many fond memories of playing here, in the surrounding forest and orchard, and along the riverbank that lay between the Barret and the Deverell holdings.

A sprawling affair, Barret Keep had been constructed in several phases since the Norman invasion. A stout, round keep was flanked by high walks and intermittent watch towers. The stone edifice loomed dull and gray until the sun lit the surface just right and highlighted hidden sparkles in the dark rock. Much larger than the small holding she had grown up in, the Barrets were a more powerful family. Lucian would properly be her father's overlord now if her father still lived.

"Did one of my sisters move into Deverell Keep?" she asked, wishing she'd had a brother who could have inherited the inviting property. She had always been so happy there.

"Nay. The king told Roarke that he would reassign it. It has been vacant for some years." Lucian flung his leg over the saddle and leaped from the horse.

Frowning, Melissande allowed Lucian to help her down. Suddenly self-conscious of her appearance, she tried to tighten her braid and to dust their travels, along with a few pine needles, from her skirts.

Already striding toward the main entrance, Lucian called over his shoulder. "I wouldn't worry about how you look, Mel. Roarke will be thrilled to see you no matter how I deliver you."

His comment unsettled her. It seemed a very inappropriate thing to say. She hurried to catch up with him, wanting a moment to speak to him before Roarke discovered their arrival.

Although she called out to him, he opened the main door as if he had not heard her. Doubly annoyed, she nearly ran to reach his side.

Two servants greeted Lucian immediately, apologizing for not noting his appearance earlier.

Now the picture of chivalrous concern, Lucian extended

his arm to her as he waited in the archway, although Melissande noted his eyes held no warmth. She took his arm, but silently fumed at him, frustrated they would have no time to talk privately before facing Roarke.

What would they say to him? How should she behave? Would Lucian expect her to contribute to the discussion?

Her fears converged into panic as a towering, princely man with striking green eyes strode toward them into the hall.

Roarke.

There was no mistaking the man she had adored as a child. Those green eyes had always struck her as sensitive, inviting as a spring day. The arrogance still lurked in the set of his chin, the proud tilt of his nose.

Only now as she stared at the brothers with a woman's eyes did it occur to her how different they looked. From the color of their eyes to the way they carried themselves, the Barret men bore no shared physical traits to mark them as kin. As handsome as Roarke might be, Melissande couldn't wait to escape his company. Surely he had turned out to be a fine man, but she could only think of Lucian and what had passed between them earlier in the day. She inched closer to Lucian, needing to feel his strength beside her.

"You are well come, my brother." He bowed low to them both, but turned his bright green gaze on Melissande. "As are you, Melissande. The years find you more beautiful than my fondest imaginings."

To her discomfort, Lucian released her. Indeed, the brute nudged her forward toward Roarke.

Faltering for words, she merely curtsied.

Apparently that was not enough for Roarke. He picked up her hand to hold it gently in his and, raising her palm to his lips, kissed her.

Why didn't Lucian say something?

She turned around to glare at him, hoping she conveyed her confusion and desperation in her expression. This was not proceeding at all as she'd envisioned.

"Welcome to my home, Melissande." Roarke smiled, his white teeth as perfect as in childhood. "I hope you will be very happy here."

She wanted to scream at him that Barret Keep belonged to Lucian, as did she, but she knew it was not her place. Mutely, she allowed Roarke to take her arm and to draw her to his side.

Her heart beat wildly. She now stood at Roarke's side, staring across the hall at Lucian, who should be saying something any moment to clarify this mess...

"Brother." Lucian cleared his throat and met Roarke's gaze. "It has cost me more than I ever imagined to deliver your wife to you."

Melissande knew her mouth fell wide open, but for all the world, she could not shut it. Betrayal slammed her in the belly.

Lucian's jaw clenched. "Now that I've abducted a convent-bred novitiate and risked her life and limb as well as my own so she might be your bride, I consider my debt to you well paid."

His cruelty, his callousness astounded her. How could he hand her over to his brother, when only a few hours ago they had lain sprawled together in a haze of passion, baring their bodies and souls to one another?

If she lived to be one hundred, Melissande would never forgive him.

Chapter Fifteen

Lucian could live to be as old as Methuselah and still not forget the anguish in Melissande's eyes when he'd given her into his brother's care.

He glared into the cold grate in his room at Barret Keep and reminded himself she had never wanted to marry, had never wanted to leave St. Ursula's. He'd forced her here anyway. Surely that betrayal accounted for the hurt in her gaze and not any regret she couldn't be with Lucian.

To think otherwise would be foolish.

He had departed the hall in haste after that, muttering some rubbish about allowing Roarke and Melissande to get acquainted again. In truth, he couldn't bear to see them together.

Now, Lucian paced the bedchamber of his boyhood with determined strides, wondering what the reunited couple discussed belowstairs.

Or maybe they did not talk. Maybe Roarke wasted no time sealing his bargain with his soon-to-be wife and even now initiated her into knowledge of her wifely duties.

The thought turned Lucian's gut to ice. If not for divine intervention, Melissande would belong to Lucian right now instead of his brother.

Damn.

Lucian would have taken her innocence then and there, on the cold hard ground in the middle of nowhere, if she had not reminded him she didn't belong to him.

We are not even married.

At the time, Lucian's passion-fogged brain had thought, for one brief instant, that she wanted the sanction of marriage upon them before he consummated their union. He had immediately started plotting where he could take his angel to make her his for all time.

Several long moments had passed before he recalled she was promised to another and no doubt meant her words as a rebuff.

On the remaining ride to Barret Keep, he'd thanked God that he had not gone so far as to despoil her. A miracle had saved him from destroying her innocence and shattering his brother's trust.

Could he help it if a part of him cursed the fact that he had come to his senses? If their relationship had been consummated this afternoon, Lucian would be wedding her tomorrow. Or tonight.

He would be warming the linens with Melissande now instead of fuming in this cold, sterile chamber by himself. With every fiber of his being he wished such were the case.

And damn it, not just because his feelings were a knot of lust for her siren's body. No, somewhere on the road between St. Ursula's and Barret Keep, Lucian had fallen in love with Melissande Deverell.

Hard.

He sank into the room's one chair and allowed his head to fall into his hands. Closing his eyes, he envisioned her, not wide-eyed with betrayal as she had been tonight, but smiling and chattering as she had on their journey to England.

Perhaps he'd first started to love her when she'd built the fire on her own the first night they camped outdoors. She had been so proud...and so quick to credit him with teaching her the skill. The fact that she even recalled moments shared as youths had warmed his heart.

Her passion for reading had further entranced him. He could pass hours listening to her musical voice and inflections for various characters as she spun tales from around the world.

The woman read Greek, for chrissake. What was not to love?

Above all, she believed in him.

The knowledge awed and humbled him. His angel had offered her faith to him at no cost. Freely, she gave him her trust.

And he had betrayed it beyond repair by giving her to a man she had no wish to wed.

The ache in his heart speared his whole body.

Dragging restless fingers through his hair, he gave up trying to think through the tangle of the day's events and emotions. Sleep was out of the question. Perhaps a ride would help. Anything to get out of Barret Keep—and away from Melissande.

Securing his sword to his hip, Lucian stormed from the chamber. Down the main stairs and across the hall, he kept his eyes trained on the front door that would deliver him from Melissande.

"You would steal away in the night like a thief?" A whispered feminine voice called to him from the shadows.

For a moment he thought—hoped—it was his conscience that spoke. Then a woman stepped from the recesses of the hall, clothed in a white linen wrapper.

Guilt and desire warred within him.

Lucian grabbed her by the arms before he realized the

torture simply touching her could wreak. "What are you doing out here? Have you no sense?" She was scarcely dressed for greeting strangers.

Anger emanated from her slight form. "I could not sleep for fear you'd sneak away before I could speak with you." She glared at him with more venom than a serpent's tooth. "I am appalled my fears were well placed."

She seemed to wait for him to speak, perhaps make some excuse for fulfilling his bargain with Roarke despite her wishes. He could not.

"You are angry."

"Furious." Her red hair leaped like hungry flames around her shoulders. Lucian had not seen it undone since…this afternoon.

He recalled the taste of her kisses, the sound of her breathy gasps as if they had just embraced. "You did not think I would really bring you here."

"Not after what happened by the creek." Her hands fisted at her sides.

That caught him off guard. Had she sought to manipulate him through her kisses? She had been the one to initiate a conversation, to touch him. "You hoped that…incident… would make me turn around and take you back to St. Ursula's?"

Judging from the way her eyes grew round as carriage wheels, Lucian guessed not. Her mouth hung open as she gaped at him. "No, Lucian." She shook her head, brow furrowed. "I thought that what happened between us counted as something very intimate."

He could not bear a discussion of their familiarity. Not now when she stood mere inches from him, her body unencumbered by a formal gown, her hair freed to his gaze.

Seeing his lack of response, she pressed forward, crossing her arms defiantly over her chest.

The gesture thrust her breasts provocatively forward. Lucian fought to concentrate on her words.

She bit her lip for a split second, then launched ahead. "I thought that when a man touches a woman in such a manner, it constituted a marriage proposal."

The blow that put a lifelong scar on Lucian's temple had not struck so deep as her accusation.

"What are you saying?" Did he want to know? Didn't he already know, in the deepest recesses of his heart?

"That you are not the man I thought you were, Lucian Barret, if you could so carelessly make love to me, then toss me aside for your brother to wed." Tears glittered in her eyes, though she fairly shook with fury.

"But we did nothing to prevent you from—"

"Nothing?" She threw her arms in the air, then let them fall with a hard thud against her thighs. "You have no honor if you can touch me as a husband touches a wife, then marry me off to someone else. And the fact that you would skulk from the keep in the middle of the night to avoid explaining yourself adds to your wretchedness."

Had she thought they made love? She was so innocent. Chances were she knew naught of what went on between husband and wife.

If Melissande said he was wretched, then by God, he had sinned indeed. Hadn't she been his most stalwart supporter up until now? "I never thought you would want—"

"Exactly." She raised her chin, proud and unbending. "You never gave a thought to me and how I might feel. Heaven forbid you should actually ask me. To do so would require conversing, which you seem to find abhorrent."

"I am not worthy of someone like you, Melissande." He longed to place his hands upon her shoulders and to lower her to a bench for a more civil conversation, but dared not risk touching her. He might never let go.

"Only because you won't allow yourself to be worthy, Lucian." A hint of compassion fluttered through her eyes, though not nearly enough to outweigh her anger. "You are too consumed with your own guilt to free yourself from it."

How could he make her see he had made the best decision? How could she think for a moment she would have been happy tied to a known murderer who had given up his home and title to hide from the truth of what he was? "Roarke is a good man."

He recognized the look in her eyes. She had possessed it once before, just before she had slugged him.

But this was a more mature Melissande. She settled for shaking her head in clear disdain. "So are you, Lucian, but it is obvious you do not want me or the trouble it would require to wed me. I will not marry your brother, however. Even if what we shared means nothing to you, you have made it impossible for me to marry another man."

Her words pummeled him with more force than any fist. He reeled from the blow, unsure how to respond without a full-scale discussion of what true intimacy between man and woman involved.

In a more honorable world, however, perhaps Melissande had the right of it. Even if he had not ruined her according to the letter of the law, he had stolen something precious. Something he had no right to.

"I will return to the convent as soon as Roarke can arrange a suitable escort." She cleared her throat, regaining a measure of the reserve all the years of convent breeding had pounded into her.

Having spoken her peace, she whirled away from him in a blur of white linen and red hair.

Lucian watched her ascend the stairs, her determined stride never pausing.

He struggled to orient himself, to regain his wits in the wake of her confrontation. Recovering from battles with the infidel had not been so taxing.

With more reason than ever to depart Barret Keep, Lucian pushed open the main door and stepped into the sultry night air. There was naught but recrimination and unhappiness left for him here.

He would return to the one place he was useful, the only place where his brutality and unworthiness were fortuitous qualities.

While Melissande tried to argue her way out of marriage to Roarke, Lucian would begin his journey back to the battlefield.

Roarke did not seem the least bit surprised that Lucian departed in the middle of the night without saying goodbye. He told Melissande as much each day when she raised the question of Lucian's whereabouts over supper. Their daily ritual was to argue first about where Lucian had gone and then about the wedding that Roarke wanted and Melissande did not.

So far they had reached no definitive conclusions on either matter.

Roarke claimed his elder brother had left because he wouldn't want to confront their mother, a feat Lucian apparently found difficult since Osbern Fitzhugh's death.

Melissande feared Lucian had left because of her. He might never come back.

Left to her own devices much of the day at Barret Keep, she spent her afternoons in the gardens or in the orchards, often traveling the riverside path that would eventually lead to her family's former holding.

As she wandered aimlessly down the trail for the umpteenth time in a fortnight, Melissande seethed that he could leave her behind so easily.

And, heaven help her, she missed him.

Melissande had enjoyed her first true friendship with Lucian. In fact, Lucian had been her best friend before she'd entered St. Ursula's. There had always been some sort of mutual empathy between them. Now there was a layer of attraction in their friendship that made Lucian's absence all the more painful for her.

Could she love him?

The question lurked in the corners of her mind and leaped out at her when she least expected it. The notion scared her to her toes, maybe because it seemed entirely possible.

Yet it struck her as wrong for a woman who had been a few weeks away from taking her final vows as a nun to fall in love with a man so fast, so simply.

When she had been on the brink of marrying Lucian, or so she thought, she had rationalized the nuptials as inescapable.

But now that Roarke wanted to wed her, Melissande protested at every turn. She cared for Lucian, more than she could admit even now, whereas she didn't feel anything but mild fondness for Roarke.

Turning back once she reached the halfway point on the path, Melissande plucked wildflowers with absent fingers.

She might like Roarke better if he had not accepted Lucian's offer of title and lands in exchange for his cooperation in keeping the details of Fitzhugh's death secret from their mother.

Why didn't Roarke have more faith in his brother's motives? Roarke sounded as though he believed the worst from the very beginning. Had he intended to enhance the view of Lucian as a murderer to put himself in a better social and financial position?

The questions niggled Melissande the longer she stayed at Barret Keep, and they couldn't be denied any longer. She resolved to learn more about the events surrounding Osbern Fitzhugh's death and the ones that followed.

Even though Lucian had handed her off to his brother without so much as a farewell, Melissande knew she owed the man more than she could repay for saving her life in the Alps and protecting her the whole way home. He had given her a taste of the bittersweet joy a man's touch could bring a woman—a gift she knew to be precious even if he thought nothing of it. Indeed, she owed Lucian simply for opening her eyes to the world and to herself.

In return, she could delve into the details of Lord Fitzhugh's death to uncover whatever truths might be buried there. It was high time she asserted herself. Instead of passively accepting everyone else's vision for her and her future, Melissande would forge her own plans and exercise her choices.

Feeling fully alive and almost happy for the first time since she'd arrived at Barret Keep, Melissande hurried home with skipping steps. Ticking off a mental list of people she wanted to talk to when she got back, she was so distracted she almost missed the uproar in the courtyard when she arrived.

One of the servants called out to her before she reached the main doors, however. Turning toward the voice, she noticed a small crowd of castle folk engrossed in conversation, including Roarke.

"Yes?" She walked toward them with slow steps, a foreboding growing at the dark look on Roarke's face.

A man-at-arms with foreign colors stood among them, sweaty and dirty as if from a hard ride.

Roarke clenched his jaw and took a deep breath. For a fleeting moment, the hard aspect of his face made him look like his brother.

He called to her. "It's Lucian."

She hastened the rest of the way over. "Is he all right?"

"He's been shot, Melissande. An arrow in the chest."

The world swayed around her, but Melissande bit the inside of her cheek to take her mind off the swirling queasiness that threatened. She could not faint now. "Is he…?"

"He's not expected to live."

As if an arrow pierced her own heart, the words sliced right through her. It couldn't be true. She lashed out at the nearest target, too overwhelmed with pain to harbor it all within herself. "How convenient that will be for you."

Roarke blanched. The crowd of servants gasped.

"If he dies, you will never have to worry about Lucian claiming what is rightfully his." She referred only to herself as a bride, but Melissande knew everyone else would interpret her words as an accusation that Roarke stole Lucian's earldom. She did not care.

"I am sure you are overwrought, Melissande," he declared through gritted teeth, scowling at the servants until they dispersed with the wind. "You obviously have no idea what you are talking about."

"Where is he?" How could she waste time being petty when Lucian could still be alive?

The man-at-arms stepped forward. "On my lord Wesley's holding close to the French crossing, my lady. He lays in naught but an abandoned crofter's cottage. We were loathe to move a man so wounded."

"You will accompany me there." She turned to the groom, ignoring Roarke's spluttered objections. "My horse, please, and do not dally. Mary," she called to a young maid, "would you retrieve the large book in my chamber and whatever healing supplies the keep maintains, please?''

Satisfied to see both the boy and maid depart with all speed, Melissande spun on Roarke. ''I have no choice, my lord. He saved me from death, and now I must do the same for him.''

He looked as if he would argue, but Melissande plowed forward, refusing to back down.

''You wouldn't want it said that you aided in your brother's death by not lifting a finger to help him, would you?''

His mouth flattened to a thin line. ''I will bring someone to relieve you this evening.''

''We need a physician.'' She shifted her attention to the man-at-arms. ''Has someone ridden for one?''

Roarke intervened. ''There is no one, my lady. Our last midwife left after—'' he eyed her warily ''—after Fitzhugh died.''

''There must be someone.'' She knew nothing of nursing. The thought that she alone could be responsible for Lucian's life or death shook her resolve.

''Here's your horse, my lady,'' the groom called just as Roarke assured her there was no medical help in the area.

Swallowing her panic, Melissande waved forward the maid who used both hands to carry the massive copy of the *Odyssey*.

She would save Lucian.

She must.

Maybe then she could return to the abbey with a clear conscience, knowing she had given back to Lucian a portion of what he had given to her.

The thought gave her little comfort as she rode to his aid.

Chapter Sixteen

Lucian hauled in another sharp breath, knowing he would not live this time. He had escaped death often enough in the past two years to realize he could no longer run from his fate.

The abandoned hut he lay in seemed an appropriate place to die. Cheerless. Alone.

After leaving Melissande he'd spent time gathering his supplies for another trip abroad. He'd been prepared to sail for the continent today, ready to leave England behind him. Justice may have been served this morn when Chadsworth's arrow had finally hit true to its mark, yet Lucian experienced none of the relief he had once anticipated.

He had always been prepared to pay for Osbern Fitzhugh's life with his own. Now that the time had come, however, Lucian felt an overwhelming urge to live.

Melissande had made him want to live again.

Thoughts of her plagued him. His callous manner of passing her along to his brother had upset her, and with good reason. Lucian wished he could go back to remove the look of betrayal from her eyes.

How could a woman as fine and pure as Melissande want *him,* with a soul as tainted as Cain's, when she could wed his upstanding younger brother? Lucian couldn't have offered for her. Could he?

The question tormented him more than the searing pain in his chest as he lay on the cold dirt floor of the shelter. He had lost the chance to make her his forever, and now it would never be regained. He wondered if she would mourn his passing.

The rhythmic drum of a horse's hooves shook the ground and interrupted his thoughts.

Perhaps his brother...

Nay. A feminine voice trilled on the summer breeze, sweet and musical as it called to him.

Melissande.

As if he conjured her there by thinking of her, she appeared in the doorway, half running, half tripping into the dim interior of the hut.

Lucian's eyes, well adjusted to the amount of light, could discern her clearly. She carried her copy of the *Odyssey* as she groped her way around the room, searching for him. Curiosity pricked his increasingly hazy mind. Why the hell would she bring a book to his deathbed?

Her hand stumbled over his elbow.

"Lucian!" Tossing the magnificent volume aside, she fell to the floor beside him. She ran her hands gingerly along his still form, certainly because she searched his body for injury and not out of the desire to touch him.

"You came." The effort to speak stung, bitter and metallic in his throat, but not for the world could he lay there in silence while the woman of his dreams manifested before him.

She peered down at him as if surprised at his words, her questing fingers pausing in their work. "I heard your wound could be fatal, Lucian."

"Not for a matter of hours, I'll warrant."

She gasped at his pronouncement, then resumed her tentative inspection of his body, blinking back tears when she reached the pile of soaked rags just above his breastbone. ''I will save you.''

Her tears wrenched his heart. He did not deserve them. Could not bear to witness them.

''Do not bother, Angel.'' He grabbed her wrist, unwilling to have her waste energy or emotions on a death that had long been destined.

''Nonsense.'' She grabbed a wineskin from around her neck, paying him no heed. ''I can save you.''

''My time of reckoning has arrived.'' He released her arm to swat away the wineskin.

''You can do your reckoning alive as well as dead, Lucian Barret. Argue the point as much as you want, but you will do it as I sew you together.'' Her brown eyes lit with an internal flame, though her voice still quivered with her tears.

Melissande scrambled away to gather the wineskin he'd tossed aside. When she returned, she seemed more resolved, more determined than ever. She wiped a stray tear from her cheek. ''I brought water in this. You do not have another, containing something stronger perhaps?''

''Aye.'' Sighing, he tugged at another pouch near his hip. He didn't have the strength to argue with Melissande on his best days. What made him think he could win a debate with her when he lay here half dead? ''I will need it if you plan to wield a needle.''

''Sorry. Your wound needs it more.'' She pulled out the stopper from the pouch and poured the contents over the injury.

Lucian could not prevent the wince of his body, but no sound escaped his throat.

"I read it in a medical text I translated," Melissande offered, her voice vaguely apologetic. "'Twill clean it."

Her words sounded blurred and far away to his ears. The alcohol in his wound had nudged him a few steps closer to unconsciousness. He wanted to talk to her, tried to speak, but pain engulfed him.

Through fading eyesight, he watched Melissande lean over his body, several strands of her hair slipping loose from its knot to fall on his chest in a silken curl.

Her breath came in light puffs over his wound as she concentrated with her needle and thread, poised to begin stitching.

When had she become so dear to him?

If he had possessed the strength, he would have drawn her head to his heart and rested it there. In his last moments of consciousness, he wished for nothing so much as to hold her one last time.

Doubt niggled the back of Melissande's brain as she tried to decide how to go about sewing a man's skin. Every other Deverell woman knew how to wield a needle. Her sisters had all been experts, but they were scattered to the four winds now, all of them married to men whose keeps were many leagues distant.

Melissande had not sewn a stitch since early childhood. As soon as the convent discovered her facility with languages, they had put her to work in the scriptorium as much of the day as possible.

Now that she no longer resided at St. Ursula's and must face real life, it amazed her how much practical education she lacked.

"It may hurt a bit," she warned him.

God help me. She prayed as she jabbed the needle into Lucian's skin, but he did not even twitch.

"Lucian?" For one horrific instant she thought he was dead. But the pulse at his neck still throbbed weakly.

Relieved he did not feel the pain of her handiwork, Melissande stitched him up quickly. Even after she finished, she continued to apply pressure to the wound, hoping that might quell the bleeding.

Hours after her fingers grew numb and night had fallen, Roarke arrived at the hut, a maid from Barret Keep in tow.

Melissande watched him struggle to see her in the dim light.

"Melissande?" He eased forward, feeling his way around the darkness to find her.

He was a good man, she decided, if a little misguided. Although he should have been beside Lucian earlier in the day, at least Roarke kept his promise and had come this eve.

"I am here," she called, not moving from her place at Lucian's side.

The maid lit a taper then, raining light and shadow upon their heads.

Roarke knelt beside her, his forehead creased with worry. "Are you all right?"

She nodded, too heartsick and weary to say more.

"Is he…?"

"He lives." For the moment. "He will live," she said more fiercely, refusing to allow Lucian's dire condition to predict his death.

"I have brought Isabel to stay the night with him." He took Melissande's arm. "You may come home with me and rest now."

She remained immobile, her fingers staunchly pressed against Lucian's chest. "I am happy to have Isabel stay with me, my lord, but I will not leave until your brother is healed."

"Think of what people will say." Roarke lowered his voice, his head bowed conspiratorially next to hers. "Surely you cannot mean to spend another night with my brother now that our nuptials have been declared."

"I mean to sit here until Lucian is out of danger—" she gave him a level gaze "—regardless of what people say."

Changing tactics, Roarke raised his head and peered down his nose at her. "As my future wife, Melissande, you will do what pleases me. I expect you to return with me tonight." Then, more gently, he added, "I will bring you back in the morning after you have rested."

She would not change her mind no matter what he said, but it surprised Melissande how vehemently she opposed his dictum of "You will do what pleases me." Hadn't she tried in vain to please him as a child, only to be teased and sent on fool's errands for him? Hadn't she been trying to please the sisters of St. Ursula's for years now? In return, the majority of them resented her friendship with the abbess or struck out at her blatantly like Sister Eleanor.

What had been the point of her endless efforts to please?

She peered down at Lucian. He had not expected her to please him. He had been happy to find pleasure in the things that suited her—like reading or, on rare occasions, talking.

"I will not attempt to please you on this matter, Roarke. I do not wish to wed you, and I will not turn my back on my heart to fulfill your commands. After Lucian is well, I wish to return to the convent."

His mouth gaped wide, though it emitted no sound.

"I am sorry I could not comply with your wishes."

He drew himself up to his full height. "You will change your mind about leaving, Melissande. We are to wed within a fortnight."

"I have never agreed to marry you."

Roarke argued the point while she tended his brother.

Melissande ate a few bites of the supper Isabel had brought her and tried to quiet him so Lucian might rest peacefully.

"Why does it matter so much to you who you marry, Roarke?" she asked finally. He could wed almost anyone with his position as earl.

Roarke tugged a weary hand through his golden-brown hair. "Lucian always fancied you to be Countess Barret. Once he gave the title to me and swore he'd never marry…"

"Lucian swore not to marry?" Why hadn't he ever told her? Was that why he did not ask for her hand after their dalliance by the creek?

"Aye. 'Twould no doubt set our heirs at odds if he were to have children. Any lad of Lucian's might feel compelled to take back Barret Keep."

"As well he should," Melissande muttered. Lucian was evidently too muddle-headed to right the mess he had made of things.

Her mind strayed back to Roarke's earlier comment… something about Lucian fancying her for a countess. She sifted through the bits of information she had, trying to force the pieces into order. "So you want to marry me, because Lucian once wanted to marry me?"

Roarke pinched the bridge of his nose as if to relieve a pain in his head. "I thought it would ease his heart to see you in the place he had once envisioned for you."

"You thought to please him by taking to wife someone he had once admired?" Could Roarke be so stupid? Somehow she didn't think so. "Or…perhaps you thought Lucian would be less likely to change his mind about granting you the title if you were to marry a woman he respected."

Roarke's grimace gave her all the answers she needed.

"Good God, Roarke, you have bumbled this." She

hoped God might forgive her for taking His name in vain this one time. Roarke's foolishness seemed to warrant an oath.

He covered his eyes with his palms, rubbing the heels of his hands into the sockets. "At some point, I really thought I was doing the right thing."

"The moment you realized you were not, you should have stopped." How could the Barret brothers have gone so far astray in her absence? They had both changed so much in ten years.

They had obviously done a lot more living than she had. Perhaps it was easy to judge from the comfortable position of a bystander.

"Mother died six months ago," he confided. "I did not tell Lucian until he returned home with you. But she babbled incoherently at the end. Spoke of things that could not be true." Roarke closed his eyes. Swallowed. When he stared at her once again, dark secrets lurked in his gaze. "I didn't think Lucian needed that burden, too. I let him think she passed peacefully in her sleep a few weeks ago."

"I am sorry." She patted his arm with her free hand. *All the more reason he is in a hurry to wed.* Without the threat of Lucian's mother learning the truth, Roarke probably feared his brother would try to take the earldom back.

"I hate to lose the rest of my family." He gestured toward Lucian, and his big hand trembled just slightly. "Did he say who shot him?"

For the first time, Melissande saw the love he bore his brother. "Nay. I did not think to ask."

"Did you see the arrow?" He peered around the dark room, lifting the taper Isabel had set on the floor.

"Nay, I—"

Holding the object aloft, Roarke had already discovered it.

Melissande gasped. She recognized it immediately. "'Tis the same as an arrow launched at him while we journeyed here, only…"

Roarke frowned. "Someone shot at my brother in the Alps?"

"Aye. But Lucian already killed the shooter. I saw him—" What had she seen, precisely? Lucian hitting a man in the head with a sword.

"Yes?"

There could be no mistaking the black-feathered arrow with its red markings on the shaft. Identical to the one in France, it could have only come from the man who'd targeted them abroad. But why would Lucian have allowed her to think he had killed the man, if he had not done so?

The answer sprang to mind almost before she finished formulating the question. It had to be part of Lucian's web of penance, his quest for the world to recognize the depths of his sins.

"Lucian made it appear as though he killed the shooter, but he obviously just knocked the man unconscious to give us time to get away." Shaken by the realization, Melissande swallowed a wave of fervent regret he had not ended the assassin's life. Perhaps deep within her she possessed a bit of warrior's spirit, as well. "Unfortunately, he protected me, but did not bother to protect himself."

Roarke tucked the arrow into the leather band that encircled his waist and stood. "I will ask one more time, Melissande. Please return home with me." He extended a beseeching hand to her, embodying all her girlhood fancies with his fairy-tale handsomeness and gallant manner.

But he lacked the rugged appeal of the man who had captured her heart. Nor did he possess the endearing scholarly disposition her warrior knight kept hidden beneath his fearsome facade.

He was not Lucian.

"I cannot. I owe him this."

Roarke studied her in the flickering candlelight, as if seeking some hidden truth. "Have you fallen in love with my brother?"

The question unnerved her, echoing the recent musings of her own mind. She could not meet his eyes, for fear he would read her indecision.

She didn't love Lucian, did she? He had pushed her away, betrayed her at the most cruel level when he'd handed her over to Roarke. How could she love a man who would so dishonor her?

"Nay."

Satisfied, Roarke nodded. "Then there is no excuse for not wedding me. I will see you as my bride, Melissande."

They were back at this again? She thought to argue, but 'twas too much for one day. She was glad to see him go, glad to be left in peace to pray for Lucian's recovery.

Not that she loved him.

Roarke had stepped just beyond the hut's threshold when a thought occurred to her.

A sudden flare of hope sparked within her breast. If Lucian had not really slain the man who trailed them in France, perhaps he had exaggerated the circumstances of Osbern Fitzhugh's death, as well.

And Roarke had witnessed the whole thing.

"Roarke?" She raised her voice, unwilling to leave Lucian's side or to release the continual pressure she had applied to his wound for hours.

"Aye?" He ducked his massive frame into the shelter once again.

"Lucian said you were present when he fought with Lord Fitzhugh."

She could see Roarke's jaw working even in the dim light. His words came through gritted teeth.

"Aye."

"Did he truly, that is, do you think he really…killed him?" Perhaps Lucian had overstated his role in the man's death.

"He may have thought to raise his sword in self-defense, but I saw into his eyes, Melissande." Roarke fixed her with the vacant stare of a man lost in memories. "I've never seen Lucian more furious than on that day. He killed Osbern Fitzhugh as surely as an assassin's arrow struck him down this morn."

Shaking his head, mayhap shaking off a ghost of the past, Roarke stalked off into the night.

For days Melissande watched over Lucian in the tiny shelter. Each night, Roarke returned, offering her escort home, but she steadfastly refused. He provided her with a horse so she might leave whenever she chose. He supplied her with food and moved or lifted Lucian whenever she asked him to.

Melissande was extremely grateful, yet their relationship grew even more strained. Roarke hounded her for a wedding date, despite her insistence that he return her to the abbey. His accusation that Lucian meant to kill Osbern Fitzhugh had created a barrier between them.

As Melissande washed Lucian's forehead five days after he had been shot, she wondered how he could be shot just inches from his heart and still cling to life nearly a sennight later. Yet Lord Fitzhugh had been wounded in his arm and he'd died within one day.

Had Lucian's attack really been so vicious? The picture Roarke painted of Lucian in his fury matched Melissande's lifelong mental image of a warrior—ruthless and lethal.

She dipped her linen cloth to clean it, then ran it along Lucian's face and neck, wondering if he could possess such a violent nature.

With wistful fingers, she brushed a stray strand of hair from his face. She knew she should not devote so much of herself to untangling the complex mysteries of this man who was determined not to have her anyway.

Yet she could not stop herself from unearthing every piece of information she could about him. Could she still blame her desire to make sense of his past on her notorious curiosity? Or did her need to know more about him go far beyond that, into regions Melissande was not yet ready to face herself?

All of this ruminating would be for naught if he died. The fear dominated her thoughts. While her musing frequently went far afield, they always came back to that one frightening truth.

Aside from the slow, steady thrum of his heart and the shallow rise and fall of his chest, there was no sign of life in Lucian. He did not seem to dream. He did not call out in his sleep. Nor did he have a fever.

He just lay there, so still that Melissande frequently lay her ear to his chest to assure herself he lived.

She often whispered prayers over him, but began to fear her unconfessed recent sins had rendered her supplications less effective. It had been months since her last confession, and heaven knew, she had strayed from her convent teachings lately.

Over the past few hours another idea had begun to niggle the back of her mind. Prayer was not helping, her healing skills didn't seem to have much effect on him, but there was one other, outrageous approach she thought of trying.

What if she kissed him?

Could the touch of her lips to his breathe life—even a will to live—back into his motionless form?

No doubt she would be disappointed. If kissing worked for physicians, surely she would have read about it in one of the medical texts she translated. Certainly Abbess Helen would say the very idea was ludicrous.

But Abbess Helen wasn't here.

The idea had taken root, and no matter how much Melissande tried to rationalize herself out of such an impulsive gesture, some contrary force within her refused to forget it.

Truth be told, she also could not bear the thought of never kissing him again. Whether he felt anything for her or not, Melissande could not deny that Lucian had aroused something within her too potent to be categorized as mere friendship.

A brief brush of her lips certainly could not harm him.

Gently she lifted his head to offer him a drink. More wine spilled to the floor than went into his throat, but she was satisfied with the effort. With trembling fingers, she wiped his cheek and chin.

Nerves harassing her, she picked up the wineskin and helped herself to a long swallow. She braced herself for courage and leaned over him.

Closing her eyes, she drifted nearer. She settled one hand on his shoulder at the same time she eased her lips to his. Just a taste, she told herself. It struck her as unseemly to kiss a man on the verge of death.

But this was Lucian, not just any man.

Once she had pressed her mouth against him, a sigh shuddered through her. Something about being next to Lucian felt utterly right—not unseemly or foolish in the least.

Growing more brazen, she flicked her tongue tentatively between his lips. It felt as heavenly as she remembered, but her rational mind taunted her. Was she such a love-starved nun that she had to extract pleasure from kissing a sense-less man?

Curse rationality. She could have sworn she felt a hitch in Lucian's breathing.

Throwing off all vestiges of logic and reason, she dipped her hand into his tunic to run idle fingers through the silken hair of his chest.

He groaned.

Melissande was so startled she stopped to look at him. He made no further movement, but she was sure she had heard him.

Desperate to succeed, she pulled his head into her lap and stroked his hair, whispering heartfelt pleas for his recovery.

When he still made no move, she lowered her lips to his once again. She forsook the more tender kisses to partake of his mouth. Hungrily, she demanded some response from him, unwilling to think she could have imagined his signs of life.

For a long moment he did not move. Then his breathing seemed to deepen.

Giddy with the kiss and the thought of Lucian alive and well, Melissande pressed the vibrant warmth of her body to his cool one, being careful not to touch the wound at the center of his chest.

Then suddenly his arm wrapped itself around her. His lips came alive under hers and he kissed her as though he thought to make her as senseless as he had been just moments before.

The drumming of her heart pounded in her ears. In the far recesses of her mind, she thought she heard a noise outside the shelter, but nothing seemed as important as Lucian's health, his touch, his mouth upon hers.

She couldn't have stopped him if she tried, although she

was desperate to look into his eyes and to assure herself he was no ghost. But the warmth of his mouth, the insistence of his tongue, held her captive.

"What the hell is going on here?" The fury of an intruder's voice yanked Melissande and Lucian apart.

They turned as one, still breathless and clinging to each other, to confront a red-faced and furious Roarke Barret.

Chapter Seventeen

"**Y**ou're still the back-stabbing bastard you were two years ago, I see." Roarke leveled Lucian with flashing green eyes.

Melissande jumped up, shaky and off balance. "It's not what it looks like. I—"

"I'll just bet it's not." He stood frozen in the doorway, his anger filling the room. "You've gotten just what you wanted, Mel." Roarke swung his gaze to her. "Our betrothal is obviously nullified."

She didn't bother to remind him they were never betrothed. He looked enraged enough to strangle her. "I am sorry."

"Not half as sorry as I'll be when Lucian comes swaggering back to take his earldom with his new bride at his side." He shook his head in disgust. "That'll teach me to lend a hand next time my big brother needs help."

Purposefully he spit on the floor before he spun on his heel and left.

As the sound of the hooves of his horse faded into the distance, Lucian and Melissande stared at one another. She noted his pale complexion and hurried to his side.

"You are not well enough for this." She struggled to

help him lie back down on his pallet, but he remained propped up on one elbow, staring at her as if she had lost her mind. "You must rest, Lucian, or you will no doubt collapse again and—"

"Why on earth would we have been kissing just now?" He looked both confused and annoyed.

Melissande flushed, embarrassment heating her cheeks and neck. "I'm not really sure."

"Recall you do not lie well, Melissande."

How could he be cornering her, his voice as vital and strong as if he just woke from a short nap, when not half an hour ago he seemed on the verge of death?

She folded her arms across her chest. "I will answer you if you lay down, please."

Glaring at her the whole way, he did as she bid.

"I thought a kiss might call you from unconsciousness. You have been lying there as if dead for five days now."

A moment of shocked silence greeted her words until Lucian absently rubbed a hand over his chest.

"I had been shot, Mel. A man needs time to recover." His voice scratched with lack of use.

Her fingers flexed in an effort to remain calm. She breathed deeply. "Yes, well, your 'recovery' looked ten paces from death."

"And so you kissed me?" He sounded horrified.

She lifted her chin, though she thought the deep blush in her cheeks probably counteracted any pretense of defiance. "Yes."

Wiping a frustrated hand through his hair, he cursed.

Melissande stiffened.

"Well, it seems I am recovered now." He tried to prop himself up and failed. "Perhaps you could ride to Barret Keep for one of the grooms to play valet for me. I should appreciate a man's help getting out of here."

The invincible warrior had spoken. Pale as a wraith, weak as a babe, he would give orders and assert his command. Memories of the way her father had treated her mother ran through her mind.

He was dismissing her. The ingrate.

If she thought he was in any danger, she would not allow him to scare her off. But he would be fine until she could send someone to fetch him.

"Very well, sir. I leave you to your rest." She gave him a curt nod and strode from the room, swallowing back the tears that threatened. He had her so confused she didn't know what to think or how to feel, but she knew his treatment stung.

She realized what she needed to do, however. When life turned this turbulent, this confusing, there was only one place to go to find a sense of peace. Although she no longer had Abbess Helen to turn to, Melissande could seek comfort in the chapel at Barret Keep.

She was already mounted on the white palfrey Roarke had provided for her when she recalled she had forgotten her book.

Lucian listened to the pounding of her horses' hooves as she thundered away, hoping like hell she wouldn't come back to witness more of his weakness. Frustrated and aching, he thumbed through the pristine pages of the *Odyssey,* trying to sort out the latest debacle of his life. Like the words in the text, his next move was inscrutable.

Only Melissande would try to cure a man by kissing him. Where the hell had she come up with that harebrained idea?

Lucian realized he loved her all the more for it. After everything that had transpired between them, he didn't think he could stop himself from adoring her if he tried.

Heaven knew, she was not to blame for the passionate

turn her healing method had taken. Lucian had floated up from the depths of a dark dream to the exquisite feel of her pressed against him. Her scent, her taste, her touch had given his senses something to latch onto in the hazy shadows that had claimed him for days.

He came alive in her arms, filled with the sense that his body could be whole and strong again. Her gift of life convinced him he was not ready to die.

The time for wallowing in guilt had passed. No longer would Lucian accept that half-death he had been walking through for the past two years.

If he ever wanted to deserve a woman as pure and innocent as Melissande, he needed to stop wearing his guilt as a battle shield and to start slaying the demons that haunted him.

Our Father, who art in Heaven...

More eloquent words eluding her, Melissande took comfort from the most simple of prayers as she knelt before a statue of Mary in the Barret family chapel four days later.

The sainted mother of Christ had been a living, mortal woman once. She had known the love of a family, the heart-wrenching joy and pain of motherhood, the contrasting demands of her heart and the holy path.

It made her seem approachable today, when Melissande's heart was torn. No priest presided here. The chapel existed as more of a spiritual sanctuary for the keep's residents and a place for visiting clergymen to preach.

Melissande felt at home immediately. Stripped of the pomp and ceremony that accompanied many of the masses at St. Ursula's, the church resonated with a quiet, personal spirituality that filled her with reverence.

"I do not know how to proceed," she confided to Mary,

her voice echoing over the stone walls. "Pray, send me guidance that I may know what to do."

"Melissande."

The feminine voice, full of maternal authority, made Melissande jump. As her heart pounded a furious rhythm against her chest, she realized the voice did not issue from Mary.

A petite woman with laughing blue eyes called to her from across the chapel. Cloaked from head to foot in coarse black wool despite the heat of the day, her well-wrinkled face attested to her wholehearted embrace of life.

Melissande thanked heaven for the speedy answer to her prayer. Relief washed over her. "Abbess Helen."

Melissande's mentor from St. Ursula's entered the nave, flanked by one of her men-at-arms to the left and by Roarke to her right. The abbess emanated as much authority as either of the men.

"You found me." Melissande rose shakily to her feet, drinking in the comforting sight of a woman who had been the only mother she'd known the past ten years.

She looked wonderful, cheeks still wind-burned from a brisk ride, her normally perfect habit and wimple a little bit askew.

"Although snow in the mountains detained our riding party nearly a fortnight and frustrated me to no end, it seems God has ensured that I would arrive just in time." The abbess hurried forward to greet her. "You seem most agitated, Melissande." Turning to the men, she nodded. "I shall be fine now, gentlemen. Thank you."

Roarke did not even spare a glance for Melissande before spinning on his heel along with the other man. She wondered if he would ever forgive her.

Abbess Helen squeezed her shoulders, bestowing a warm

smile upon her. "I can fairly feel the tension flow from this keep, child. Do you care to tell me what is afoot here?"

Melissande warmed to the woman's rare touch. The convent did not encourage demonstrativeness, but Melissande thrived on the attention the abbess gave her now. "Of course. Won't you have a seat?" Melissande steered the nun toward a pew. "I must confess I am surprised you came all this way."

Abbess Helen chuckled as she took her seat. "You know I never do anything in half measures, Melissande. I could not give up until I found you."

"You got my letter?"

"A few weeks after you sent it, I believe. Would that we could have caught up with you and saved both of us the travel, but we lost much time due to the mountain snow."

Melissande felt the blush steal over her cheeks as she thought of several times along the way when she would have been mortified to have been discovered unawares by the abbess and her troop. "We had to change paths midway when an assassin stalked us."

Abbess Helen crossed herself. "I had no idea you were in such serious danger."

Thinking of the man who guarded her, Melissande smiled. "I was well protected."

Briefly, Melissande recounted her tale, omitting the more intimate details of her relationship with Lucian. Oddly, those details stood out foremost in her mind as she thought back on the journey.

She had no choice but to admit her recent mishap with Roarke, however. Her new status as his unwanted bride meant she could leave Barret Keep right away.

"I brought nothing with me, except for my—the convent's—book," Melissande explained. "Since I have nothing to pack, I am ready to depart anytime."

The abbess regarded her skeptically. "You say this Roarke Barret no longer wishes to marry you because of the devotion you demonstrated toward his wounded brother?"

"Actually, I—" Would Abbess Helen reinstate her as the primary guardian of Emilia, Andre and Rafael if Melissande admitted what she had done? She had no choice but to tell the truth, of course, yet the words did not trip easily from her tongue. "I kissed his brother."

"Ah-hh." The abbess frowned. "This is most serious, Melissande."

"It was all a mistake." Had it been? "I didn't mean to—" She could not complete the thought for it would have been an outright untruth. She had meant to kiss Lucian.

"We have much to sort out, Melissande. I can see why I felt called to journey all this way for you, child." She smiled at Melissande and tucked an errant red curl behind her ear. "I had no idea your hair had grown so long again. You look lovely."

Melissande smiled at the abbess's praise. It was not so much the compliment that pleased her as the gentle touch of the woman's hand. Losing her mother at a tender age had made Melissande more needy for such simple kindnesses. "Thank you."

The abbess stood. "I will need to interview all parties involved to determine the best course of action."

"Excuse me?"

"Obviously we need to make sense of this tangle before we do anything rash. I will speak to both of the Barret men and get everything sorted out in no time. All will be well, my dear."

If the abbess learned the full extent of Melissande's sins, she could never go back to St. Ursula's. "But—"

"Do not trouble yourself. I will not disturb your patient until he has rested a few more days." She stretched her arms by her sides. "I am afraid I could use a few days' rest myself before I face the journey back. But when everyone settles down a bit, I'm sure I'll discover just what needs to be done here."

Nervous and at a loss for words, Melissande watched her depart. Her life rested in Abbess Helen's hands, as it had for a decade. The thought both disturbed and comforted Melissande as she toured the small chapel.

There was some sense of relief to have difficult decisions lifted from her shoulders, but could Melissande be happy with what someone else decided for her?

She had to make sure the abbess did not wheedle the truth of what transpired between she and Lucian on the journey home. If the pious woman knew Melissande had lost her innocence to him, Abbess Helen would not allow Melissande to care for the abbey orphans anymore.

She would just have to get to Lucian before the abbess did. Certainly he would be happy to do whatever he could to ensure Melissande left England forever.

Although she should have taken reassurance from the notion, Melissande couldn't suppress the urge to cry.

Lucian had been situated in his chamber at Barret Keep for nearly a week when a timid knock broke his concentration on the Greek letters late one afternoon.

Roarke's serving wench was the most humble little mouse Lucian had ever met. "Come in, Isabel!" he shouted, even though he knew his recent habit of growling at whoever ventured into his space probably didn't make the girl feel any more at ease.

He felt her presence the moment the door swung open.

Not the timid mouse, but the woman who haunted his dreams. Heaven only knew how, but he could feel the woman even across the room. She sang along his nerves and warmed his blood at twenty paces.

"Melissande." He longed to hide the book. It embarrassed him to be caught with it—as if he were missing her and fondling the one part of her he possessed.

He cleared his throat. "I am teaching myself Greek," he announced. It was partly true, anyway. She didn't need to know he'd missed her.

Melissande closed the door behind her.

The intimacy of that act caught him off guard. He shoved aside the book, wincing at the burning in his shoulder as he moved too quickly. "You wanted to...talk?"

He hoped she wanted to refresh her memory on how incredible he could make her body feel. He wanted to see that peculiar flush in her cheeks, the wonder in her brown eyes.

"Do you really think you can learn Greek on your own?" There was wonder in her voice, but not exactly the kind his lust-hazed brain had envisioned.

"I have deciphered several of the letters from memory. I recalled the first few lines of the story best, though not perfectly, and I've translated some of the words accordingly."

She looked so impressed he had no choice but to pull out the volume and show her. She sat beside him on the bed.

"The opening words were 'Sing in me, Muse,' so I know for sure all of these letters." He pointed to his roughly scratched list, along with the letters that still puzzled him.

"You could have just asked me." She chastised him

with her eyes. "I would have been happy to translate the first page for you."

She smelled so good—a little like the kitchens, a little like the chapel. He could discern both the scent of baking bread and sweet frankincense about her.

What a beautiful contradiction she was.

"I thought it best we did not spend any more time together." He closed the book again and slid it to the far side of the bed. Without the Greek tome to focus their attentions on, they suddenly seemed much too close together.

"That is why I am here, as a matter of fact." She plucked at her surcoat, a rich burgundy garment that accurately conveyed the boldness of her spirit.

He lifted a curious brow, but said nothing; instead he wondered where she had obtained new attire.

"I don't know if you have heard that Abbess Helen arrived here some days ago."

He hadn't heard, thanks to Isabel for never opening her meek little mouth. "She is here to drag you back to the Alps?"

"I want to go, Lucian."

"To catch your death this winter? Or to work yourself to exhaustion in the scriptorium so you might scrounge a few moments to play with the orphans you love?"

She tossed him a disdainful glare. "You and I both know the abbey is the best place for me. I have no desire to wed a warrior knight who kills for a living, and neither you nor Roarke want me here. Therefore, it will suit all of us if we can convince Abbess Helen to take me back in my capacity overseeing the children."

"You think I kill for a living?" Lucian remembered a time when she believed in him. Had she changed her mind?

"You freely admit that you do, much as you despise it." Her eyes softened to liquid honey as she gazed at him.

"Although you have taught me that there are redeeming aspects of a warrior, I can also see that you will be entrenched in bloody warfare all your life as a permanent penance."

Lucian didn't quite know how to respond to this new Melissande. She was a combination of the cool reserve she had learned at the abbey and the bold girl of his youth who was not afraid to speak her mind.

"Anyway, remaining here is out of the question, so I've come to beg a favor from you."

Even more interesting. Maybe now she wanted him to refresh her memory on how incredible he could make her body feel. "And what favor might that be, Angel?"

Her breath caught at the endearment. Lucian could see the flutter of nervousness that trembled through her.

"I need you to omit a few things when Abbess Helen comes to interview you about our relationship."

"You want me to lie to a holy woman?"

"Nay!" She caught her bottom lip between her teeth. "I would just ask you to skip over some of the more—" she blushed, hesitating with her answer "—intimate parts."

"'The honest obtains God's favor, the schemer incurs His condemnation,'" Lucian quoted, allowing some perverse demon within himself to needle her. No doubt he had been convalescing for too long that he deliberately quarreled with Melissande to keep her in his chamber a bit longer.

"'The trustworthy keeps things hidden,'" she returned, crossing her arms over her chest in smug triumph.

Lucian couldn't suppress his grin. How had he ever thought it a burden to listen to Melissande talk? His heart had thirsted for a hint of her musical voice over the past few days. "In exchange for my silence, Lady Melissande, you must be willing to give me something."

She went still, staring at him with wide eyes. Lucian longed to wrest a kiss from her, but settled for something almost as satisfying.

"You will finish the *Odyssey*." He thrust the book in her hands, gratified by the brief flash of disappointment in her gaze. Had she hoped he would ask her for a kiss? Did she think about the time they shared by the creek half as much as he did?

"I've told you the tale is rather…romantic at the end." She took the heavy volume from his hands.

Perhaps he was ready to admit there could be happy endings for a warrior hero. Although Lucian could never hang his battle sword above the hearth in retirement, he understood the desire to escape to a more peaceful existence.

Hadn't he sought to ensure Roarke would never have to know the torment of killing by making him the next earl? Lucian would not wish the guilt and nightmares on anyone. "I want to hear it anyway."

Melissande settled in a chair beside his bed and read for hours, providing Lucian with time to study her.

She did not wish to wed a warrior, yet Lucian knew he could never let her return to St. Ursula's and an early death to lung fever. Melissande deserved to know the joys of motherhood, the love of a family.

Roarke would understand once Lucian spoke to him.

Or so he hoped.

Lucian had sent missives to his brother three times in the past few days, none of which were answered except for a terse note informing Lucian of a few more details surrounding their mother's death.

Although saddened to learn of her passing, Lucian knew she had been in failing health ever since their father returned from an earlier crusade. His formerly open, spirited mother, had become a woman full of secrets after her husband's return. What disturbed him most, oddly enough, was the fact that she had died before he ever revealed the truth of Osbern Fitzhugh's death to her.

Maybe he never would have, but now he'd never know. The chance to be honest had passed him by and he would carry yet another sin to his grave.

He couldn't lie to Abbess Helen, no matter what Melissande asked. For that matter, he didn't think he could equivocate to Roarke, either.

Lucian did not deserve her. Yet, watching her eyes fly over the lines of Greek, her mouth quickly spouting the words while her clever mind translated them all, Lucian knew he desired her above all things.

He might never be worthy of her, but he would lay down his life for her. And, in light of the years she suffered in the Alps, he would make damn sure she was never cold again for so much as a moment.

"Are you quite sure you're listening, Lucian?" Melissande asked suddenly. "You don't want to miss Penelope's clever trick."

Indeed he didn't. His mind resolved about his course of action with the Abbess, Lucian turned his full attention back to the story. Penelope was about to test the identity of the man who claimed to be Odysseus, returned to her after their twenty-year separation. Testing the man's reaction, Penelope told her maid to make up the old bed her husband had built and to move it outside the bedchamber.

In a fit of anger, the stranger raged at Penelope and Melissande stood to mimic the impassioned diatribe. "No mortal in his best days could budge that bed with a crowbar. There is our pact and pledge, our secret sign, built into that bed—my handiwork and no one else's!"

It seemed Odysseus had constructed his home around an

olive tree and, after cutting it down, had carved the standing stump into an elaborate marriage bed.

She finished the tale then, which thankfully had one more battle scene before the end, redeeming the story in Lucian's eyes.

When she completed the tale, however, it was not the battle that Melissande spoke of.

She sighed, gazing up at Lucian with wistful eyes. "The bed was the centerpiece for their home, its roots extending into the earth to provide the whole foundation for their family."

"Thus she knew the man to be Odysseus," Lucian observed.

"He was the only one who knew about their bed."

"Does it not strike you as odd that she did not recognize him sooner?" Lucian was not certain that he liked the brief romantic turn the tale had taken. A warrior ought to have a more welcoming homecoming than to be put to the test by his own wife.

"I did not recognize you at first, either, and it had been only ten years since we'd seen one another," Melissande countered.

Night had fallen as they'd talked and read. The keep had grown quiet since the evening meal, which neither of them had missed. Tapers flickered in their sconces, no doubt lit by the silent maid who often waited upon him.

Lucian realized they had not spent such time alone since their journey. He had missed the intimacy of talking to Melissande, a closeness as potent as their kisses.

"I deliberately concealed my face from you."

"But people change, and in far more significant ways than their appearance." Melissande's glance seemed to probe the depths of his soul.

How could a woman be so wise and yet so innocent?

"You changed, too." Lucian recalled how he had spied on her through the convent enclosure, waiting for confirmation of her identity. "I didn't know it was you until after you finished reading to the children."

Melissande grinned, the happy memory chasing shadows from her dark eyes.

"When your young charges wrestled you to the ground, I heard your laughter and glimpsed a lock of your hair. Then, there could be no mistaking the girl I remembered." Lucian reached to tug at an errant curl that had worked its way loose from her silver circlet.

Melissande blushed. The urge to pull her into his arms battled with his need to explain his plans for her future.

He hated to upset her, but he would not allow her to return to the Alps under any circumstances.

A sharp rap at his door halted his confession.

"Yes?" Lucian called, his gaze locked on Melissande.

"'Tis Abbess Helen, my lord," an efficient feminine voice returned. "May I have a word with you?"

"St. Ursula's sainted brow," Melissande whispered as she leaped from her perch on his bed. "Hide me!"

Chapter Eighteen

"Come in, Sister."

Melissande could not believe her ears when Lucian blithely invited the abbess into his chamber. What was he thinking?

The door swung wide and the nun bustled in, a rather sheepish Roarke close at her heels. The abbess's gaze landed squarely upon Melissande. "Ah! Melissande. I hoped to find you here."

Melissande fidgeted with the sleeve of her gown. "I thought to help Luc—that is, Sir Barret—pass his convalescence with a story." She held up the *Odyssey* in self-defense, hoping the flickering candlelight did not illuminate the heated color of her embarrassment.

Abbess Helen cast her an indulgent smile while Roarke glared at his brother.

Lucian gestured to the wooden bench some feet from his bed. "Please have a seat, my Lady Abbess."

Although Abbess Helen took her seat with grace, Melissande and Roarke were left standing awkwardly on the fringes of the narrow chamber.

"Lord Barret," she addressed Lucian, although everyone else in the room knew the title belonged to Roarke. No one dared to correct Abbess Helen. "It seems I have stumbled into a most troublesome situation here at Barret Keep."

"I'm sure my brother, the earl, will find a way to make your stay more pleasant, Sister." Lucian bowed his head in courteous deference to Roarke.

Melissande fumed inwardly, still disturbed that Roarke would steal away Lucian's inherited right.

"Unfortunately, he and I have talked at length and cannot rectify the unhappy problem to which I refer." She looked pointedly at Melissande. "That is, what to do with my young charge, Melissande Deverell."

Melissande bristled at the notion that she needed to be taken care of. For years she had been taught to accept the teachings of the elder nuns, to do as they commanded without question or complaint.

But just now, the urge to argue on her own behalf tempted her sorely.

"She will be well cared for, I assure you," Lucian remarked.

It took a long moment for his words to penetrate Melissande's brain. When they did, his betrayal hit her with the force of a blow. She stepped forward.

"I do not wish to remain here," she asserted, striving to be civil for Abbess Helen's sake, but seething with anger at Lucian. How could he force her to remain here and wed Roarke?

"Well cared for by whom, my lord?" Abbess Helen ignored Melissande's interjection and lifted a skeptical brow in Lucian's direction. "Your brother has told me he cannot marry her. And given the fact that it is *you* who ruined her reputation, I cannot in good conscience force him to wed her."

Heat flooded Melissande's cheeks. She hastened to interrupt again. "But I wish to return to the convent, Abbess Helen."

The powerful nun and the warrior knight did not acknowledge her. They stared at one another in a silent battle of wills.

Melissande wanted to rage at them both, but with her whole life hanging in the balance, she feared alienating the abbess.

"What are you suggesting, Lady Abbess?" Lucian's question hissed through the chamber.

Melissande leaned forward.

"You ruined her reputation, even if your kiss was most innocent. Because of your rash act, your brother will no longer accept her, and I certainly cannot bring her back to an abbey where three impressionable young children are in her charge. I deem it your responsibility to determine an agreeable fate for her. You're the one who abducted her and spent months on the road alone with her."

"Nay!" Melissande stamped her foot, glaring a warning look at Lucian before she pleaded with the abbess. "Do not separate me from the children. They need me so much and—"

Lucian clamped warm fingers about her wrist. "I will wed her," he announced.

Melissande swung on him, livid. "You will do no such thing!" Who was he to decide her fate for her?

"Be reasonable, Melissande," the abbess coaxed, laying a comforting hand on Melissande's shoulder. "There is really no choice—"

"There is most certainly a choice!" Melissande raged, raising her voice in Abbess Helen's presence for the first time in her life. To no avail, she attempted to withdraw her wrist from Lucian's grip. "Take me home to St. Ursula's where I belong."

The abbess eyed her long and hard. "And are you prepared to swear, despite the proof of your affection for Lord Barret and the weeks the two of you spent alone together, that you have never been…intimate with him?"

Oh, Lord.

Melissande's rage dissipated as guilt stole through her.

Vivid memories of the day by the creek with Lucian assailed her. She had eagerly given him her innocence, had sacrificed her future at the abbey for a few stolen moments in his arms.

They all waited, staring at her.

She could not tell an outright lie to Abbess Helen. Besides, the time had arrived for Melissande to grow up. No matter how much easier it was to blame Lucian or the abbess for her predicament, Melissande knew her own passion and curiosity had led her to this.

Are you prepared to swear…you have never been intimate with him?

This was one bit of mischief-making Melissande could not deny. And heaven knew she didn't lie well.

"I cannot," Melissande responded finally, knowing her flushed cheeks answered more tellingly than any words she might devise.

The abbess drew a sharp breath.

Lucian's gaze remained on Abbess Helen. "We will wed at once." After a final squeeze of Melissande's hand, he released his grip on her fingers.

Set in grim lines of determination, his bleak visage conveyed to even the most innocent of human observers that Lucian's heart was not in a wedding.

Tears begged for release from beneath her downswept lashes, but Melissande would not grant herself the luxury of crying.

"Then it is settled," Abbess Helen noted, drawing Melissande to her side. "I would like to witness the nuptials before I depart so that I might leave with a peaceful heart. Would that be admissible, my lord?"

"I am not the lord here, my Lady Abbess, but I welcome your presence."

Abbess Helen stood, nodding her approval. "I will take care of the banns to promote a hasty marriage. Would tomorrow be too soon? Shall we say noon?"

Melissande nodded, too overwhelmed to speak.

She would never see her children again. And it would not be, as she had once foolishly hoped, because Lucian had fallen in love with her and wanted her to be his wife.

No. She would be separated from the orphans because she had acted on impulse one too many times and now paid the price in marriage to a hardened warrior who lacked a heart.

Roarke approached his brother as the abbess readied herself to leave. "If I might have a word with you, brother."

Melissande saw Lucian nod, but all their movements seemed disassociated from herself, as if she were far removed from this time and place.

The foundation on which she had built her life seemed to have dropped out from under her.

"Come, Melissande." The abbess called to her from where she stood beside the door. "We have much to prepare for tomorrow."

The abbess's words jolted Melissande from her musings. Resolutely, she followed her longtime mentor.

Although Melissande could not stop her marriage, she vowed she would never allow Lucian to rule her as she had been ruled all her life—first by her father, then by the abbey.

Starting now, she would reclaim her life as her own.

* * *

Lucian watched Melissande walk away, her spine stiff and unrelenting. Apparently his offer of marriage came too late. While he hadn't expected her eternal gratitude, he had hoped she would be a little less angry about his proposal.

His gaze fell upon Roarke as his younger brother approached. At least Roarke could be counted on to support Lucian's decision.

Roarke cleared his throat. "I am leaving Barret Keep, Lucian," he announced. "Forever."

Lucian shook his head, hoping he hadn't heard his younger brother correctly. "What?"

"I cannot be happy here any longer." Roarke met his gaze evenly, as if he somehow stood taller than he had in a long time.

Lucian could not give his younger brother's latest flare of temper any more attention than absolutely necessary. He combed his fingers through hair that had grown too long over the past months. "I am sorry about Melissande, Roarke, but I will take her away from here so you will not be vexed by our presence. You will find a woman you are happy with a bit closer to home."

Roarke shook his head. "Nay. I will not. I spoke at length with the abbess over supper, and I realize I am not happy with what I have made of my life."

Good God, what had the meddling holy woman wrought now? "Do not let a busybody nun talk you out of a—"

"That is unfair to Abbess Helen." Roarke reproached him with his glance. "I feel fortunate to have recognized why I am not happy while I am young enough to change it. I have been disturbed by a few things mother said before she died, disjointed ramblings I need to research before I settle down. I will leave a few days after your wedding to make my way in the world as a landless second son."

Lucian threw off the bed linens and stood to face his brother. This was not like Roarke at all. Hadn't the younger Barret coveted the earldom and all the benefits of the first-born from the time he was a child? "You have lands! I promised them to you, Roarke. Do you think I would ever go back on my word? If you want to grant me something, I can be your vassal at the old Deverell Keep."

Roarke folded his arms across his chest. Lucian realized for the first time his brother had grown every bit as broad of chest as he.

"I know you are far too honorable to request your rights back, Lucian. But this is not about you, it is about me. And the ravings of our mother on her deathbed." He cast Lucian a look. "I did not want to believe it at the time, but the more I piece together her whispers, the more I fear…we may not share the same father, Lucian."

Lucian shook his head, determined to dislodge the thought. "What is this madness? We were raised together. Fostered together. I can think of no woman more honorable, more noble, than our mother."

How dare Roarke suggest such a thing?

"It is only a thought, I dismissed it as well at the time, but since it preys upon me still after six months, I have no choice but to try and disprove it so I may rest easy at night. I will have the satisfaction of making a name for myself outside of Northumbria, perhaps in the Holy Lands."

"So you can die before you make a name or find a home for yourself?" Lucian could feel the blood of his anger pound against the place in his chest where the arrow had pierced him.

"My battle prowess may not be so lacking as that, brother." He turned toward the door, but paused when he reached it. "No matter what you think of my plans, I dispatched a letter to the king yesterday, telling him of your return and my departure. You are already the earl, Lucian, as you have always truly been.''

What was Roarke thinking? How could he blithely throw away his future? ''Roarke, wait—''

''You must admit,'' Roarke interrupted, grinning, ''Melissande was destined to be countess here.''

Before Lucian could protest any further, Roarke slipped out the door. Lucian sank to his bed as the door shut behind the sibling he had loved and struggled with since childhood. Dear God, what if there were some truth to Roarke's words?

Impossible. Roarke was worse off now than if Lucian had never given him the title. Struck by some noble urge to seek his own fortune in the world, Roarke might be gone for years…might never return.

And Lucian now possessed everything he had always dreamed of having. His earldom restored, his lands prospered, his beautiful bride awaited him on the morrow, and surely a family could not be far behind.

Yet a bitter ache robbed him of all joy the rewards should have bestowed. His brother harbored details that would set any man's world on its ear.

Worse, a killer still stalked him to mete out justice for Lucian's past sins. With so many people depending on him for protection, he stood to lose much more than just his life to Osbern Fitzhugh's avenger.

Although in all likelihood, the man who shot him was Peter Chadsworth, the larger threat still loomed. One day, Damon Fitzhugh would return from war and demand satisfaction for his father's death.

Lucian had to make sure the woman he loved was protected when that day came. No matter what Melissande thought of his proposal to marry her, Lucian knew he would take his vows very seriously.

To keep her safe, he would have to live his life as the warrior knight Melissande reviled.

As much as Melissande loved to talk, she grew weary of the endless niceties she was forced to exchange with the hundreds of well-wishers who attended her wedding feast.

More days had passed since the abbess's decree that Melissande and Lucian should wed. Yet, somehow the inhabitants of Barret lands had assembled an elaborate feast. Lucian seemed to grow stronger by the moment, his health improved by walks about the keep and—much to Melissande's dismay—trips to the practice yard where he swung slow arcs with his sword.

Ever the warrior.

Now their lives were joined after a few simple words intoned by the local priest. She'd barely absorbed the fact that her wedding day had arrived when she was whisked off to the celebration amid much song and strewing of flowers. Still, no amount of frivolity could take away the fact that she'd wed a man of dark, brooding passions. A man who had scarcely acknowledged her despite her lovely blue gown, a simple beaded surcoat that had belonged to Lucian's mother.

Now she sipped the last of her wine while the villagers danced, her gaze tripping over the festivities in search of her husband.

For reasons she did not fathom, Lucian had been reinstated as earl, making their wedding an even more significant event. While all the outlying tenants paid their respects to the new Lord and Lady Barret, Melissande puzzled over the sudden turnabout between Roarke and Lucian. She had tried to query Roarke about the matter, but he had turned as closedmouthed as her husband.

Strange things were afoot.

She raised her cup in the direction of the server, perhaps indulging in more wine today than she ought. But as new mistress of her own destiny, Melissande had made a pact with herself to answer only to her conscience and God from now on, despite the vows she took to obey her husband.

Sipping from her refilled horn, Melissande sought Lucian, never a difficult task since he and Roarke towered over the other men present.

She stabbed a bit of wedding cake onto her knife, musing over her bizarre new circumstances.

Never had she expected Lucian to offer for her. After he'd given her to Roarke, Melissande knew he did not return the feelings she had developed for him.

Why had he offered for her now? The abbess had maneuvered him, to a certain extent. But Lucian could have easily demanded she return to the convent.

His reasons for marrying her were too obscure for her to understand, especially after she downed her third glass of wine. Or was it her fourth?

Gazing at Lucian while he spoke to one of his tenants, Melissande sought reassurance that he was still the same man who loved to read and could speak Sanskrit.

Such a man would be gentle with her on their wedding night, would he not?

She knew better than to expect the tender treatment he had lavished upon her by the creek's edge. Lucian would be too annoyed with her for cornering him into a marriage he did not want to treat her to such exquisite passion.

Just recalling the incredible wealth of sensation the man could arouse in her made her cheeks flush.

Or maybe it was the wine.

Melissande set down her cup, hoping to cool the nervous anticipation that skittered through her no matter how many times she told herself not to expect any tenderness from Lucian on their wedding night.

Hadn't he been cool to her all day?

Lost in conflicting thoughts of her husband, she jumped when Abbess Helen took her by the arm.

"Dreaming of your groom, my dear?"

Melissande spluttered an incoherent reply and the nun laughed heartily. Melissande wondered if the good sister had not indulged in a few too many cups of wine herself.

"Do not be abashed, child! 'Tis only natural." She tugged Melissande forward through the crowd. "I will help you prepare yourself for him."

Melissande gulped. "Is it that time already?"

"Aye! Well past it, judging by the looks you two have been exchanging. Come with me." Abbess Helen drew her up the stairs, forcing Melissande to pause at the gallery overlooking the hall to wave to her guests one last time.

A cheer went up in response, and then all eyes turned to Lucian.

Like the dutiful, practical man he was, he lifted his cup to her in salute, earning more cheers and shouts throughout the hall.

Melissande knew his good humor to be an act, however. She had spent enough time alone with Lucian Barret to recognize the degrees of his brooding moods.

"Do not look so glum, my dear," the abbess clucked as she drew Melissande into the master chamber Roarke had already vacated. "I hear a wedding night is great fun at the hands of a man who cares for his wife."

"He does not care for me," Melissande muttered, allowing the abbess to unlace the simple beaded surcoat that served as her wedding garment.

"Of course he does, child, or he would not have been kissing you when Roarke discovered the two of you." The nun hung the tunic and retrieved a lightweight night rail from within the small wardrobe.

Melissande gasped at the sight of it, never having possessed such a fine and impractical piece of clothing. It surprised her a bit that Abbess Helen, of all people, would own a blatantly seductive garment. "Where did you get it?" She fingered the gossamer-thin material, tracing the intricate pattern scrolled over the bodice.

"Many of the sisters arrive at the convent with some of the finest clothes in Christendom." She winked. "We are just not allowed to wear them."

"You brought this all the way from St. Ursula's?"

The abbess helped Melissande slide the garment over her head, then smoothed the wrinkles with gentle fingers. "When I received your note, I did not know what to expect when I finally caught up with you. It seems to me that when a woman is abducted by a man, a wedding is always a possibility, and you know I don't take any chances when I pack."

"Whose was it?" A contrary part of Melissande longed to know which sister had brought such an uncompromisingly romantic piece of froth with her to the abbey.

The abbess sobered. "Sister Adelaide, a sweet young woman who was dismissed from St. Ursula's before I arrived, apparently."

Melissande remembered too well. "She was forced to leave because a boy was enamored with her and would not cease throwing notes and trinkets over the enclosure wall. Her family could not afford to take her back."

"I heard later that his family could and did, however, so give her no more thought." Abbess Helen fussed with the ribbons at Melissande's waist and neck. "She has been happily married for almost nine years."

Melissande clapped in delight, relieved the young

woman's story had a happy end. "You checked up on her when you arrived."

"The rumors of how the sisters tossed her out did not sit well with me, so I made sure she was happily settled. Adelaide gave me this gown as a token of her appreciation." Abbess Helen gave Melissande a sheepish grin. "I am a bit of a romantic myself, so I was very tempted by this garment. But I never once donned the gown."

On impulse, Melissande hugged the woman who had been both mother and inspiration to her. "I will try hard to do well here."

"Try hard to be happy, Melissande. Your joyousness has the power to infect all those around you." Abbess Helen stroked Melissande's cheek with maternal affection.

"Nay. My husband will never know joyousness, my Lady Abbess. He does not truly care for me," she confided, unable to halt the confession her pride told her she should have kept hidden.

"He has not learned to love and forgive himself, Melissande. He cannot possibly offer love to another until he first heals the unhappiness he wears like a shield." The abbess guided Melissande to the huge master bed and tucked her into the rose-scented linens. "You might help him do that, Melissande. 'Twould be a good place to start."

Melissande pressed a kiss to the abbess's hand, her heart lighter than it had been for weeks. "I will."

She would have done anything the abbess asked of her, but this quest appealed particularly to Melissande. The wise woman who reigned supreme over a hundred diverse, gossip-prone women had not gained her position by accident. A shrewd eye for human nature and a tender heart had won the nun an abbey full of staunch supporters.

Melissande would heed her advice well.

"Now enjoy your wedding night, child." Abbess Helen

backed toward the door, smiling as she left. "I wish to see the happy flush of love upon your face before I leave, Melissande, so I will still be here on the morrow."

As the door closed behind her, Melissande wondered how long her mentor would be willing to stay to see that sign of love. It seemed Melissande was destined to live without it.

Although she promised herself she would find a way to help Lucian overcome his guilt to triumph over the past, she intended to guard her heart until that time.

Her convent home was already lost to her, and she no longer had a home or family to return to in England. She had also lost the love of her children and the joy of watching them grow to adulthood.

She had no intention of losing her heart to a hardened warrior who could never share his in return.

Chapter Nineteen

Lucian stared into his drinking horn and fought to concentrate on his conversation with Roarke. His brother deserved his full attention. Too bad the only thing on Lucian's mind at this moment was his wedding night.

Ever since the abbess had led Melissande from the hall to retire, Lucian's thoughts focused solely on the bedchamber where his wife lay.

His wife.

He could scarcely believe fate had granted him Melissande for a bride. For as many years as he could remember, Melissande had been the secret dream of his heart. Now she belonged to him.

How long must he wait to tread those steps to the master suite and claim the prize he thought he'd never obtain?

"...when Damon Fitzhugh arrives."

Roarke's mention of Lucian's mortal enemy jarred him from his daydreams.

"What did you say?" Lucian studied his brother, wondering if he knew something Lucian did not.

"I am trying my best to warn you despite your obvious lack of attention." Roarke clapped a hand on Lucian's shoulder. "It is whispered that Osbern Fitzhugh's son is on his way home from the Holy Lands at last. You would do well to watch your back, brother.''

The precariousness of Lucian's newfound happiness hit him with the force of a Saracen blade. Damon Fitzhugh would soon seek revenge for his father's death.

Normally, Lucian had every confidence in his ability to defend himself. But this would be a battle in which he was morally wrong. Surely God would contend on Damon's side when Lucian's enemy came to call. Where would that leave Melissande?

Lucian could trust only one man with her fate. ''You will come back for Melissande if anything should happen to me.''

''You will not be defeated, brother.''

''Nay?'' Lucian quirked a brow at the confidence in Roarke's tone.

''You have overcome even death to take your rightful place here.'' Roarke slid his hand from Lucian's shoulder and straightened. ''You were fated to rule the Barret lands.''

''Nevertheless, I would have your word that Melissande will be protected if I should die.'' Her safety was too important to be left in the hands of fickle fate. No matter what doubts plagued Roarke about his place in the family, they would always be linked by brotherhood in spirit.

''I pledge my life to her service.'' Roarke met his gaze and, for the first time, Lucian saw a hint of the regard his brother still bore for his wife.

Lucian nodded, acknowledging the vow at the same time he prayed he would never need to call upon it. He could not abide the thought of leaving Melissande in anyone's care but his own.

''You have waited long enough, by the way,'' Roarke added.

Lucian's gaze swung from the door of the master chamber to his companion. "What?"

Roarke laughed. "I am sure she is ready by now."

Lucian could not restrain his own grin. "Then I shall not idle with the likes of you any longer." Slamming his horn onto the nearest server's tray, Lucian bid Roarke farewell and bolted for the stairs.

Shouts and whoops of goodwill drowned out his thoughts as he launched onto the gallery. Roarke led the wedding guests in a noisy toast to his brother's fertility.

After a quick bow to their generosity, Lucian backed toward the door where Melissande awaited him. Anticipation and love for his wife made him slow his pace. This would be her first time, after all, though his naive bride thought she had already experienced lovemaking. He had no doubt she had been well satisfied the day they'd kissed by the creek's edge. If he were to maintain the passion he had kindled in her that day, he would need to initiate her into the rites of marriage most tenderly.

As his hand hovered over the door handle, he considered that this might be one way to win a bit of his wife's affection.

Not for the world would he miss out on such a chance.

He stepped into his future and, for tonight at least, shut the door behind him.

"Lucian?" Melissande's heart picked up speed as the huge, shadowy form of her husband entered the chamber.

She had not waited in the bed for him long, but the few moments alone in the massive chamber had given her plenty of time to grow nervous.

Of course, she knew what to expect from the marriage bed after their encounter by the creek. But knowing what was expected of her made the butterflies in her belly flutter more furiously.

Intimacy between a man and wife meant disrobing. Melissande had bared almost her whole body to Lucian the day they made love.

Now that Lucian would be sleeping with her, would he remove all his clothing, as well?

The thought both intrigued and worried her.

She had never seen a naked man before.

Melissande watched him as he slid off his boots and padded across the floor to the bed. The scar on his temple caught the firelight, a white streak of lightning in the dark sky of his bronze face.

Yet the scarred visage and rock-wall chest of her warrior husband did not frighten her tonight. His strength beckoned her, begged her to touch and to test the hard muscle of his powerful body.

Eagerness to be close to him sent a pleasant shiver of expectation down her spine.

"You are cold?" Lucian reached the bed and sank beside her.

Melissande shifted against the pillows to see him better. He gazed down at her with gentle concern.

"Nay—" she began, then wondered what he might do to warm her. "Maybe a little."

Lucian dropped a finger to her exposed neck and drew a languorous line down to the ribbons of her gown. "'Tis no wonder when you are garbed in naught but an airy bit of silk."

He deliberately wound the silk ribbon about his finger, and another chill tingled through her nerves.

"The abbess gave it to me for tonight."

Lucian raised a brow in amused surprise, then pushed

the linens down to bare a bit more of the garment. Cool air fanned over her body, no match for the heat of his gaze.

"She has my utmost gratitude."

Leaning over her as if to study the intricate pattern of embroidery at her bodice, Lucian traced the swirls in the complicated weave with his thumb.

Mesmerized by the circuitous dance of the touch, Melissande's eyes drifted shut.

"Very beautiful," he commented, his mouth mere inches from her breasts. The caress of his breath drew the crests beneath to tight peaks against the fabric.

She sighed languorously as he began the trek with his thumb again, then cried out when he ceased his progress where one of the woven decorations curved around her nipple. "What, Angel?"

Melissande dragged open an eyelid to see him gazing at her as if she were a sweet confection to be devoured. She was willing to bet the man knew all too well what she wanted.

For now, she craved his touch.

Deep inside, she also yearned for his heart.

Willing to settle for a thorough sensual exploration tonight, Melissande threaded her fingers through the dark hair that touched his collar and tugged him nearer to her straining bodice.

His mouth settled upon her, heating her tender flesh right through the filmy barrier of gossamer fabric.

Molten pleasure sizzled in her womb. Her body arched toward his mouth and the source of her delight. Hungry to experience his kiss without impediment, Melissande wriggled her hands free to brush away the moist silk.

Lucian paused long enough to peer up at her with a mixture of lust and...humor, mayhap?

"My bride is more eager than I could have hoped."

She was not sure if he teased her. Ineffectual as it seemed when she was already half naked, she lifted her chin in proud defense. "You have taught me a kind of pleasure that I am impatient to experience again."

He dropped a kiss on the curve of her neck, breathing his warmth into her hair. "Tonight I will teach you the rewards of patience." Another kiss circled her ear.

A sensual thrill shuddered through Melissande. "If ten years in the convent cannot make me patient, my lord, I do not think you will accomplish the feat in the course of a night."

Lucian skimmed his fingers down the inside of her arm, barely brushing the underside of her breast with his hand. "When the prize is wondrous enough, Melissande, even you will wait for it."

"But I have sampled the wonder of the prize, Lucian—" she felt the blush creep over her cheeks as she admitted it "—and it is because the reward is so good I find I cannot wait."

He cradled her face in his palm and stroked her cheek with one broad thumb. "Angel, you don't know the half of it."

How could that be? If there were more to the intimacy between a man and a woman, Lucian had plenty of opportunity to tell her before now. "But when we were by the creek—"

Lucian toyed with a lock of her hair, idly teasing the strand over her neck and breasts. "When we were by the creek, we committed only the precursors to lovemaking. There is much more to the wedding night than that."

The bout of butterflies returned, and with it, overwhelming inquisitiveness. "More?"

"Much more."

"But what if—"

Lucian raised his fingers to her mouth. "Melissande, I have made a vow to cherish your sweet voice and your incessant chatter, but I do not think I can uphold it tonight."

She might have been incensed had he not chosen to quiet her offending lips with his own.

Questions faded from her mind as Lucian savored her mouth in a thought-stealing kiss. Her blood heated by slow degrees as his body moved against hers, molding her softness to the hard muscle that covered every inch of him.

The knot in her belly began to tighten, reminding her of the miraculous rapture Lucian could ultimately bring her…only now she knew it wasn't the ultimate pleasure. What more could there be to intimacy than what she'd already experienced?

Excited to find out, Melissande pressed herself still closer to him, sealing their bodies in a passionate tangle. Calling on her limited knowledge of lovemaking, she inched her leg up the length of his leather braies until she could wrap it about his waist.

His leg fell between hers, brushing deliciously near the center of her growing need. He groaned at her brazen act, but obligingly increased the pressure of his thigh against her.

Something else moved against her as he did so…something rigid that pressed into her belly with as much force as his thigh pushed into her feminine softness.

Curiosity mingled with passion, driving her to more desperate measures.

She whimpered her impatience, needing more from him than the slow torment he seemed insistent on wreaking.

She reached for the tie at his waist to undo the leather encasing the lower half of his body, ready to unveil what mysteries of the male form it kept hidden.

Just as her finger slipped between supple leather and warm flesh, Lucian manacled her wrist in one strong hand.

"You might not be ready for that, Angel." He raised his head to whisper hoarsely across the sultry space that separated them.

"For what?" she whispered back, hearing as much anxiety in her voice as interest.

Gently he changed his grip upon her wrist, no longer imprisoning her but guiding her toward the mystery she hoped to unveil.

As her hand fell upon the unyielding object in the front of his braies, it moved.

Melissande yelped, her hand leaping away from whatever it was that seemed to have a life of its own. Her gaze flew to Lucian's face.

Lucian's chuckle dissolved into a groan.

"What is it?" She sensed her cheeks flushing, felt horribly ignorant. Never had she been more intensely aware of the disadvantages of being raised in a convent.

She watched Lucian make a valiant effort to suppress the grin still twitching his lips.

"'Tis me, Angel." He reached for her hand again and she allowed him to settle her fingers around the hard length of him.

This time, Melissande did not pull away when he moved, but allowed her fingers to curve around him as much as the leather separating them would allow.

"'Tis how I will consummate our marriage this night."

Still amazed Lucian could possess a part so incredibly foreign, Melissande tested and measured him with her palm, already putting together a new mental image of lovemaking.

"You mean you will…" She could not quite articulate the picture that entered her mind. Although she had seen animals engaged in such crude behaviors, she would have never, in her wildest imaginings, thought that man and woman would join in such a manner.

She looked helplessly to Lucian. "And I will—"

"Receive me."

"St. Ursula's slipper." The vision coalesced in her mind's eye. Now she knew what happened. Abruptly she let go and shook her head. "I cannot."

Lucian wiped his hand over his forehead, massaging the scar at his temple. "We are not truly married until the deed is accomplished. 'Tis the ultimate sealing of the wedding vow."

She considered it for a moment more, tempted to indulge in more kisses but not at all tempted by this coarse new version of marital relations. "Perhaps we could just continue as we did the day at the creek."

Lucian eyed her for a long moment, finally pulling her close. "Aye, we will. But I am no longer content to stop there, Melissande. What we did before is merely a pleasurable prelude. It does not fulfill the promise of the marriage bed."

His words did little to persuade her. "But—"

He tightened his grip upon her, his eyes lit with new determination. "We cannot make a baby unless we approach this my way."

Her heart expanded and softened at the idea. "A baby?"

"Aye!" The half grin reappeared to tease at his lips. "There can be no babes without the completion of the marriage act."

A vision of herself filled with Lucian's child eased her fears. What would it feel like to carry a babe in her belly, a new life nestled beneath her heart for nine moons?

She steeled herself. For a child, she could undergo most anything.

Perhaps, too, this consummation of wedding vows might be a way for her to give something to Lucian. Her heart had grown so irreversibly attached to him. If only he would commit himself to his family rather than a life of battle, Melissande could finally allow herself to love him.

Maybe tonight she could show him a measure of the love that awaited him if he would only reconsider his warrior ways—his sense of responsibility for the whole world that weighed upon him as tangibly as chain mail.

Willing herself to relax, she snuggled closer to her husband, confident he would handle this troublesome ordeal of baby-making. "All right."

Relief poured through Lucian a he released a breath he had not realized he'd been holding.

Thank God.

He would never have proceeded without her acquiescence, but it would have tortured him to wait for her.

As she burrowed into the shelter of his arms, he reminded himself how much he coveted her affections. He would not risk her tender feelings to satisfy his long-suppressed desires.

Thankfully, she was as passionate as her hair was red. It shouldn't take too much effort to draw out her innate curiosity and to entice her irrepressible fingers back to his body.

Ruthlessly he bit back the primal urge that surged through him as he took in her slender thighs, her bared breasts. Instead, he tipped her chin up to gaze upon her, focusing his attention on her wide brown eyes and delicately quivering lips.

"Come kiss me, Angel."

Her siren's body teased his to painful proportions as the length of her sweet self rubbed over his chest in the slow journey to his lips.

Yet he did no more than kiss her, calling forth the banked hunger he knew still lay within her.

And, dear God, but she warmed to him in no time. Her restless hands soon wandered his chest and shoulders—always careful not to press upon his wound—her impatient body wriggled against his.

Yanking the forgotten night rail down her shoulders, Lucian dispensed with her scant garb to bare her completely. His eyes feasted on the sight, especially the delightful balance between her rosy nipples and the shield of red hair at the juncture of her thighs.

Gritting his teeth against the temptation to sink himself between those fair legs, Lucian laved one generous breast and then the other with his tongue.

When he trailed kisses down her navel and to her thigh, Melissande's breathy whimpers turned to little moans, half eager, half fearful.

He debated pausing, taking more time to arouse her, when Melissande rolled her hips in an invitation she probably hadn't consciously meant to deliver.

Lucian blessed his wife's impatience.

Gladly he parted those silky red curls to kiss the heated jewel of her womanhood.

He barely had a moment to savor her when she came apart in a broken cry that inflamed him almost as much as the honeyed response that signaled her readiness for him.

With infinite care he tasted his way back up her body, reveling in the flush of heat that covered her skin, the erratic heartbeat that pounded through her.

Pulling off his tunic with his uninjured arm, he poised himself above her, wishing desperately he did not have to hurt her.

Her eyelids remained closed, her face still relaxed into the lines of joyous rapture she had only just experienced.

Taking advantage of her momentary lack of awareness, he unlaced his braies, thinking it might be better if she didn't grow fearful all over again. She was ready now.

He kissed her cheek, her neck, the shell of her ear, all the while shifting her legs apart to minimize the pain she would feel. His heart pounded as though it would erupt with wanting her, his manhood strained past the point of torment.

"Melissande," he whispered in her ear.

"Mmm?"

"Lovemaking hurts the first time." He cursed himself when her eyes flew open, but he thought it only fair to warn her. "After that, it is only pleasurable, like what we just did."

She fidgeted beneath him, trying to move her legs together again, but she was impeded by the stalwart barrier of his body.

"Can you trust me, Angel? That it only hurts this first time?"

She relaxed a little, then nodded.

"Good girl." He brushed his lips over her, encouraged for their future together. She trusted him. Perhaps one day, she would learn to care about him, battle sword and all. "Now put your arms around me."

Dutifully, she wrapped both arms about his neck and gazed up at him warily.

The taste of her still lingering on his lips, Lucian could not wait a moment more.

He slid one finger inside her to test the breadth of her sheath. Although gratified at the joyous sigh Melissande emitted at his touch, he couldn't help but worry at the implications of her snug grip around him.

His feat would not be easy, but he couldn't deny he also looked forward to it.

"'Tis for a babe," he whispered as he removed his finger and eased himself within her.

Melissande's eyes widened in surprise as he hit the obstacle of her innocence. Sweat beaded his brow from the constraints he had put on his body.

In this instance, however, he knew the deed would hurt less if done quickly. Looking down into those trusting eyes, he willed her to understand, then drove himself the rest of the way inside.

He captured her cry with his mouth, wishing he could absorb her pain so easily. He fought to stay still within her, hoping to accustom her to his presence before he moved again.

When he could stand no more, he withdrew carefully and rocked into her again and again, too delirious with his own pleasure now to hold back anymore.

"Lucian!"

He heard his wife cry out, and he wanted to stop, but heaven help him, he could not.

"Lucian..." Melissande called his name again as he hurtled over the edge of desire, spending himself between her thighs in the ultimate sealing of their sacred vows.

He yanked his eyes open to peer down at her—to beg for forgiveness if necessary—and saw her face frozen in ecstatic pleasure.

Only then did he realize her own body quivered in the aftermath of passion.

The urge to laugh bubbled in his throat. He had worried so much about her and all the while his lusty, convent-bred bride had been lost in the throes of fulfilled desire.

She sighed his name once more before her breathing slowed into the even cadence of asleep. Warmth curled through him, as potent and gratifying as the passion he had just spent.

He withdrew from her slowly, then pulled her head to his chest, cradling her as if she were a child. He covered her cheek with his palm, allowing his fingers to stray into the damp curls at her temple.

Now he knew why Odysseus fought so long and hard to return to his wife.

Lucian would battle any odds to protect the precious gift Abbess Helen had entrusted him with. He could not allow Damon Fitzhugh to rob him of a lifetime in Melissande's arms.

Not now when he sensed he might be able to one day win her love.

Not now that after two years of penance and pain, guilt and remorse, Lucian had, at long last, come home.

Chapter Twenty

Melissande pried one eyelid open in spite of the relentless sunlight that penetrated the master bedchamber. Her first thought was of her husband.

Languid pleasure flowed through her veins. The man had introduced her to delights she had never imagined, then cradled her against him as if she were more precious than gold.

All night she'd dreamed of him. Between dreams, Lucian had held her and kissed her hair, whispered endearments and promises of forever.

She couldn't wait to see him, to be sure she hadn't really dreamed the heaven she'd found in his arms last night.

But where was Lucian?

Raising up on an elbow, Melissande scanned the room for signs of him. His clothes and sword were gone, though his side of the bed still held the huge rumpled imprint of his warrior's body.

The other side of the bed also held a tiny scroll tied in white ribbon.

Melissande reached for the small piece of parchment opened it. A bold, masculine scrawl covered the missive.

''The rose dawn might have found them together still had not gray-eyed Athena slowed the night when night was most profound, and held the dawn under the ocean of the east.''

It was from the *Odyssey*. The passage was a loose translation of the moment when Penelope and Odysseus were at last reunited.

That Lucian would even recall the passage surprised her. The fact that he would convey the same message to her, as if he loved her as deeply as Odysseus loved Penelope, made her want to weep with joy.

Love and hope blossomed in Melissande's heart at his sentimental act. Her world-weary warrior had penned her a poem on their first morning together.

Although her husband wasn't there to witness the monumental occasion, for the first time ever, Melissande was speechless.

Obviously, Lucian sought to please her. Perhaps now that he was the earl, he would consider retiring his sword and remaining on his lands. Was there a chance he could forsake his trade of killing now that he possessed a wife and had obligations to land and family? Would he consider making their marriage a true partnership in which she could have a voice in how they raised their children?

She pressed the parchment to her heart. Recalling Abbess Helen's advice, Melissande wondered if there was a way to help Lucian heal his past and to allow him to face his future. What could she do to help him overcome the guilt that had haunted him for two years?

An inspired idea rousted her out of bed and sent her scurrying about the chamber for fresh garments. Her body protested the activity after the love play with Lucian the previous night. But she could not afford to laze about in bed when there was a chance she could help her husband forgive himself.

Bubbling with anticipation—of running into Lucian, of implementing her clever scheme to benefit him—Melissande dragged a comb through her hair and covered it with a sheer veil and circlet. She could braid it later, after she set her plan in motion.

For nostalgia's sake, she pulled the forest-green kirtle from Linette's mother out of the wardrobe and over her white tunic. The gown brought back so many happy memories. She could almost smell the campfires from her nights on the road with Lucian.

She raced out the door and down the stairs to the great hall, hoping to find the man who could help her execute her new stratagem. She found him seated at the dais table, her husband lounging to his right.

"Good morning," she called to the Barret brothers, blushing a little to see Lucian after the night they had shared.

Roarke managed a pleasant greeting, but Lucian looked nearly as tongue-twisted as she felt. Did he regret leaving her the poem?

"I have come to seek a favor of you, Roarke, if you have a moment." She did not want to speak to him with Lucian present. He would never agree to her plan.

Lucian stood hastily, as if glad for an excuse to leave her. Melissande bit her lip, worried things were not as well between them as she thought.

Her husband walked around the table to where she stood. Melissande grew both nervous and hopeful as he neared.

He clasped her shoulders in his broad palms and a jolt of awareness surged through her. Memories of their wedding night assailed her, making her long for dusk to fall again so they might be together.

"You're beautiful," he whispered huskily, his lips hovering over hers. Somewhere in the back of her mind, she heard Roarke begin to hum loudly.

Lucian noticed the dress. Pleasure simmered through her at his blatant attention, although the look in his eyes made her distinctly aware that he itched to relieve her of the garment.

She would have thanked him for the poem, but he kissed her before she could reply.

When he released her, she swayed on her feet.

"Until tonight." With a half smile, he turned and stalked from the hall, leaving her to recover her senses on her own.

"You look…well-rested this morning, Lady Barret," Roarke observed.

Melissande shook off the sensual fog that clouded her brain to shoot her new brother-in-law a withering look. "I am, thank you."

Roarke laughed, then shoved aside Lucian's breakfast plate. "I do not mean to tease you so early in the day, Mel. Come sit down."

After plucking some fresh quinces and a slab of bread, Melissande joined him. She hoped his good humor indicated there were no hard feelings about her wedding Lucian.

"I am sorry to hear you are leaving—" she began, wanting to make peace before she asked favors.

"Do not be." He patted her hand. "It is past time I grew up and sought my fortune. I honestly look forward to it."

"Truly?"

"Aye. In a way, I have you to thank for giving me the impetus to go."

That did not make her feel much better. "Because you saw me kissing Lucian."

"Because you made me realize I have nothing of real

value to offer any woman, nothing I can be truly proud of.'' His eyes darkened at the words, revealing an emptiness she had not suspected lurked inside him.

She offered him a bite of quince. ''Perhaps, if you are indebted to me, you will not begrudge me a small favor.''

''Name it.''

''I need to locate the midwife who cared for Osbern Fitzhugh before he died.''

''Melissande, I don't think—''

''There's no way Lucian's blow to Fitzhugh could have killed him so fast.'' She latched onto Roarke's arm, willing him to see the sense of her argument. ''You saw how Lucian clung to life for days after being shot in the chest, right near his heart. If Lucian could hold on so long with such a serious wound, why would Osbern die so soon after a glancing blow?''

''Infection?'' Roarke looked a little less sure of himself.

She shook her head. ''Not likely. Lucian told me the midwife gave him something to ward off infection.''

Roarke studied her, his eyes searching hers for answers she couldn't give.

''I just need to talk to her, Roarke. Please.''

Although Roarke remained quiet, Melissande knew she'd won by the slump of his broad shoulders. ''I don't know what you can possibly hope to accomplish.''

Impulsively she kissed his cheek. ''Your brother's salvation.''

He touched the place where her lips had been. Melissande hoped she had not offended him.

''It is a good day's ride from here,'' he warned. ''And I hear she does not practice healing anymore.''

Melissande stood, satisfied the first leg of her plan was under way. ''That doesn't matter.''

"I don't know that I'll be able to convince her to come here with me," he called as she moved to the door.

She paused and glanced over her shoulder, eyeing Roarke with an objective gaze. He was an incredibly handsome man, though that came as no surprise since he was Lucian's brother. Melissande had forgotten how appealing she had found him when they were children. "I'd be surprised if you've heard many a feminine refusal in your day, brother."

With a wink, she hurried off to her next errand, but not before she heard Roarke mutter, "Only one."

Lucian struggled to ward off thoughts of Melissande all day long. From the moment he had extracted himself from her arms to pen a hasty love note, he had daydreamed of his wife nonstop.

Now, as the sun set low on his first full day as a married man, he couldn't wait to get back to her. He handed his horse to a groom and cut the quickest path to the keep, anxious to find Melissande.

After consulting with his brother that morning, Lucian had ridden out to seek Damon Fitzhugh. Not one to wait docilely for his fate to come to him, Lucian was prepared to greet it straight-on.

Pausing to wash his face and hands at a small well, Lucian ruminated over the dismal outcome of his day's wanderings. Rumors abounded that Damon Fitzhugh was within a night's ride of his home. Lucian had also learned Peter Chadsworth was in Northumbria as a guest at Fitzhugh Keep.

Much as he desired to put this business between he and Damon behind him, Lucian was not ready for hand-to-hand combat. The wound in his chest had healed nicely, but the days abed had left his sword arm slower than usual. Now was not a fortuitous time for facing his former friend in battle.

Lucian knew he could not delay the meeting, however. His love for Melissande would not allow him to go about life trapped in guilt and remorse any longer.

Before he could fully realize the joys of marriage and reveal the extent of his feelings for Melissande, he needed to know their future together would last.

Their marriage would give her absolute security and financial independence, even if Lucian died tomorrow. But confiding his love for her would only hurt her if he were to meet an untimely end at Fitzhugh's blade.

Lucian longed to secure Melissande's love, but she would never grant it as long as he continued to wield a sword. And he had no choice but to wield it for at least as long as Damon hunted for him.

No. Melissande must not know the depth of his feelings for her yet, not until the threat of Damon could be eliminated.

Maybe then he would consider exchanging his chain mail for the refinements his new position afforded him.

Maybe.

Much as he wanted Melissande to love him, Lucian didn't relish the thought of forsaking his whole life's training. How could she condemn knighthood in such a broad sweep?

When he reached the hall, Melissande was nowhere in sight. Nor was his brother, for that matter.

After signaling to a server, Lucian wove through the trestles to the men-at-arms' table. He approached the biggest man, Roarke's closest friend. "Collin, where's my brother this eve?"

The man wiped his mouth on his sleeve before responding, carefully juggling the two ladies seated on his lap. He spoke over the blonde's curly head. "He left the keep on an errand for your lady, my lord."

Lucian wondered what Melissande could possibly need outside the keep. "And do you know the whereabouts of my lady?"

Collin shook his head and returned to his evening's entertainment while the server Lucian had called stepped forward.

"Lady Barret asked to dine in the master's chamber, my lord," the boy offered. "She is abovestairs."

Perfect. Now they would not have to sit through the lengthy protocol and niceties of supping in the hall. Lucian could seduce her all the sooner.

After ordering a second plate to be brought up to him, Lucian climbed the steps to the gallery, more eager than ever to see his wife.

He ignored the pessimistic voice that kept wondering if this would be their last night together.

His hand started for the door handle, then paused. He knocked instead.

"Lucian?" Her voice chimed through the heavy oak.

Was it his imagination or did she sound hopeful? He pushed the door open, surprised at the wave of heat that assailed him as he did.

In spite of the mild temperature out of doors, a merry fire crackled in the hearth. Melissande sat near to the blaze, her feet much too close to the hot cinders for his comfort. Why would she risk burning her toes, unless…

Panic seized him. Could she have suffered a relapse from the lung fever? "You are ill, wife?"

She turned to smile at him, her grin more full of warmth and cheer than the leaping flames. "Nay…just decadent, I suppose."

Understanding soothed his racing heart. She was well.

Lucian promised himself he would whisper countless prayers of thanksgiving when he went to chapel the next morning.

He trusted Melissande could get along in life without him, but not for the world would he want to suffer being left without her.

Lucian strode closer, then pulled her to her feet to stand before him. She was vibrant, full of life and vigorous health. "You are reliving youthful days of good cheer in front of a fire." He recalled her sadness at being deprived such pleasures in the abbey. "I am glad. You never have to deny yourself comfort in our home."

Melissande caught his hand in one of her own and pressed her cheek to his palm. His words soothed her soul, eased her spirit.

How blessed she was to marry a man who understood her so well. Lucian seemed to have more insight to her mind than she did herself at times.

She considered broaching the topic of the children. Emilia, Andre and Rafael were never far from her thoughts. Yet, spying the grave seriousness in Lucian's eyes as she stood to face him, she thought her request might keep another day. After witnessing Lucian's considerate treatment of her, she had reason to hope he would consider a partnership where their children were concerned.

"I have missed you," she told him finally, at a loss for any other words to convey the complex feelings of her heart. This much, at least, was true.

Although she could have told him she feared she had fallen deeply in love with him, Melissande could not risk her heart until he confirmed his intentions. She had been abandoned before by a man she loved, her father, the man who had promised her to a convent even though she had begged him not to send her away.

Even after ten years, she had not recovered enough to risk such rejection again. If her father could reject her, a gentle man who had promised to adore her no matter what, how could she trust a warrior knight who had not uttered one word of love?

He tipped her chin to peer down into her eyes. "As I have missed you, Angel." With one hand he pulled the circlet from her head and threaded his fingers through the hair she had never gotten around to braiding.

"Will you go away again soon?" She had not meant to ask so bluntly, but her lips seemed to have a will of their own since she'd left St. Ursula's.

His brow furrowed. "As lord of a sizable holding, I will spend much time visiting my vassal knights and overseeing the use of our lands."

"That is not quite what I mean." Melissande could be more than content with that sort of life. She could be ecstatic. She took a deep breath, stealing herself for the inevitable disappointment her next question would unearth. "From your note this morn, I gathered you would not return to battle again."

Tension quivered through her, steeling her for his response.

"I am a knight, Melissande." He gripped her shoulders as if willing her to understand. "Not a miller or a priest, but a warrior. Battle is the obligation and reality of my life."

A violent death would also be his reality, Melissande thought, eyes burning with unshed tears. She wanted a family, and a man who would return to his children day after day. Lucian, it seemed, wanted something else.

She searched her mind for some semblance of cool logic that would appeal to her practical husband. "Yet you didn't slay the man who shot at us in the Alps. You set him free and gave him the chance to nearly kill you in England. Surely that proves you possess a merciful nature."

Something flashed in his eyes, a passionate emotion at odds with the reserved man she knew. His hands fell away from her shoulders. "My merciful nature killed my foster father, Melissande. No matter that I prided myself on being able to control my temper with one of the most unpredictable men in northern England. I lost it that day."

"But maybe—"

"Maybe I wanted him dead." He looked at her levelly, his eyes cold and flat. "For one moment, as I recalled the way he'd humiliated all of his foster sons at one time or another during a drunken rant, I think I might have willed his death."

She struggled for the right words to console him. "Everyone thinks a horrible thought sometimes. That doesn't mean you acted upon it."

"Didn't I?"

She shook her head, refusing to believe he was right, trusting her instincts that he wasn't. "No matter how hard you try, you will never recreate that moment in your mind exactly as it happened. Perhaps your sense of guilt is embellishing what happened so that you may lay the blame fully upon yourself, but it must have all happened so fast. You can't spend your life punishing yourself for this, Lucian."

He quirked a brow, a humorless smile crossing his face. "In that you are right, Angel. Sooner or later, Damon Fitzhugh will shoulder the burden of meting out justice."

Fear knotted in her belly. Despite the heat of the blaze in the hearth, the chamber seemed to have lost all its warmth. "Damon." She'd forgotten about Osbern's son. "But he is in the Holy Lands, is he not?"

"He will return."

He left unspoken the rest of the thought—that only one man would walk away from that confrontation. When Lucian next greeted his childhood friend, he would be forced to draw his sword against him.

"You will be faced with a difficult choice when he returns, my lord." An impossible choice.

Her throat grew tight, imagining the horror of that moment. Would she be left a widow after that fateful day? Or would she be left with a warrior husband whose battle victory would ensure the defeat of her marriage?

Her only hope rested on the shoulders on a runaway healer. She prayed Roarke would find the midwife before it was too late.

Lucian closed the distance between them. His intent gaze heated her flesh, stirred her blood, despite her fears.

"We cannot live in fear of the future." His hands found her waist, then shifted lower to curl around her hips.

Her heart kicked up a notch, her body attuned to his slightest touch. "Neither can we hide from it."

He pulled her against him, allowing her to feel every muscled nuance of his body. The leather of his braies slid against the thin silk of her night rail, igniting a deep hunger for him.

"We shall not hide." He teased her lips with his, chasing her fears to the corners of her mind, calling forth her desire in its place. "We shall await it together." He nipped her lower lip gently with his teeth, then soothed that place with his tongue.

Warmth pooled in her belly, then flooded her limbs. She prayed time would work on their side, couldn't stand to think about the consequences if it didn't. "In the meantime, we will discover one another and strengthen one another," she assured him between kisses, giving her fingers free rein over his shoulders, his arms.

Melissande absorbed the feel of him, drank in the taste of him, wishing just this once they could make time stand still. If only Athena could hold the dawn under the ocean, the way she had for Penelope and Odysseus.

But she would take this one night to hold Lucian in her arms. And she would greedily take every night hereafter until Damon came and their dreams of a future came to an end.

"I will give you a babe before then," he promised her, running one splayed hand over her belly.

Tears burned her eyes, but she refused to let them fall. She framed Lucian's face with her hands, trailing one finger down the imperfection of his scar. "I would like that. I would like *all* of my children here with me."

He rained kisses over her throat, but she felt his nod in the curve of her shoulder. "I will see what can be done, Melissande."

Hope curled through her at the thought of seeing the abbey's orphans again. Would Lucian truly retrieve her children? Perhaps he meant to fill her life with a family, knowing he might face death before he could give her all the sons and daughters she craved.

As much as the notion tore at her heart, she couldn't resist his primal invitation, his slow seduction of her senses. Lucian was with her, here and now.

His hands grew restless at her bodice. He tugged the silken ties open and plundered deep into her neckline to cradle her breast. The rough heat of his palm sent a shudder coursing through her.

He rubbed his cheek against her hair. The day's growth of beard prickled her scalp. "How do you feel today?" he whispered.

She leaned back to peer up at him. "Frightened of what

lies ahead, but I am quite content to be in your arms to-night.''

A grin tugged at his lips. '''Tis not what I meant.'' He allowed one hand to trail down the inside of her thigh. "How do you feel in the aftermath of your wedding night?"

"Oh." Heat climbed her cheeks. "I feel very well."

He stroked one broad palm over her hair, skimming the length of it to rest on the small of her back. "I did not hurt you?"

She found it difficult to meet his gaze, but she didn't falter from speaking her mind. "You brought me only pleasure."

The low growl that emanated from him vibrated through her and thrilled her to her toes. He hoisted her into his arms and carried her to their bed, depositing her in a nest of warm linens.

The hearth fire leaped and crackled, casting a heated glow around them. Melissande held her arms out to her husband, eager to pull him into bed beside her.

"It is too soon for you, wife," Lucian mumbled as he trailed kisses down her neck.

"It is not nearly soon enough for me, my lord." She edged her fingers into the collar of his tunic, tugging the ties apart as she went, reveling in the breadth of his chest.

She could feel Lucian's smile against the column of her throat.

"You are dangerous, woman."

"You have no one but yourself to blame." Was she too brazen to raise the hem of his tunic, to splay hungry fingers over the muscles of his chest? She prayed not, because her husband was too tempting to resist.

"And how do you arrive at that conclusion?" He assisted her by pulling the tunic over his head, then turned his attention to kissing the straps of her night rail off of her shoulders.

"You are the one who went searching for the bold and brazen Melissande." She shimmied out of the night rail, only too happy to press her bared body to Lucian's. "And I believe you have found her."

She interpreted his throaty groan as acquiescence. The low growl reverberated right through her, inspiring a wave of shivery tingles all over her exposed skin.

"I want that woman." Lucian's hands sought her belly, her hips, her thighs. And lingered. "In fact, I want all the sides of you. Every part of you."

The words soothed her spirit while inciting her body. His fingers worked minor miracles, causing tingles to course down her spine and flash fires to sizzle up her legs. Her back arched, seeking the solid strength of him. She couldn't possibly be close enough to this man that turned her inside out.

The blaze from the hearth cast him in shadows above her. Golden light danced over his skin, highlighting taut sinews sprinkled with dark hair. Her fingers followed the flickering light, skimming all the places that warm glow touched. Heat radiated from him as if the fire originated within, his whole body simmering with need.

"I have thought about this often today," she admitted, hunger swirling through her as liquid desire coursed through her veins. "I had no idea marriage could be so…fulfilling."

He grazed kisses over her breasts, his tongue lavishing her with the kind of attention she'd been dreaming about all day. "I vow to fulfill you as often as you like, wife."

Pleasure hummed through her as his kisses slowed, strengthened. He palmed her thigh, spreading her legs with warm, calloused hands. She gripped his shoulders, willing him to touch her *there* where she needed him so desperately. Bending to whisper in his ear, she confided her wish.

"I think I would like it right now."

His groan rumbled through them both, the sound vibrating against his lips as he kissed her. Still, he seemed to agree to her request as his hand dipped between her thighs. Cradled her.

Her whole body melted against that broad palm.

He found her innermost core with his finger and gently teased her with gentle strokes.

"Yes," she agreed mindlessly, ready to give this man all that she had, all that she was capable of. She shifted her legs to give him further access, trusting him to give her everything she wanted in return.

Heat gathered in her belly and between her thighs. Desire tightened into a spiral, ready to spring at any moment. Her breathing quickened, her heart hammered.

She was so close to that glorious release that when Lucian lowered his head to grant her that most intimate of kisses, she flew apart in a million directions, the sensations rocking her body with more force than ever before.

He entered her before the glorious sensations subsided, and the thrust of his body only added to the magic of the exquisite feeling.

She dug her fingers into his back, her ankles locking around his waist, holding him deeply inside her until he refused to be held any longer.

"I will take you there again," he promised, his words a ragged whisper in her ear. "Do not fear."

She loosened her grip upon him to run her fingers over his naked chest. "If I don't take you there first, my lord."

In answer to her wriggling beneath him, he allowed her to sit on top of him, rolling their bodies so they might exchange positions.

Melissande marveled at the new opportunities this granted her. She tested his reaction to her every move, delighting in the power she seemed to hold over the mighty warrior knight.

When she had decided he'd waited long enough, Melissande used her new knowledge to bring him to the brink of fulfillment.

"Too dangerous," he announced hoarsely. He flipped her underneath him once again to fully claim her body in the moments before he spilled his seed inside her, bathed her in the life-giving force she craved almost as much as his love.

He made love to her all through the night, sometimes with the fierceness of a warrior and other times with the thoroughness of a scholar. Still, their time together was tinged with the knowledge that it wasn't forever, that their time together was borrowed.

Just before she fell asleep, she considered how perfect life would be if the threat of Damon Fitzhugh did not hover between them. But until Lucian faced his past, there could be no future for their marriage and no hope for love to grow between them.

Chapter Twenty-One

"My Lord Roarke wishes to see you, my lady," the maid Isabel whispered over Melissande's still bleary-eyed form the next morning.

Melissande chastised herself for sleeping late yet again. The sun shone into the narrow slits in the wall above the bed despite the occasional ominous rumble of thunder.

"Thank you, Isabel." Melissande struggled to sit up as the maid scurried out the door. If Roarke wanted to see her, it could mean only one thing. He'd found the midwife.

Eager to converse with the healer, Melissande bounded out of bed and promptly winced. Her night with her husband left an ache in her body, though not nearly so keen as the one in her heart.

She tugged on a dark yellow surcoat from the small chest of items Abbess Helen had brought for her and made quick work of her hair by wrapping a single braid around her head to hold the rest of the strands from her face.

Melissande shoved open the door and headed down the stairs, praying the healer held a key to Lucian's past—a key to their future together. If she could somehow prove he did not bear full responsibility for his foster father's death, perhaps Damon Fitzhugh would listen to reason.

Moreover, perhaps Lucian would be ready to give and to receive love. After the last two heaven-sent nights she and Lucian had shared together, Melissande desperately wanted to capture forever with her husband.

With any luck, the midwife could help Melissande to do just that.

Entering the great hall, Melissande stopped short to see the woman Roarke had brought to Barret Keep. Small and fair, with snowy curls peeking out from a modest linen cap, the healer would have been exceedingly pretty if not for the mulish frown creasing her lips and the heavy rope girding her waist and arms.

Melissande hurried over to them, prepared to take the younger Barret to task. "By St. Ursula's wimple, Roarke, why is she bound?"

"She turned six shades of pale and ran when she saw me coming, my lady." Roarke turned narrowed eyes on the midwife. "My guess is she stole something before she left Barret Keep and is afraid I've found her out."

A surge of excitement shot through Melissande. She had a much better idea why the midwife ran. But unless Roarke halted his intimidation tactics, Melissande doubted they would uncover the truth.

As thunder rumbled outside, the great hall was cast in abrupt shadows. The sudden darkness provided a baleful backdrop to Melissande's hopeful mood.

"Regardless, she is my guest now." Melissande adopted an authoritative manner that would make Abbess Helen proud. "Would you untie her please, so she might join me to break our fast?"

Roarke studied Melissande for a long moment, perhaps attempting to discern her motive, but finally began to loosen the bonds.

"When you finish there, would you be so kind as to

dispatch a maid to the abbess? I am sure she would like to join us.'' Melissande smiled brilliantly, hoping Roarke would not balk. She wanted to give the recalcitrant midwife the impression that Melissande was in charge.

Melissande had to discover the truth of the elder Fitzhugh's death so that Lucian could forgive himself for the past. She needed to discover what the midwife knew.

Now.

Roarke cocked a curious brow in her direction, but only bowed politely. ''Anything else, my lady?''

''Would you mind checking on the whereabouts of my husband, please?'' Melissande hoped he was close at hand in case she was able to extract new information regarding Lord Fitzhugh's death.

Roarke stepped closer, as if he would deny her highhanded commands. He flashed a wicked grin intended for her eyes alone. ''I am, as always, your humble servant.''

He strode from the room, clearing his throat in a gurgle that sounded suspiciously close to laughter, but Melissande's guest did not seem to notice. The woman stared out a narrow window at a summer rainstorm whipping through the courtyard.

Melissande gauged her opponent now that they were alone. Although the young woman made a show of lifting her chin and maintaining a reserved demeanor, Melissande could see the flicker of fear in her sky-blue eyes.

After a lifetime spent getting into one mischievous mess after another, Melissande could well read the mantle of guilt when worn by another.

If Melissande could adapt the tactics Abbess Helen used when questioning a wayward novitiate, maybe she could convince the young woman to share her secrets.

''You know,'' Melissande began, mentally flipping through the Book of Proverbs as she filled two cups of watered-down wine from the sideboard in an effort to loosen the woman's tongue. "I just happened to read a lovely passage." Smiling, she handed one of the cups to the former midwife. "Perhaps you are familiar with it? 'The truthful witness saves lives, whoever utters lies is a deceiver.'"

The healer's hands trembled as she accepted the wine. "I never meant to be deceptive, my lady." Her soft voice hinted at an inner strength her delicate form lacked.

Melissande froze. "Then you and I must talk at length. I am Lady Melissande of Barret Keep. How shall I call you?"

"I am Alisoun of the Woods." Her blue eyes pinned Melissande with a gaze at once suspicious and proud. "I may have sinned by keeping my secrets, but I swear to you I never meant to hurt anyone."

Melissande's heart thrummed so noisily she feared she would miss the young woman's words. "You speak of Lord Fitzhugh?"

Alisoun responded with a tight nod, her body rigid.

Relinquishing her wine to the sideboard, Melissande knelt beside the woman and covered Alisoun's hand with her own. "You will come to no harm if you confide in me."

Alisoun shook her head and cast a pleading look toward Melissande. "I do not care for myself, my lady. But I have children who depend upon me."

Melissande's heart softened in sympathy. "I will not allow them to come to harm, either, Alisoun."

"I would never have run in the first place if I didn't fear for them," Alisoun whispered, her voice hoarse with unshed tears. "But after Osbern…rather, after Lord Fitzhugh died, I could not be certain that the children would be safe."

Melissande tried to imagine what lengths she would go to if her own children were in danger. Perhaps more accurately, she tried to imagine what she *wouldn't* do. She could not think of a thing.

"Too many lives depend upon the truth now, Alisoun. I can help you keep your children safe." Or Lucian would. Her warrior husband could protect anyone.

But it was up to Melissande to safeguard him.

Alisoun nodded. "You are right. I know in my heart you are right." She squeezed Melissande's hand, the action spurring the tears to stream down the woman's cheeks. "It seems I have kept my secrets long enough."

Lucian had been tempted to stay abed with his wife this morning and forego the quest to meet his destiny with Damon Fitzhugh.

Had he listened to his selfish heart, he would still be languishing next to Melissande instead of fighting his way through the sudden storm that drained buckets of rain upon him.

He had been on his way to the Fitzhugh holding when the storm hit and foiled his plans to meet Damon. Much as Lucian wanted to settle the differences between them, whether by word or sword, he refused to enter his enemy's home dripping like a wet rat.

'Twould hardly further Lucian's fierce reputation to ask his host for a dry linen before meeting him in combat.

Damon might not arrive home until tomorrow. Even if he did appear earlier, he certainly would not seek out Lucian in this wet wrath of Poseidon.

Now, Lucian had won yet another day's reprieve to enjoy his wife. Another day to plant his seed in her belly and to give himself the satisfaction of knowing that, if he died at

Fitzhugh's hand, Melissande would at least carry the babe she'd always craved.

Between his heir and the surprise he had asked Roarke to acquire for her, Melissande would be secure without him.

Of course, Lucian had no intention of going down without a fight. Although Damon was reputed to be one of the best swordsmen in England, Lucian's new intense will to live would no doubt render him a credible opponent.

More than anything he wanted the peace of mind that he could have a future with Melissande, despite his warrior livelihood. Couldn't she see the need for men who were willing to die for their beliefs? Their land? Their families?

He longed to reveal his love for her, whether she returned it or not. He would spend a lifetime winning that love in slow degrees.

His thoughts inflamed with images of his sweetly sensuous wife, Lucian hastened his mare into the Barret stables and wiped the excess rainwater from his face.

Lucian cared for the horse himself, there being no groom in sight due to the weather. He dried and hung the tack on the stable wall.

Engrossed in his task and lulled by the steady din of thunder, Lucian heard no warning of a stranger's approach.

"Barret." A man's voice penetrated the tumult.

From the deep bass of the sound, coupled with the edge of cool hatred, Lucian knew who he would face when he turned around.

"Fitzhugh." Lucian exhaled the name along with two years' worth of pent-up guilt. Instead of repentant, Lucian felt oddly relieved as he swung about to greet his former friend.

Feral eyes gleamed back at Lucian. Lean and hard, Damon Fitzhugh looked every inch the brutal warrior. The squared jaw and thin line of his lips did nothing to relieve the impression. Rainwater sluiced from his hauberk to pool on the dirt floor.

Lucian saw for the first time how Melissande might have arrived at her impression that all knights were a blood-thirsty, intimidating lot. If Lucian Barret felt a small taste of apprehension, he could only imagine how his convent-bred wife must feel in the presence of such thinly disguised violence.

"I have been looking for you." Damon reached across his body to rest his hand on the hilt of his sword.

Lucian simmered with the heat of the coming battle. He knew Damon would not walk away until he slid his blade deep into Lucian's chest.

"For the wrong reasons," Lucian returned.

All of Melissande's insistence that Lucian was innocent of murder had fallen on deaf ears, until now. As he confronted the man who most desperately needed to hear the truth about his father, Lucian realized he had not purposely killed Osbern Fitzhugh. He'd acted in self-defense. He was only a man—subject to human error.

"For the best reason of all, Barret," Damon corrected him, drawing his sword. "You murdered my father."

Lucian's mind recalled another day when he faced a violently angry Fitzhugh holding a sword. Only this day would not have the same brutal end. He could not allow it.

"I raised my sword to ward off one of his fits of temper, Damon." Lucian's natural instinct when facing a furious man with a sword was to draw his own weapon. His hand itched to do just that. But some faint hope in his heart refused to let him. "He plowed right into my blade trying to come at me."

Damon's fingers clenched, white-knuckled, on the hilt. Lightning flashed behind him, illuminating his hulking silhouette in the open door. "Such a glancing blow would not have been mortal, Barret. You are not so inexperienced a fighter as to expect me to accept that.''

''Wounds can be fickle, Fitzhugh. I did not deal your father a fatal blow. 'Twas some infection or illness that set in afterward.''

''He died that same night, Barret.'' Damon's nostrils flared with his rising fury.

With a sinking heart, Lucian knew Damon would not believe him—did not want to believe him. And who could blame him? Lucian had refused to believe it for two years.

They would be forced to fight and Lucian would either kill or be killed.

Melissande would either hate him for engaging in mortal combat or mourn him for losing.

Damon stepped closer. ''My father was strong as a bull and we both know it. He could have fought off a petty wound with a few stitches and some attention from that sweet little midwife.'' Damon took a deep breath. He seemed to grow even larger as he stood there. ''Now draw.''

Good God, Lucian did not want to. Damon had once been his close friend. Besides, Lucian's injury from the arrow was too fresh. His body was not yet ready to combat one of the best knights Christendom had to offer. ''Damon—''

''Draw!'' Fitzhugh barked the word, his tension and anger radiating through his drenched garments.

If Lucian had thought it might help his cause to stall, he could have chastened Damon with the news that Peter Chadsworth had tried to kill him. Damon was a good knight and an honorable man, and he would not want to fight a man who was not at full capacity to defend himself.

It would also gall Damon to know simpleminded Peter had been corrupted with his lord's mission for revenge.

But ultimately Damon would not be robbed of his revenge. And Lucian's sense of honor demanded he fight.

He drew.

Hands steady, heart hardened against his former friend, Lucian raised his blade. He hoped God and Melissande would forgive him.

With a vicious clash of steel against steel, the battle of Lucian's life commenced.

Melissande's feet flew toward the stable before she made a conscious decision to go there.

There is a battle going on out in the stables, my lady, we think it's...

Melissande hadn't needed to hear the rest of the server's words. She knew exactly who fought out there and why. Who else but Lucian would be wielding a sword a mere fortnight after getting shot in the chest?

Rain soaked through her tunic and kirtle before she realized she should have grabbed a cloak. Mud spattered her skirt as she tore through the soaked grass to the planked home of the keep's horseflesh.

A thousand thoughts plagued her as she ran. Vaguely she marveled that her mind could sort through so much information in such a short span of time.

She berated herself for not dragging Alisoun, the midwife, out into the storm. The young woman possessed the answers that could halt the fighting.

Another corner of her brain feared she would be too late, that Lucian would be dead by the time she arrived. He did not have the benefit of fighting full-strength because of his recent injury. Her heart wrenched at the thought, spurring her feet to such long strides she fell in the mud.

Barely registering the cold layer of dirt caked on her gown, she hauled herself up. She had almost reached the stable when a man came tumbling out of the building and sprawled on the ground at her feet.

Melissande screamed, even after she realized the fallen knight was not Lucian.

Stunned, she turned to see her husband edge his way out of the planked building, his eyes never leaving his opponent.

She couldn't believe her husband, still healing from his bout with death, could knock down a man the size of the giant at her feet.

A jolt of pride took her by surprise.

She had spent all her convent years disdaining the vainglorious Crusaders who frequented St. Ursula's table. She had been sickened by their obvious bloodlust, offended by their boastful tales.

But Lucian had shown her a new side to a warrior.

Never prideful or eager to kill, he was a protector because of his God-given strength and an innate sense of justice.

For the first time Melissande appreciated exactly who her husband was and what made him that way. Warrior protector or scholarly speaker of Sanskrit, Lucian Barret embodied all that was fine and noble about a man.

"Get back, Mel," Lucian shouted, his eyes still trained on his quarry.

The other knight, who Melissande recognized as Damon Fitzhugh grown to manhood, scrambled to his feet.

As their swords crashed together, Melissande realized she had lost her chance of intervening. Mayhap she had even stolen Lucian's moment of advantage over his hulking opponent.

"Wait!" she screamed, her cry of no avail. She saw the intense concentration on their faces as they circled each other in the pouring rain. These men would not halt their battle for her.

She turned to call for Roarke, prepared to shriek her throat hoarse, when she spied him striding through the rain, tugging Alisoun along behind him. The abbess hurried two steps behind them, one cloak about her shoulders, another draped over her head.

To Melissande, the mismatched threesome looked like avenging angels come to her rescue. Between them, they could put a stop to this insanity.

They had to.

"Hurry!" she cried, wondering why Roarke walked as if he had all the time in the world.

She flinched as the swords rang in a discordant crash, wondering how much longer Lucian could fend off his huge—and healthy—opponent.

Roarke arrived at her side and squeezed her shoulders as she watched the men struggle. "He can hold his own ground," he confided.

"We cannot just let them battle it out!" she called back, striving to be heard over the clamor of the storm. "He could be killed."

"If Lucian would not stop for your sake, Mel, he sure as hell won't throw down his sword for me."

As they debated their options, Abbess Helen marched past Roarke and jumped straight into the fray, unarmed but for the silver cross about her neck. This she held proudly before her, as if to ward off any evil spirits that dared to tread near her.

"Cease in the name of God and our Sainted Ursula, gentlemen, or prepare your souls for His wrath," she shouted effortlessly, as if she were accustomed to laying men low with the power of her voice.

Both men halted, their swords frozen in midair.

Warrior knights were no match for the abbess.

"I know your quarrel is deep and well-founded, my lords." She nodded respectfully to both of them. "But I have news that may alter your dispute."

Long accustomed to following Abbess Helen's lead, Melissande knew her cue. She strode forward, arm-in-arm with a trembling Alisoun.

"All will be well," Melissande whispered, squeezing the girl's hand.

"You found the midwife," Lucian noted, his gaze jumping from Melissande to Alisoun. "She knows something?"

Damon made an impatient gesture, his fingers flexing on the hilt of his sword. "I am sorry, Sister, but I cannot—"

Abbess Helen gave him a scathing look. "There is enough time for killing, sir. You might give a few moments to hear the girl."

The rain continued to beat down on all of them. Melissande felt her dress adhere to her skin with the persistence of a leech. She wished they could settle this indoors, warm and dry, but Damon Fitzhugh did not look as though he would be amenable to any more manipulation.

"I killed him," Alisoun blurted, her poor body shaking convulsively.

"Not deliberately," Melissande amended, wrapping her arm about the woman's slender shoulders.

Damon's gaze darkened, settling on the former midwife. "How so, woman? Do you mean to tell me you wielded the sword that bore my father's deathblow?" He glared at Lucian.

"I was not meant to be a midwife. I had so little experience," she cried. "I—I tried to staunch his bleeding with what I thought was woundwart." She looked helplessly at the abbess, blue eyes full of tears that were obvious even through the driving rain. "After I applied it, I realized it was wormwood. The labels looked the same and I was so frightened by all the blood.''

Alisoun collapsed in a sobbing heap against Melissande's shoulder, whispering apologies no one else could hear.

''What the hell does that mean?'' Damon asked, frustration radiating from his body along with the steam of his recent exertions.

''Wormwood can be deadly,'' Melissande explained, ''especially in concentrated amounts. She applied the herb quite liberally, thinking it was something else.''

''Jesus!'' Damon ignored the abbess's flinch. ''My father was not struck down in combat with a man, but rather—'' he looked scathingly at the pitiful mass of coarse clothing and blond hair that now streamed haphazardly over the midwife's shoulders ''—by this mite of a woman?''

He stepped toward Melissande and Alisoun.

The menace in his gaze terrified Melissande. She knew too well how brutal a warrior knight could be.

Lucian edged in front of her, planting himself between danger and the women. ''I still struck the blow.''

Melissande wanted to bury her head in the crook of his arm, to revel in the sense of protection her husband had always imparted.

How had she ever viewed Lucian as a cold-hearted killer?

''But she killed him with her vile treatments.'' Damon's big hand shook with rage when he pointed a finger at Alisoun.

Melissande froze as Damon raised his sword high over his head, his face a mask of fury. For a moment, it seemed he meant to cleave Alisoun in two.

Swearing an ungodly curse, Damon turned and smashed the blade deep into the trunk of a sturdy maple tree. The air echoed with his oath while the sword seemed to reverberate with the awful power of the swing.

Although Melissande breathed a shaky sigh of relief, a nervous tremble shuddered through her in the aftermath of such violence.

"She was barely more than a girl," Lucian remarked quietly.

"Then maybe you shouldn't have called her to aid my father." Damon yanked his blade from the tree trunk, his words slightly more calm than they had been a moment ago.

"I am still ready to defend myself," Lucian assured him, stepping forward.

"I called Alisoun," Roarke interjected. "I knew your father enjoyed her…company."

Damon squeezed his eyes shut, lifting his hand to rub over the sockets.

"Perhaps we had best sort this out inside," Abbess Helen suggested, laying her fingers on Damon's arm.

"Nay." Damon stepped away from her, his gaze falling swiftly on Lucian. "Not yet."

The huge knight hefted his blade once again.

Melissande's heart sank. How could he still want to kill Lucian after all this?

Lucian straightened, his sword in its scabbard at his side, but seemingly unafraid.

In a ritual Melissande had not witnessed since childhood, Damon Fitzhugh lowered his massive body to one knee and turned his sword around so he might hold the blade.

"Lucian Barret, I swear my fealty to you this day, before these witnesses, and claim you as my sovereign lord."

Curiously, a smile crooked the corner of Melissande's lips even as a tear formed in her eye.

Her sire had humbled himself before Lucian's father in

this way year after year to show his allegiance to the earl. But the sight of her slight father, with his scholar's demeanor and cleric's righteousness, bowed before another man had not made such an impression.

To see a knight as magnificent as Damon Fitzhugh kneel in deference to her husband sent a shiver through her.

At last Lucian was restored to the glory of his birthright, hailed as lord by a man who'd called him enemy the day before.

Melissande had not felt so much pride since she watched little Andre learn to read.

Lucian Barret, soaked to the skin and more regal than she'd ever seen him, gripped the hilt of Damon's sword with both hands. ''I accept your pledge, Fitzhugh, with glad heart.''

A sense of peace washed through Melissande, more cleansing than the pouring rain. Happiness could prevail in her household now, if only Lucian would allow it.

As Abbess Helen crossed herself and Roarke awkwardly patted Alisoun on the back, Melissande thanked God she had arrived in time to safeguard her husband's life.

Lucian pulled Damon to his feet. They exchanged quiet words for a moment before Lucian clapped him about the shoulders in the fashion of an old friend. ''To the keep!'' he shouted.

Later that night in the privacy of the master bedchamber, Melissande smiled to herself as she recalled that moment.

''Damon is an honorable man,'' she observed, combing through her damp hair while her husband stripped off his garments.

Good heavens, but Lucian did curious things to her heart. And her pulse. And her knees.

Melissande sat on the bed to disguise the tremor that

shook her every time she looked at all that raw male power unveiled. Tonight, she would tell him the words that had echoed in her mind all day.

Now that she had seen Lucian at his most warrior-lethal, Melissande knew she would no longer revile his power to kill. She respected his judgment and restraint to use his might only where needed. His warrior spirit was superbly controlled by a brilliant mind.

Moreover, Melissande had realized that his strength, his battle prowess, were part of what made her sleep so soundly at his side. With a man like Lucian Barret to depend on, she need never be afraid again.

Lucian would protect her, now and always.

And she loved him for it.

"I will be sad to see the abbess leave," she remarked absently, though her mind already envisioned various ways and times to tell Lucian she loved him. "And your brother, too."

Naked but for the leather braies that encased his legs, Lucian plucked the silver comb from her hand and laid it on a small chest. "We will see Roarke again soon enough."

Melissande blinked. "I thought he itched to wander the world?" Lucian had confided Roarke's conversations with their mother before her death, along with his reasons to suspect his parentage. The news greatly upset Lucian, but didn't really surprise Melissande. The men bore little resemblance to one another, their characters as different as their countenances. Still, she hoped Roarke would find peace in his travels along with the answers he sought.

Lucian enjoyed this moment—had looked forward to it ever since his fight with Damon Fitzhugh had ended peaceably. He wanted it to be perfect.

Settling himself beside her, he pulled her body against

his. "Roarke *will* wander…as soon as he does a small favor for me."

He could almost feel the curiosity zinging through her. Melissande sat up to look at him.

"What favor?"

"He is picking up my wedding gift to you."

"A gift for me?" Her brown eyes shone with pleasure. Her red hair seemed to dance in the soft candlelight. "Oh, Lucian!" She clapped her hands like an eager child. "What is it?"

Lucian relished every moment of her excitement, wanted to spin out the joy of the news, but found his own enthusiasm wouldn't let him dangle the surprise before her much longer.

"If I tell you, it won't be a surprise," he warned.

Her hands flew to his shoulders, hands clenching his flesh. "Don't you dare keep me in suspense, Lucian Barret."

"He rides to St. Ursula's with the abbess," Lucian admitted, savoring her puzzlement as her brow furrowed.

"Abbess Helen does not need his escort…" she started, then her breath caught. Her gaze narrowed. "He is retrieving something for me?" she asked.

Lucian could see the pulse flutter at her throat. Her hope was palpable.

"My gift is your children, my lady."

She smothered him with a bear hug that knocked him flat on his back. She squeezed him so tightly it took him a moment to catch his breath.

"Rather our children, Mel," he corrected himself, smiling as he wiped a strand of her hair off his face. "That is, if you agree to share them with me."

For a long moment she did not speak. She remained burrowed into his shoulder, her arms still squeezing his neck.

"Angel?" Then he felt the shudders that racked her slender body. "Melissande?" He pushed her off of him so he could see her face, lifting them both upright again.

Tears streamed down her cheeks. Her brown eyes were ringed in bright red.

"Oh, Lucian, I love you so." She sniffled, wiping a hand over one drenched cheek. "Even before you told me about the children, I loved you. I can't believe you would do that for me, for them."

Lucian's mouth went dry as he staggered with the weight of her gift, so tender and unexpected. He had longed to share words of love with her this night, but he hadn't dreamed of hearing them back from her. At least not yet.

He took a deep breath and handed her his heart. "Angel, I've loved you since you were in braids."

Her eyes widened.

"Since you were old enough to start pining over my brother."

She grinned sheepishly.

"More precisely, since the day I taught you to fish."

Lucian smiled to see he had rendered her speechless. He decided, much as he had grown to adore her sweet voice, he liked this new power of quieting her, too.

"Truly?" she finally squeaked, her cheeks tinted with pink.

He slid his arms around her, more complete than he had ever been his life.

"Truly." He kissed her tears away one by one, brushed her hair from her face. "And I plan to show you just how much in the months before the three little ones arrive."

He traced a path down her neck with his finger, fascinated by the hitch in her breath, the quick flutter of pulse through her veins.

"Four little ones."

Lucian paused. "Four?"

Her grin grew wide. "Well, with any luck there will be four by spring." She trailed her hands over his chest, her eyes lighting with the trace of mischief he loved. "If you work at it, that is."

Melissande had challenged him.

Cupping her face in one hand, Lucian rubbed his thumb over the soft fullness of her lower lip. "Angel, I swear to do my devoted best."

* * * * *

Be sure to watch for Joanne Rock's sizzling miniseries, SINGLE IN SOUTH BEACH, *which will be returning to Harlequin Blaze in May 2004. And don't miss Roarke's story, coming only to Harlequin Historicals in late 2004.*

From Regency romps
to mesmerizing Medievals,
savor these stirring tales from
Harlequin Historicals®

On sale January 2004

THE KNAVE AND THE MAIDEN by Blythe Gifford

A cynical knight's life is forever changed when he falls
in love with a naive young woman while journeying
to a holy shrine.

MARRYING THE MAJOR by Joanna Maitland

Can a war hero wounded in body and spirit find
happiness with his childhood sweetheart, now that she
has become the toast of London society?

On sale February 2004

THE CHAPERON BRIDE by Nicola Cornick

When England's most notorious rake is attracted to
a proper ladies' chaperon, could it be true love?

THE WEDDING KNIGHT by Joanne Rock

A dashing knight abducts a young woman to marry his
brother, but soon falls in love with her instead!

HEAD FOR THE ROCKIES WITH

Harlequin Historicals®
Historical Romantic Adventure!

AND SEE HOW IT ALL BEGAN!

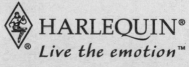

PICK UP THESE HARLEQUIN HISTORICALS
AND IMMERSE YOURSELF IN THRILLING
AND EMOTIONAL LOVE STORIES
SET IN THE AMERICAN FRONTIER

On sale January 2004

CHEYENNE WIFE by Judith Stacy
(Colorado, 1844)

Will opposites attract when a handsome
half-Cheyenne horse trader comes to the rescue
of a proper young lady from back east?

WHIRLWIND BRIDE by Debra Cowan
(Texas, 1883)

A widowed rancher unexpectedly falls in love with
a beautiful and pregnant young woman.

On sale February 2004

COLORADO COURTSHIP by Carolyn Davidson
(Colorado, 1862)

A young widow finds a father for her unborn child—
and a man for her heart—in a loving wagon train scout.

THE LIGHTKEEPER'S WOMAN by Mary Burton
(North Carolina, 1879)

When an heiress reunites with her former fiancée,
will they rekindle their romance or say goodbye
once and for all?

Visit us at www.eHarlequin.com

HARLEQUIN HISTORICALS®

COMING NEXT MONTH FROM

HARLEQUIN HISTORICALS®

- **ROCKY MOUNTAIN MARRIAGE**
  by **Debra Lee Brown,** the third of three historicals in the
  Colorado Confidential series
  After discovering she'd inherited a saloon from her estranged father,
  a straitlaced schoolteacher travels to Colorado. When a mysterious
  gambler takes a shine to her, will she open her heart to love?
  HH #695 ISBN# 29295-3 $5.25 U.S./$6.25 CAN.

- **THE NORMAN'S BRIDE**
  by **Terri Brisbin,** author of THE DUMONT BRIDE
  Thought dead and killed in battle, Sir William De Severin is in truth
  alive and lives as a mercenary. When he finds a noblewoman left for
  dead in the forest, he nurses her back to health...but will this mean
  confronting the life he had long abandoned?
  HH #696 ISBN# 29296-1 $5.25 U.S./$6.25 CAN.

- **RAKE'S REWARD**
  by **Joanna Maitland,** the sequel to MARRYING THE MAJOR
  After five years of enforced exile, the black sheep of the Stratton
  family has returned to England, determined to have his revenge on
  the countess who ruined him at cards. But the countess has acquired
  a surprisingly beautiful companion who isn't fooled by his charming
  facade....
  HH #697 ISBN# 29297-X $5.25 U.S./$6.25 CAN.

- **MAGGIE AND THE LAW**
  by **Judith Stacy,** author of CHEYENNE WIFE
  Desperate to recover a priceless artifact, a young woman travels out
  west, only to learn that if she wants it back, she'll have to steal it! But
  how can she when the town's oh-so-handsome sheriff won't let her out
  of his sight?
  HH #698 ISBN# 29298-8 $5.25 U.S./$6.25 CAN.

KEEP AN EYE OUT FOR ALL FOUR
OF THESE TERRIFIC NEW TITLES